Ron Nichols

ASALI SOLOMON received a Rona Jaffe Foundation Writers' Award for the stories later collected in *Get Down*, her first book, which was a finalist for the Hurston/Wright Legacy Award for Debut Fiction. In 2007, she was named one of the National Book Foundation's 5 Under 35. Solomon teaches English literature and creative writing at Haverford College. She lives in Philadelphia with her husband and two sons.

Also by Asali Solomon

Get Down

Disgruntled

Disgruntled

Asali Solomon

PICADOR • FARRAR, STRAUS AND GIROUX • NEW YORK

DISGRUNTLED. Copyright © 2015 by Asali Solomon. All rights reserved. Printed in the United States of America. For information, address Picador, 175 Fifth Avenue, New York, N.Y. 10010.

picadorusa.com • picadorbookroom.tumblr.com
twitter.com/picadorusa • facebook.com/picadorusa

Picador® is a U.S. registered trademark and is used by Farrar, Straus and Giroux under license from Pan Books Limited.

For book club information, please visit facebook.com/picadorbookclub or e-mail marketing@picadorusa.com.

Designed by Abby Kagan

The Library of Congress has cataloged the Farrar, Straus and Giroux edition as follows:

Solomon, Asali.
    Disgruntled : a novel / Asali Solomon.—First edition.
        p. cm.
    ISBN 978-0-374-14034-2 (hardcover)
    ISBN 978-0-374-71295-2 (e-book)
1. African American girls—Pennsylvania—Philadelphia—Fiction. 2. Philadelphia (Pa.)—History—20th century—Fiction. I. Title.
    PS3619.O4335 D57 2015
    813'.6—dc23   2014027442

Picador Paperback ISBN 978-1-250-09463-6

Our books may be purchased in bulk for promotional, educational, or business use. Please contact your local bookseller or the Macmillan Corporate and Premium Sales Department at 1-800-221-7945, extension 5442, or by e-mail at MacmillanSpecialMarkets@macmillan.com.

First published by Farrar, Straus and Giroux

First Picador Edition: March 2016

10 9 8 7 6 5 4 3 2 1

For Andrew, sputnik

Young, gifted and black,
It's where it's at.
—Donny Hathaway

The Way It Was

In the first grade at Henry Charles Lea School in West Philadelphia, when Kenya told kids that she celebrated Kwanzaa, no one knew what she was talking about. By the third grade, led by the tiny tyrant L'Tisha Simmons, the kids were calling her an African bootyscratcher and chanting to a conga line rhythm:

You don't get no pre-*sents*!

You don't get no pre-*sents*!

In fact, she did get presents on the last morning of Kwanzaa, seven days after Christmas. By the fourth grade Kenya was down to one friend.

It wasn't just the Kwanzaa problem. And anyway, she could have lied about Kwanzaa like she suspected Fatima McCullers did—Fatima, whose dad had dreadlocks and who always said "Christmas" and "Santa Claus" with a wavering inflection. It was also that she couldn't eat any pork, including the bologna sandwiches that were the everyday fare of the lunchroom—something to do with her father muttering that white people forced slaves to eat hog guts—though as far as Kenya could see, white people loved bologna enough to give it both a first and a second name. It was that she wasn't allowed to watch *Gimme a Break!*, *Good Times*, or *Diff'rent Strokes* because, according to her mother, watching black people on TV acting the fool was worse than not watching any at all. It was that she was forbidden to actually speak the Pledge of Allegiance and had been directed to mouth it with her hand not actually touching her chest. It was that she had to call her father "Baba," and when she'd asked if she could call him "Daddy" like other people, it had triggered what seemed like days of lectures, during which Kenya learned to hate the phrase *other people*. It was that while her parents said grace like normal people, they directed it to the Creator instead of God. It was that she was never *ever* allowed to say *nigger*, even during the step where they had to say *nigger boy*. In fact, when she first heard someone say it in school—L'Tisha Simmons in the third grade—Kenya said "Ooooooooooooh!" expecting everyone to join in. They didn't. Even Aliyah, the pale girl from Sudan (actual Africa—but no one called *her* a bootyscratcher!), with a long rope of hair, was laughing at her, and when Kenya pointed at L'Tisha, explaining, "She said the n-word!" they laughed even harder.

Kenya's one friend was Charlena Scott, who went to Lea and lived a few blocks away from her. She made Kenya look normal during the times of the year when no one was thinking about Christmas. Her parents were adherents to some offshoot of the Seventh-day Adventists, and so she wore old lady's cat-eye glasses and long, dark skirts. Aside from the fact that she and Kenya were both forbidden to watch *The Dukes of Hazzard* (Charlena because it came on after nine o'clock, Kenya because according to her father it "declawed" the racist South), they had little in common. They were both "advanced" readers, but Charlena was more advanced than Kenya and had her own private reading group. She and the teacher, Mrs. Preston, drank cherry soda and casually conversed about the chapter book they were currently enjoying.

The point of being friends with Charlena was to have a partner for lunch, someone Kenya could walk with on the zoo trip, talk to at recess, someone she could sit with on the sidelines of Double Dutch, trying to make watching look fun. Charlena couldn't manage Double Dutch in her pioneer-length skirts and Kenya couldn't manage it at all. And sometimes when her father couldn't pick her up from school, Kenya had to go to Charlena's, because Charlena's mother got home earlier than either of Kenya's parents. Given the UNICEF poster–African wood sculpture–exotic-incense-smelling eccentricities of her house over on Irving Street (less tree-lined and prosperous-looking than Charlena's block), the arrangement was a relief.

Charlena always wanted to play *Star Wars*—one of the few movies that she'd seen. At least she claimed she'd seen it; her grasp of the plot seemed tenuous. She always insisted on being Darth Vader, declared Kenya Princess Leia, and said if Leia didn't kiss Darth Vader, Luke would be tortured.

Kenya hated to break character during these games, which offered a thrilling escape from real life, but she also hated Charlena's peanut butter–apple juice kisses, which were made worse by her heavy Darth Vader breathing. She played along the first few times, but she finally tried to fight back.

"I will keep my honor," declared Kenya, ducking the kiss. "And if you torture Luke," she cried, "I will swear to God a vengeance on your head!"

"No!" Charlena said in her own, rather than her Darth Vader, voice. "They have to kiss!"

Kenya gave in. When Charlena didn't get her way, the fun evaporated in a damp cloud of gloom. It was also true sometimes that Charlena would occasionally break away mid-kiss and fly off to pout for mysterious reasons.

"What is your problem?" blurted Kenya one afternoon after a particularly nauseating session of tongue kissing had failed to cheer Charlena.

Charlena sighed theatrically. "Nothing."

Bored, but not quite ready to do math worksheets, Kenya watched Charlena fritter with the slats of the mint-green blinds and stare out onto the street. Kenya viewed the blinds with her usual sense of longing. For reasons that were never explained to her, and to the consternation of their neighbor Mrs. Osgood, her own parents had kept the boards on the bottom front windows that had "come with" their small row house.

Kenya tried again. "Come on. Tell me what's wrong."

"Do your parents ever fight?" Charlena asked, turning slowly from the window to face Kenya.

"Sometimes," Kenya said, her face suddenly burning. Did her parents fight? Not all the time, but when they did . . . She recalled two Thanksgivings ago, when her father's "wino philosopher" friends, as her mother called them, mysteriously showed up around dinnertime and her mother broke a wooden spoon on a pot.

Charlena's eyes welled up. "I think mine are going to get a—a—divorce!"

Kenya sucked in air sharply. While many of the Lea kids

were being raised by single mothers and grandmothers, an actual divorce seemed cataclysmic. It was something so dramatic they made movies, TV movies, *and* specials about it. In one of the movies her parents had for some reason allowed her to watch, there was a horrible courtroom scene where a judge made a sobbing boy choose which parent he liked better and which one he'd see only on weekends. He chose to live with his mother—and then his father died in a car accident.

Charlena started to cry and all Kenya could think to do was swat at her back. It was what her father would have done. She tried to picture her mother, but she would feel ridiculous crushing Charlena, who was nearly a head taller, into her skinny chest.

"I bet it's going to be okay," Kenya said, wanting to ask more about Charlena's parents and how they fought. She thought again about that Thanksgiving. She had been in the dining room, listening both to her father making a point about the decline of black music, playing snatches from record after record, and to her mother's voice from a distance, "Johnbrown, Johnbrown, *Johnbrown* . . ." Kenya had yelled, "Baba," but he couldn't hear her. A few moments later, the spoon was in splinters and everyone heard her mother call her father the worst curse Kenya knew. In the heavy silence that followed, two of the winos fled. The stuffing, usually Kenya's favorite, tasted like chunks of dust that year. No one had mustered the courage to tell Sheila that there were bits of wood in her hair. Maybe Johnbrown had stayed in touch with those friends, but Kenya never saw them again.

"What makes you think it's going to be okay? You're just

saying that," Charlena accused. "You don't even know my parents."

"Isn't divorce against your religion?"

"I think so."

"They're so strict with you. They have to be like that with themselves, too."

"Well," said Charlena. "Maybe."

But in fact, Kenya thought it was only right that Charlena's mother should leave her father. She was beautiful in spite of the plain white blouses, long, dark skirts, and bun she had to wear because of her religion. Her skin looked like fudge; she had long, thick hair and spoke in a soft voice. Charlena's father, on the other hand, was tall with patchy hair, rusty skin, and a permanent frown.

As for her own parents, Kenya wasn't worried. Maybe they fought, but she couldn't imagine life without them fighting. She was sure that they couldn't imagine it either. They were her only family and each other's as well.

Johnbrown and Sheila were only children, which was the sole feature linking their childhoods.

Sheila was raised by her mother in the Richard Allen projects, which loomed high and gloomy over North Philadelphia. When her mother was heavy with Sheila, the father gave her twenty dollars and then disappeared. According to photographic evidence, Sheila's mother was a thick, dark-skinned woman who had none of the shine of Sheila's eggplant complexion, though she did share Sheila's bushy eyebrows. It was hard to see if she, too, had Sheila's gapped-tooth grin, since this grandmother never smiled in the pictures Kenya saw. Kenya thought she could understand why. The woman had worked two cleaning jobs and ironed for people in the building. She also took in a slightly older foster daughter, to help raise Sheila, and that girl turned out to be a hood. But both the mother and the foster daughter (who eventually came to hate each other) devoted themselves to making sure Sheila was fed and clothed and did her homework; she even got to go to the movies one Saturday a month. Compared with other girls in Richard Allen (and her "sister," Melvina), Sheila's life was leisurely. She did a laughable amount in the way of chores, and did not have to work a part-time job. She loved school, hated being poor, and spent her time at home studying and any free time at school running errands for the guidance counselor. She clawed her way onto the honor roll and stayed there until she had a full scholarship to college.

Sheila graduated from Franklin & Marshall College, one of three black students in her class. As if her work on earth was finished, the grandmother whom Kenya would never meet died of a heart attack in an ER waiting room three weeks later. Shortly after that, Melvina went to prison for knifing a woman said to be her lover. No one came to see Sheila eventually graduate from library school.

Johnbrown was raised in Bryn Mawr, right outside of the city, about a million miles from Richard Allen, by his mother, an elementary school teacher, and his father, one of five black pharmacy owners in the greater Philadelphia area. In pictures that Sheila had rescued from Johnbrown—and the trash—so that Kenya could see them, her paternal grandparents smiled faintly from fair-skinned faces under slick-looking limp hair. Kenya's paternal grandfather had suffered a fatal stroke when she was three, and Johnbrown hadn't spoken to his mother since the funeral. Of his parents, he would say, "They were not good people." Kenya knew that they had enforced some odd rules: for example, he was not allowed to sing at meals, and he had to pass a smell test to leave the house each morning. He would not say much more than that.

"Did they beat you?" Kenya asked him.

"No," he said.

"Did they yell all the time?"

"No."

"Did they send you to work in a factory like Oliver?"

"Ha, ha."

"Mo-om," Kenya wailed. "Make Baba answer me."

"This is between y'all and y'all," Sheila said. "It's his childhood."

What made these conversations even more maddening was that Kenya knew her father's mother and she seemed nice enough. In what Kenya later recognized as the second greatest act of treachery in her parents' marriage, every year around the holidays, Sheila would tell Johnbrown they were going shopping and instead she and Kenya went to visit Mrs. Curtis.

Kenya remembered visiting Johnbrown's mother around the time she was five. Quickly taking in the plastic-covered couch and the formal dining room that beckoned beyond, she said, "Hello, Grandmother," in a slightly British accent and bowed. The older woman laughed, but also looked pleased. "Please call me Grandmama," she'd said.

Johnbrown said his parents did not like children, and that his mother became a teacher because she wanted to "crush their young spirits." But it seemed to Kenya that Grandmama liked at least one child very much. She grabbed Kenya's face with cold, fat hands and kissed it, blowing an interesting wind that combined rot, perfume, and the peppermint balls she sucked when she wasn't smoking long, thin cigarettes.

"How are *you*?" she'd ask, settling into her throne-size brown velvet chair as Kenya and her mother tried not to make weird noises on the couch's plastic slipcover. "What are you learning in school? And tell me the interesting stuff, don't bore me, you know." Then she'd listen with great concentration as Kenya talked about the excruciating difficulties of long division and named all of the planets in the solar system.

Mostly, Sheila and Johnbrown's mother talked about dull things like the price of gasoline, the need to be careful on winter ice, and the doings of the president. It was always just before Kenya's mother sighed that it was time to be going that Grandmama would ask after Johnbrown.

"You know, Mrs. Curtis," Sheila said once. "He is the same."

"I think about him every day. And, Sheila, when will you call me Eveline?" Grandmama responded.

"What do you think about?" Kenya piped in. "What do you think about him?"

"Kenya," her mother said, the name a warning.

"That's okay, Kenya," Grandmama said, pronouncing her name *KEEN-ya*, as she always did. "I guess I just wonder when he will take responsibility for his life. He's so stuck on this business about being black, like he's the first person to have that problem. I wonder when he will do right by the both of you."

After she finished speaking, she reached first for a cigarette from a lacquered box on the coffee table, then instead for a peppermint ball in a yellow glass bowl. Kenya watched her, listening to the ticking of a clock that must have been there all along. She wondered if it had gotten louder. Her mother stared off into space. Sometimes when Kenya recalled this conversation later, she remembered her mother saying, "But he is a good man." Sometimes she remembered her saying nothing at all.

At the end of every visit, Johnbrown's mother reached into her bulky maroon purse and handed Sheila a slip of paper. When Kenya learned that it was a "check," and what a check was, she learned to look away.

Sheila had what she called "a good job" working at the public library on Fortieth Street near the University of Pennsylvania. But when kids at school asked about Johnbrown, Kenya had two choices if she wanted to tell the truth. She could say he was either a housepainter or a philosopher. She had considered saying that he was dead, but she felt terrible about that.

Though he often gave speeches to Kenya about the importance of doing well in school, Johnbrown did not believe in the ability of Western institutions to educate oppressed peoples like him. He had attended Cornell University, an Ivy League school, but only, he would remind everyone with a sneer, to escape the draft. He'd planned to leave once the war ended, but he lost the chance to drop out when he was expelled for participating in a failed attempt to take over the administration building.

After that he worked in a milk bottling plant, sold knives, and even sorted mail for a few months. But those jobs were too constraining. Saying he wanted to pursue "a life of study," he took up rather sporadic house painting. On the days when Johnbrown wasn't painting a house, he followed a schedule taped to his wall that began with predawn calisthenics. The rest of the day was blocked out for meditation, reading philosophy in a book-choked spare room, and working on The Key. The Key was a contemporary work of black philosophy that would also be a way of living for nonblack peoples who were enlightened. It would draw on Classical thought, as well as West African and Native American ways of knowing. It would unite Du Bois, Ellison, Cleaver, Muhammad Ali, and Malcolm X. It would be bigger than Karenga, who thought small, definitively refute Freud, and make Spinoza a household name in the community. Only when he finished The Key would Johnbrown go back to school and get what he called "a square job." ("Do you know what cats used to call jobs in the fifties?" he asked Kenya. "What?" "Slaves." "You calling me a slave, Johnbrown?" said Sheila. *Cats have jobs?* thought Kenya.)

They had a nice stereo and a very large record collection, but not much else. Even though she never had guests, Kenya was embarrassed by their old black-and-white television. Sheila made her slender frame glamorous with thrift store trips, the rich-smelling oil that she bought from street vendors on Fifty-Second Street, and endless variations on a part-cornrow, part-Afro hairstyle. She took Kenya shopping for clothes at the dungeon-like House of Bargains in the summer and at the nightmarishly bright Marshalls at the start of each school year. Occasionally, there was a trip to the glorious Plymouth Meeting Mall, where Kenya was allowed one item of clothing (often, though Sheila didn't know it, a flimsier version of a blouse or skirt that L'Tisha had worn) and one scoop of ice cream (Kenya nearly dreaded this part, so great was the agony of deciding between mint and butter pecan). There was no bright new outfit for Easter, which they did not celebrate.

Kenya had no aunts or uncles or cousins; she didn't go to family barbecues or reunions. But there were the Seven Days, a group Kenya's parents had started with their friends. The name came from something in *Song of Solomon*, one of the few books both Sheila and Johnbrown loved. In *Song of Solomon*, there was a group of black men who killed a white person for every black person they'd heard of being killed by a white person. If the black person had been killed on a Monday, the Monday man undertook the revenge, killing a roughly equivalent white person, say, a little girl, in a roughly equivalent fashion. Just as they were about to strike the blow, they would say, "Your Day has come."

("Don't talk to her about that, Johnbrown," Kenya's mother said when her father told Kenya this story, his eyes glinting with mischief.

("This doesn't scare Kenya. Wait, you scared, Monkey?"

("No," she lied. *Your Day has come*, she would sometimes say to herself in the dark of her bedroom, shivering with delicious terror.)

Provided she had washed up and put on her pajamas, Kenya was allowed to sit in on Seven Days meetings at her parents' house, which usually happened two Saturday nights a month. She loved the feeling of being in a crowded living room, which, with its boarded windows, low-wattage lamps, and huge plants, felt both cramped and cozy. She listened or dozed on her mother's shoulder, sometimes not waking up until the next morning in her own bed.

Kenya's parents and their friends did not kill anyone. Each of them devoted a day in their week to doing something for "the community." Kenya's father went to welfare and Social Security offices to advocate for women with crying children, frail seniors, people who were a little slow—anybody who needed help navigating piles of paperwork. He annoyed employees, most of whom were also black, by passing out mimeographed flyers about asserting civil rights in a hostile bureaucracy.

After she'd graduated college, Sheila had sworn off all contact with Richard Allen; too depressing, she'd said. As a Seven Day, she went back once a week. Johnbrown was the one who pushed her, going on about how much Sheila would have liked to meet a beautiful professional black woman like herself when she'd been a girl. ("I would have loved that," Sheila said, "especially if that woman would have bought me some new clothes.")

On her day, she knocked on doors and gave out books the library was getting rid of and made lists of repairs, for which she harassed the Housing Authority. Sometimes she would round up a group of women and children to ride downtown with her and press their demands in person. For a brief time, because Johnbrown's idea of her as a mentor did appeal to her, she also tried to make friends with some of the teenage girls—especially the ones with small children. She invited them to come to the library and take out children's books to read to their kids. This didn't last, though. "I don't understand them," she admitted to Johnbrown. "I lived there but I was never a girl like *that*." Something told Kenya not to ask what she meant.

Yaya, who worked as an accountant for the city, was Kenya's mother's best friend. Her Seven Days contribution was using personal and sick days to volunteer at the large, shabby childcare facility where her "triflin'" sister worked. Yaya read to the children and bullied the teachers into turning off the soap operas they watched on the television sets designated for *Sesame Street*. Kenya knew from her own mother that only a certain kind of black woman watched soap operas, and she knew this because in those pre-VCR days, her mother hid from Yaya the fact that she breathlessly read summaries of *The Young and the Restless* in the daily newspaper and scheduled days off around watching it.

Yaya's large and mostly silent husband, Alfred, who delivered mail, did home repairs for struggling single mothers. Johnbrown's college friend Robert, who had a law degree but worked in a health food store, gave legal advice. Earl, a Vietnam veteran taking divinity night classes who quietly continued to refer to God when others invoked the Creator, operated a mobile ministry that moved from corner to corner of Southwest Philly, delivering boys to the Church of the Advocate. He believed that liberation theology would keep them out of prison and out of the army.

Nate Camden, who insisted on being called "Brother" Camden, was Kenya's least favorite Seven Day. A short, pudgy psychology professor at Temple University, he always came to meetings with red eyes and wearing the same faded black sweatshirt and pants.

("You shouldn't judge folks like that, Monkey," Johnbrown said when Kenya asked if he ever changed his clothes.

(Sheila snorted. "Well, is she allowed to judge the smell of his one outfit? I sure do.")

But that wasn't the only problem with Brother Camden. It was that he seemed to want to "get in Kenya's world." He badgered her for watching *The Muppet Show*. ("Where are the black Muppets?") Another time he said that the Now and Laters she was eating, which were a special treat, had killed male rats and made the females sterile.

("You mean clean?" asked Kenya.

("Enough, Camden," said her mom.

("Well, she *shouldn't* be eating that crap," said Johnbrown. "You ever see that kind of candy in a white neighborhood store? They trying to poison us.")

And so of course it was Brother Camden who suggested that Kenya officially become a Seven Day by taking on a repugnant task. He had come early for a meeting, and while he'd appeared to be deep into one of his homemade-looking books, making low noises and scribbling notes, it seemed he had also been listening to Kenya talk to Sheila about an unfortunate boy in her fourth-grade class named Duvall. When it was his turn to report on what he'd done that week, he said, "I think maybe Sister Kenya should befriend Brother Duvall for her first act as a Day."

"But—" Kenya said, looking at her father, who seemed distracted. His week as a Day had gone badly; he had argued with the security guard at the welfare office, who'd told him to get a real job. ("After you," Johnbrown had said, taking off before the guard called the police.)

"But," Kenya said again, "I can't just . . ."

"Yes?" said Sheila.

"Duvall talks slow and he eats his tuna fish sandwich with his mouth open and you can see little balls of bread! Even Mrs. Preston is mean to him," Kenya said, immediately realizing her mistake.

"We all have a purpose, young sister," said Brother Camden, fixing her with one of his beady eyes. The other floated in space.

"Brother, I don't know that it's your job to assign Kenya a purpose. But, Kenya, that sounds like all the more reason," said Sheila, while Johnbrown nodded vigorously.

Kenya's favorite Day was Cindalou Waters, a pale dumpling of a woman from North Carolina who had only recently joined the group. Cindalou was the first black person Kenya had met with freckles; she also had what Kenya was forbidden to refer to as "good hair," too soft to hold an Afro. Where Brother Camden smelled faintly homeless, Cindalou came into the living room on those Saturday nights in a delightful cloud of strawberry scent, saying "Hi y'all doin'?" and pronouncing everything "wunnnnduhful."

Sheila had met Cindalou at the library, where she'd come nearly every week for months, checking out all of the history books about black people that she could carry away. Cindalou was somewhat of an exotic for Kenya's mother. Sheila didn't have family in the South, had not spent the requisite summers down there with cousins that the rest of her generation reminisced about. Even Johnbrown had stories about mean chickens in Georgia and his great-uncle-with-a-shotgun. Sheila had only a secret love for *Gone With the Wind*, of which no amount of race pride reeducation could cure her; she had *Gone With the Wind* and a soft spot for Cindalou Waters.

Kenya could tell that Johnbrown, on the other hand, did not seem to care for Cindalou. His face would often fall flat when she spoke, or else he would wear a tight smile. Kenya wondered if it was because she was so light-skinned. Despite being a greenish-tan color himself, with slanted eyes that ignorant black people admiringly called "chinky," and perhaps because of his parents, his views about fair-skinned black folks were firm. (Once Kenya had asked him what he would be if he couldn't be black and he had said, "Light-skinned.")

"Why doesn't Baba like Cindalou?" Kenya asked her mother one day as they were driving to school, a few months after Cindalou had joined the Days.

"What makes you think he doesn't like her?" Sheila asked.

"I don't know," Kenya said, trying to put her feeling into words. The ride was short and they were already in front of the tall school building with grated windows, the schoolyard full of running, screaming children who made Kenya want to go home and crawl under the bed.

Suddenly Sheila said, "I'll level with you. Your father does not care for Cindalou."

Kenya tried not to act excited, but she loved it when her mother "leveled with her." It did not happen often.

"Why not? Why doesn't he like her?"

"Well," said her mother over the sputtering idle of the car, "you know, a lot of men don't like you to have your own friends. Even good men."

Kenya thought about that as she walked into the schoolyard, where the classes were lining up. She was so wrapped up in the riddle of it—that her father, who had Robert and Earl and his wino philosophers, would deny Sheila Cindalou—that she walked right over to Fatima McCullers when she called out to her. She didn't notice until it was too late that Fatima was huddled with L'Tisha, as if plotting some meanness. Aliyah, the white-looking Sudanese girl, often their audience, stood there as well in one of her oddly formal dresses, pink with a white sash.

Kenya walked over, careful not to trip over her feet. "What?" she said, putting a hand on her hip.

L'Tisha took her traditional morning Blow Pop out of her mouth and said something so quietly that Kenya couldn't make it out.

"Huh?" she said, trying to sound more snotty than confused.

L'Tisha spoke again, saying something that sounded like "boogeddy-boo." Fatima and Aliyah elbowed each other and laughed. Nearby, Kenya could see Duvall trying to curry favor with some of the cooler boys in the class, showing them some small metal object, surely last year's prized Christmas present.

"I can't hear you," Kenya said, trying not to whine. She scanned the yard for Charlena, who was nowhere to be found, worrying that she would not have a line partner.

"I thought you understood African!" L'Tisha yelled. Aliyah clapped her hands while Fatima held her belly and emitted a fake laugh. Duvall giggled. In that moment, the most Kenya could do as a Day was to not kick him in the stomach.

Every day of that grim week L'Tisha was nearby, muttering "boogeddy-boo." And so, as was often the case, the Seven Days meeting was the thing Kenya most looked forward to. On Saturday night, Kenya washed up quickly after dinner and hovered by the windows, waiting for everyone to arrive.

Yaya and Alfred came first, bearing a bottle of wine for the libation and Alfred's personal six-pack of beer, which he only occasionally shared.

"Hey, Good People," said Yaya on her way into the kitchen to see Sheila. Alfred quietly muttered something to Kenya that sounded like *Hunchwa* but seemed to be "Hello."

"Ho!" said Johnbrown. He fought with one of Sheila's massive hanging plants to rifle through the records on the shelf underneath it. He liked to play music as the Days were arriving. Tonight it was a howling jazz record, ironically titled *Music Is the Healing Force of the Universe*.

"Baba, that was terrible," Kenya said when it ended. Finally the Days had all gathered and she was tucked between Cindalou and Sheila on the scratchy plaid love seat, which had been Sheila's mother's only piece of living room furniture back in the projects.

"I'm gonna have to agree," said Cindalou. "I'm gonna have to say that is the opposite of music."

"Well, what I'm gonna have to say is . . ." began Johnbrown with a thin smile.

"Oh, here we go," said Yaya. She sat on the arm of the easy chair where Alfred sat, while the other men, Earl, Robert, and Brother Camden, sat on the large couch, trying their best not to touch one another. Johnbrown preferred to stand, sometimes pacing, sometimes lean-sitting on the radiator.

"We ain't even done the libation yet," said Sheila.

"I take it back," said Cindalou.

Johnbrown opened and closed his mouth; he seemed chastened by the missed opportunity to give a lecture.

"From the Creator, for the martyrs," Robert said.

Anyone could start the meeting by intoning the libation. Robert, who liked to move things along, often did. Sheila always opened and poured the glass of wine. Now she passed it around. Each—except Kenya—drank from it and poured it into a bowl that was passed along as well.

"From the Creator, for Malcolm X," said Sheila.

"From the Creator, for George Jackson," said Yaya.

Denmark Vesey, Fred Hampton, Patrice Lumumba, Nat Turner. Everyone had a favorite martyr; most were names Kenya had known since she was very small. Most of the people named were black, but Yaya liked to mention "the *white* John Brown" when she was in a certain kind of mood. Brother Camden also sometimes broke tradition by mentioning what he called Indigenous Peoples.

"From the Creator, for Geronimo," he said tonight.

"From the Creator, for Martin Luther King," said Cindalou.

A deflated-ball disapproval sound left Kenya's father's mouth.

"Johnbrown," warned Sheila.

"I'm sorry, sister," he said to Cindalou. "Pay me no mind."

"Did I say something wrong?" she said.

"JB, I'm not sure I ever understood what your problem with the brother was," said Earl. "He spoke out against the war. He spoke up for workers' rights."

"I just feel like . . . a martyr with a McDonald's commercial?" said Johnbrown. Kenya could tell he was trying to seem calmer than he was. Johnbrown could get very excited about the topic of Martin Luther King and how overrated he was. Kenya noticed that Martin Luther King, Jr., was the only one of the martyrs she had learned about in school.

"That's not his fault," said Sheila. "He's not *in* the commercial. And the reason is that he got shot to death minding his own business."

"Maybe we should move on," Johnbrown said.

Cindalou hadn't said anything. Now she eyed Johnbrown, her lips twisted slightly. "Should I say somebody else?"

"Girl, don't you listen to this nonsense," said Sheila. "Just pass that glass over here." The two women grinned at each other over Kenya's head. (Still, after that meeting, Cindalou stuck to Medgar Evers.)

Johnbrown liked to keep everyone guessing with the martyrs he himself named, and he also liked to do his offering last. That way he could begin the meeting with a long story about a democratically elected Latin American president that the CIA had secretly murdered, or a black scientist who'd died on the steps of a segregated hospital.

At the same meeting where Cindalou ventured King, Johnbrown mentioned his favorite martyr.

"From the Creator, for Julian Carlton," he said.

"Now, who is that?" murmured Cindalou.

It was then that Kenya realized she didn't know who he was either. His name had been coming up for some time but had run in with the other ones whose deeds had been animatedly explained to her. Now she steeled herself to follow the intricacies of a story involving the Michigan State Police or FBI task forces.

"What, you mean you don't know the name of Frank Lloyd Wright's butler?" asked Sheila, rolling her eyes.

"That doesn't make his sacrifice any less," said Johnbrown, "that he was a butler. In fact it makes it more."

"Brother, go on and tell us your gruesome story again," said Yaya.

"So this was a brother from Barbados," said Kenya's father. "He turned up in Wisconsin in . . . 1904, to work for this famous white architect, probably the most famous American architect. Obviously after slavery, but in terms of the way black servants were being treated . . . anyway, he went to work for this white man in the middle of nowhere, this guy who everybody thought was a genius, who was, of course, incredibly arrogant. He was so arrogant that he left his wife and five kids—"

"That's the worst part of this whole story to me," said Sheila.

"And five kids," Johnbrown repeated, "and he built this house to live with his mistress, who also ran off from her husband with her kids. Anyway, one day the architect was out of town and the mistress, who probably treated him like crap, fired the brother. I mean, in those days you could only imagine why he was getting fired. I mean, even today some of these insane mammers I work for—" *Mammers* was Johnbrown's substitute, Kenya knew, for *motherfucker* (which she sometimes whispered to herself on the toilet, to see if the sky would fall).

"So he got fired and then he killed everybody," finished Sheila.

"How did he kill them?" asked Kenya. They all turned to her as if they'd forgotten she was there.

Johnbrown looked at her. "He set the house on fire and then stood in the main doorway with an ax in case anyone tried to escape."

"You mean he chopped them up?" Kenya said. She saw her mother looking at her father. He looked back.

"Yes," he said to Kenya.

"And what happened to him?" Yaya asked. "Did Wright's wife give him a medal?"

"Well, it's confusing. He tried to drink acid, but it didn't kill him. And then he supposedly died of malnutrition in prison. My guess is they beat him to death."

"And this was better than integration?" said Cindalou, who had been listening with wide eyes.

"First of all," said Johnbrown with a dramatic sigh, "folks act like King did everything on his own, when you got your Bayard Rustin and Fannie Lou Hamer and a bunch of other nameless folks who made all of that happen. And second of all, as someone who grew up with white people, I'm not convinced that desegregation is the answer to our problems."

"But chopping up white people is?" asked Robert.

Alfred made an emphatic noise that sounded like *urumph*, indicating that he thought Robert had scored some kind of point.

Johnbrown said, "Look. You can't tell me that a mass murder doesn't say more than a mass march. What the brother understood was the power of rage. I'm guessing that more regular outbursts by seriously disgruntled black employees would achieve more than three hundred sixty-five days of peaceful marches."

"Sure," said Brother Camden, "you got point seven of the ten-point platform: self-defense. Where did that get us?"

"The Panthers were onto something, but didn't quite get there. Think about their paramilitary costumes and their formations and what-have-you; they weren't different enough from the police. Fascist chic. What I'm talking about is anarchy. Black anarchy."

"Like the riots?" asked Cindalou. "We watched that on TV back home and thought y'all had truly lost your minds up here."

"Maybe you wouldn't have thought that if we'd torn up white people's neighborhoods. Because that's what *I'm* talking about."

After they honored the martyrs, they talked business, accomplishments, and goals. But that was dull and Kenya always hoped that they would rush through it to get to the part where they gossiped about local and national events: talking trash about Frank Rizzo, the illiterate thug former mayor, and Ronald Reagan, the Hollywood menace; making sardonic comments about the fact that it was actually *1984*. Then they gossiped about "movement people" in Philadelphia, arguing about who was a poverty pimp, a drunk, or an FBI agent. They usually finished off by insulting one another: Robert, the nonpracticing lawyer, was cheap as a broke Jew; Sheila, being from the projects, was niggerish ("Kenya, don't you ever say *nigger*"), with a switchblade strapped to her leg and government cheese under the sink; Yaya was waiting for the revolution so she could loot Wanamaker's for designer clothes; Alfred, so he could loot the beer distributors; Earl they teased about kids he'd left in Vietnam; they rarely mocked Brother Camden, because all he ever said was "Y'all crazy" with a smile that looked painful to maintain.

For months after she joined the Days, nobody ever made fun of Cindalou. She wasn't like the others. She was a waitress in an Upper Darby diner and hadn't even gone to college long enough to get expelled. But then one night Johnbrown paused in a rambling lecture about something he'd researched for The Key about differences in gravity based on proximity to the equator and wasn't it interesting that even the experience of gravity was related to race—and Cindalou snapped, "Prep School, *puh-leeeeeze*! Give somebody else a chance to talk."

Johnbrown flinched.

Everyone knew, but no one talked about, the way Johnbrown had grown up. It was like calling Robert out for being gay, something even Kenya knew and no one mentioned.

"I went to public school just like everybody else, sister," he said in a tight voice.

Kenya's mother laughed lightly. "We know, honey. You went to Lower Merion."

Yaya cleared her throat. "Excuse *you*. I went to Catholic school. My parents had ambitions for me." Then she winked at Kenya.

Johnbrown ignored Yaya. "Look, it was no fuckin' picnic walking around black on the Main Line back then. Or now," he said, trying to sound calm.

"You didn't hear that, Kenya," said Yaya. "All you heard was 'picnic.'"

"Whoa, now. Sorry I raised these painful memories," said Cindalou with wide eyes. "I had no idea."

Kenya had never met anyone like Cindalou. You wanted to laugh at almost everything she said, and though she was very earnest, it seemed as if that was her intent. Talking to her was like being tickled. All she had to say was "Hey, Kenya" to make her giggle. Kenya tried to stifle a laugh as Cindalou apologized to her father.

"No worries," said Johnbrown. "At least I didn't go to school in a one-room shack with a dirt floor."

"Ba-*ba*," Kenya gasped.

Cindalou laughed. "That's okay. I did go to school just like that. We had to have a dirt floor for our teachers, who were chickens, of course." Even Johnbrown chuckled.

Brother Camden's presence was unpleasant, but there was only one person who could truly ruin a Seven Days gathering for Kenya.

Johnbrown, in a certain kind of mood, would remain silent for most of a meeting. If spoken to, he would respond slowly.

Then, at the end, he would ask, "Do you all really think that what we do is enough?"

Sometimes he waited for one of the others to tell the story of someone they knew getting their head busted by the police, or harassed by white folks on the job. Just as the story seemed to wind down, he'd say, "*That's* exactly why we need to bring the fight to them Julian Carlton–style. Just burn it all down."

Johnbrown, before he conceived of The Key, while he was between crap jobs, was the one who had come up with the Seven Days, and later he seemed to forget that Sheila nearly had to wrestle him to the ground to get him to read the Toni Morrison novel. He thought the organized murdering in the book was brilliant, an ideal combination of what he saw as Eastern discipline and black anarchy, but, as he saw it, the times did not quite call for that.

His original idea had been a combination of service and confrontation. In addition to the volunteering, he wanted to stage raucous demonstrations at the suburban houses of city slumlords. He wanted to block streets in the Northeast or in the Irish Catholic part of Southwest Philly, where the white people regularly harassed black pedestrians; to patrol the neighborhood borders of South Philadelphia, where black met Italian; to picket racist unions and sabotage the Mummers Parade, the white trash blackface spectacle that was the city's sole indigenous tradition.

Johnbrown had several ideas, but perhaps his favorite involved provoking the police. For as long as she could remember, Kenya's father had owned a gun, which lived in the basement in a locked metal box that she had imagined but never seen. Johnbrown wanted all of the Days to own handguns—"legally, of course." His idea was that they should take their guns to the local police station to stage their right to bear arms—but without the "fascist theatrics" of the Panthers. But no one else was interested in spending their evenings in the city jail or getting their heads cracked with billy clubs. It might have also been the case that no one trusted Johnbrown at the police station with a gun. In any case, the Seven Days had become what they were.

When Johnbrown started his "burn it all down" talk, the others would become sullen as they listened to him rant about how even though Philly now had a bullshit black mayor, it was still Rizzoville. "And why," he would ask, his voice climbing octaves, "are we putting ourselves at the mercy of those ignorant racist thugs y'all call the police?" This was Yaya's cue to pick up the hat she was endlessly crocheting and unraveling, and Alfred's to stare thoughtfully into his can of beer. Kenya's mother had a special sigh and a dark expression for moments like these. In the end, Johnbrown usually wore himself out and things continued on as they had before.

One Saturday night, after a particularly gloomy spell of several days, Johnbrown announced, "It's no secret that I think it's time for us to *really* talk about what's going on in this city, this country, in 1984. Yeah—1984. Does that ring a bell for anyone here?" His pouty tone reminded Kenya of the afternoon not long ago when Charlena had been upset about her parents' fighting.

"Look, we're doing what we can. Just give it up, John," Sheila snapped. He'd appended *brown* to his name when he was kicked out of Cornell. Kenya's mother left it off when he seriously displeased her.

"Maybe we should hear him out," said Cindalou.

Sheila continued. "Look, if y'all want to go moon the local precinct—"

"Aw, Sheila," laughed Yaya. "That ain't right."

("Umph!" agreed Alfred.)

Johnbrown stood up abruptly, rustling the huge corn plant beside him. "Moon the police station? Oh, fuck that! Who started this whole thing?" he yelled.

Suddenly Yaya stood as well, and Kenya found herself slung over her shoulder, receding backward away from her father's bulging eyes.

"Who started this whole thing?" Johnbrown yelled. "I mean, what the hell were y'all doing with your lives when I came up with this? Going to the disco? Pledging the alumnae chapter of Wine Psi Fi?"

Behind her door, Kenya heard her mother's voice getting louder, her father's going high. "It's not like I can't hear them," she said to Yaya, rolling her eyes though her chest was tight with terror.

"That's okay," Yaya said. "It's better as background noise. So what's your favorite bedtime story?"

It was very difficult for Kenya to carry on a conversation with Yaya and still listen to what her parents were saying, but she couldn't help being indignant.

"My mother is a *librarian*. I read my own books!" she said.

Yaya grinned. "Well, excuuuuuse me. I forgot you were a genius."

Kenya's face burned. She bragged about her reading but

she was no Charlena. It had always seemed to her that if she was going to be so unpopular at school, the reason should be that she was so smart it put others off.

"I'm just playing with you," Yaya said. Then she perused the stacked orange crates that held Kenya's books and few remaining toys. "How 'bout I read this one to you anyway?" she asked, picking up *The Lion, the Witch and the Wardrobe*, a book that her parents had fought about. "Atonist" bullshit, her father had called it, using his mysterious epithet for Christians, Jews, and Muslims.

Kenya had just begun reading the Narnia books. She nodded, and in the brief silence before Yaya started, they both heard Sheila's voice snap across the word *brat*. Yaya had to leave eventually, and Sheila and Johnbrown Curtis argued into the night while Kenya fell asleep clutching her stomach.

The fight over bringing it to white Philadelphia was the only real disagreement among the Seven Days. But it was not the only battle that Kenya's parents fought. Though she really only began to pay attention because of the talk with Charlena, there had been two main kinds of fights for as long as she could remember.

One was always initiated by Sheila, and it began with her saying something like: *I'm supporting this family financially and the least you could do is the dishes I don't care what Karenga says I'm not married to him and I don't know where your fucking (sorry, Kenya) socks are.* These fights occurred more frequently after Kenya went with her mother to the library downtown, where they listened to a woman named Audre Lorde read poems that did not rhyme.

"I don't go in for that gay stuff," Sheila told Johnbrown, "but everything else that sister said is all right by me."

"She's probably an FBI informant. A lot of those people are," Johnbrown said.

"She certainly informed me about why I'm not ironing your shirts or pouring your cereal anymore."

"What people?" asked Kenya, but no one answered.

Shortly after that conversation Sheila moved from cooking an unpredictable array of fatty, fancy meals into a rigid dinner schedule featuring flavorless baked fish on Mondays accompanied by a glop of spinach, and hot dogs with a gross salad on Saturday nights.

"I'm not a housewife and I'm not the cook," she announced defensively when Kenya and her father poked at their iceberg lettuce. "Eat until you're full."

Kenya considered it a mercy that their tradition of Sunday-morning pancakes remained.

There was another ancient fight, this one always started by Johnbrown. It was *You Don't Need Me Anyway*. Shortly after Charlena had confided her fears about her parents' splitting up, Kenya was up in her room practicing jacks when *You Don't Need Me* broke out. It was because of Charlena's parents' imminent divorce that she ran downstairs yelling, "We need you! We need you!" and grabbed her father's leg. He ignored her, bulging his eyes in the direction of her mother, who said, "Upstairs, Kenya."

"Stop fighting!"

"We're having a discussion," her father said through gritted teeth, trying to shake her off.

"I won't go until you stop having it!"

"Oh yes you will," her mother said, folding her arms, and of course she was right. "And don't be sitting up there at the top listening to grown folks talk!" she called, but she didn't need to yell, because Kenya could hear her very clearly from her perch at the top of the stairs.

"Just don't get a divorce," yelled Kenya, before going into her room.

"We can't," her father's voice floated up. Then he laughed. She heard her mother laugh, too, then say quietly, "You think you're funny, Johnbrown."

The shame of being alive was a phrase Kenya would hear in her father's voice; it wafted in and out of her consciousness like the chorus of a song. What he meant by this it took her years to understand, since just as often he said, "Sure, that's nothing to be ashamed of." Things that were "nothing to be ashamed of" included bodily functions, growing up poor, as her mother had, and feeling lonely, as her father had when he was a child. And of course, though both white folks and some black—like his parents—tried to make you feel it, there was certainly no shame in being black. But during the time of her supposed stewardship of Duvall (which only amounted to her trying not to hate him) and the time of joylessly making out with Charlena, Kenya came into increasing consciousness of how fitting it was that Johnbrown had provided the language for this shame. After all, he and Sheila had created a world of opportunity for her to experience it.

In December of Kenya's fourth-grade year, Sheila decided that she would use her library connections to stage a Kwanzaa presentation with the Seven Days at the library on Fifty-Second Street, a few blocks away from their house. When it came time to start on that Saturday afternoon, the small Programs Room on the first floor suddenly looked big as a ragged handful of families scattered themselves among the rows and rows of chairs. Kenya counted technically more participants than Seven Days, though it certainly didn't feel that way. And then, on the border between presenter and participant, there was an enthusiastic drunk in a bright red wool cap with a surprising amount of knowledge about Kwanzaa. "Ujima!" he shouted as Sheila lit a red candle, before she'd even had a chance to name the principle. "Ku-uuuuuuuuu-maaaa-baaaaa!" he growled, giving the word an extra syllable. Sheila ignored him, her jaw growing steely. Johnbrown stared into the middle distance.

As her parents and their friends took up a chant that Yaya had designed to help the day care kids memorize the principles, Kenya's eye was suddenly drawn to the cracked-open door. There stood an openmouthed L'Tisha Simmons and her mother. The two sported the same ponytail, spiky with escaping bits of straightened hair, and even though L'Tisha was only nine, they also wore matching leather pants. At L'Tisha's side was her minion Fatima.

Kenya could see herself in the girls' eyes, sporting an orange, yellow, and brown dashiki and a forehead-straining vertical braided hairstyle that was her mother's imitation of an

African mask. The chanting and clapping were not loud enough to drown out the sound of L'Tisha and Fatima laughing, or the sound of L'Tisha's mother admonishing the girls for having *no class.*

L'Tisha's laughter was the soundtrack to the shame of being alive; it burned Kenya's stomach and cheeks even when L'Tisha was clearly not laughing at her. There had been one time, which Kenya recalled desperately as the Kwanzaa presentation dragged on, one incredible time when L'Tisha had laughed because Kenya made a joke. Before Duvall became her charge, she had said his breath smelled like cheddar cheese and L'Tisha had howled. Kenya had floated for the rest of the day.

Actually, Kenya wasn't sure which was worse, being laughed or gawked at, or simply being in a place where shame coated the walls, floor, and ceiling. In February, a week after she turned ten, Kenya's parents took her to a Black History Month celebration that had been advertised in *The Philadelphia Tribune.* It was at a poorly heated community center in North Philadelphia where Johnbrown had gone to the occasional Black Marxist meeting. Kenya's fingers grew stiff with cold that night as she watched presenter after presenter make the same joke about the shortest month of the year. A giant man wearing a beret and a green army jacket who reminded her of Brother Camden brandished a flyer about salmonella poisoning and re-purposed kangaroo meat in the chicken at McDonald's. Then a spotty filmstrip about a black junkie named Charlie got chewed up in the projector. Taking up the theme of the destroyed film, a black-clad man did a mime performance about being trapped in a box. The box, he said, was heroin. Finally, two women in colorful bikinis jumped around to some Africanish disco music. As their dance was winding down, they invited people from the audience to get up with them. Many of the men went, including Johnbrown, who jutted his hip bones forward and waved his hands in the air. Sheila's mouth closed in a line. One of the women's tops fell open and a thin breast jumped out. As the minutes passed, Kenya veered wildly between the desires to laugh and to cry; she fought a mounting nausea.

At least L'Tisha wasn't there laughing and saying "boogeddy-boo." But she was there in school the afternoon Duvall raised his hand the way he always did, abruptly and with the force of a rocket.

"Mrs. Preston, my stomach hurts and I really have to go to the bathroom."

"Boy, you just went to the bathroom!"

"I know, but my *stomach hurts.*"

"Duvall has to fart!" yelled a boy whose intriguing name was Aaron Hurt.

"Aaron said I had to fart," said Duvall.

"Boy, you do have to fart!" snapped Mrs. Preston. "Go do it in the bathroom!"

Without meaning to, Kenya gasped at the teacher's meanness. She looked around to see if anyone had heard. There was L'Tisha, three desks away, smiling.

As Duvall ran out to the bathroom clutching the seat of his pants, Kenya heard quiet singing: "Kenya and Duvall, Duvall and Kenya, doin' it, doin' it, doin' it . . . ." It was as if the class knew that Kenya was supposed to speak up for Duvall even though she certainly hadn't and, despite what Brother Camden and her parents said, she certainly never would. It was as if the class was punishing her for being a coward.

The song caught fire and followed Kenya for days. She had to weep in front of Mrs. Preston to make it stop.

The spring of that year, 1985, brought small victories. Kenya finally eked her way into Charlena's reading group. But so had a boy with large yellow teeth named Allmon, which dampened the triumph. Kenya did, however, beat them both at the spelling bee. She tried her best to be humble about it, because it seemed that this was the stylish way to win.

Sheila had gotten a promotion and a raise. Her boss, Susan Zabriskie, a white lady who was obsessed with animals but couldn't even commit to bringing home a hamster, was talking about quitting her job and moving out to the country so she could raise chickens. If this happened, Sheila would practically run the Research Department. For his part, Johnbrown said that he was really "closing in on The Key" and would soon start talking to publishers.

But in May the city gave Johnbrown fire for his fuel. With the blessing of Philadelphia's first black mayor, the police attacked a row house full of back-to-the-land black people who were aggravating their neighbors in West Philly, about twenty blocks from where Kenya lived. They were part of a group called MOVE, who wore dreadlocks and had all taken the last name Africa.

"I knew that couldn't go on forever," Sheila said early in the evening as the news reported the standoff in progress. "This isn't a holler in Kentucky. You can't use your backyard as a toilet and build a bunker on your roof."

"It's BS the way the city treats those people," Johnbrown

said. "It's straight-up persecution and it's Atonist bullshit. I mean, I don't agree with shitting in your yard, but all they're trying to do is live like a traditional African family. It makes a lot of sense to share child raising and resources."

Sheila looked amused. "You want to bring some more Africans up in here?"

Johnbrown shrugged. "Maybe you'd complain less about housework if you had more family to help you out."

"Any extra Africans coming in here are sleeping in your study. Then we'll see."

As the night grew deeper, Sheila lost her ironic demeanor, her eyes growing wide and wet before the television. The police tried to force MOVE out by dropping explosives on their home, but no one came out. The house caught fire, and Kenya and her family, as if pinned to the couch, watched it burn.

"Oh my God," Sheila whispered. "My God." Finally Johnbrown got up and began pacing in front of the screen and into the kitchen. Kenya was sent to bed.

When she woke up in the morning, sixty-five houses had been burned to the ground. Eleven of the MOVE people, including five children, were dead. One woman and one boy had escaped.

For weeks after, into the summer, the Days picked the event bone-clean. Strangely, Johnbrown was quieter than usual, even though the others implied that he'd foretold it.

"You tried to warn us," said Earl. "I knew Goode was bullshit, but genocide?"

"It's like a war. It was like a war," said Robert. "Maybe we *do* need to do more."

"We need to do *something*," said Cindalou. "I mean, getting a piece might not be a bad idea. I mean, last time I checked, it was still Klan members on the city council where I'm from, and there's been no black people burned there in fifty years."

"What can we do?" asked Yaya. "They might think we're doing something wrong over here and come burn *us* up."

Despite his powers of prophecy, in the wake of the MOVE attack, no one wanted to hear Johnbrown devote his libations to Julian Carlton.

"I don't want to step on any toes here," said Earl, "but maybe we should rethink our reverence of a man who used an ax on children."

("Urumph," said Alfred.)

"I'm not revering that part of it," said Johnbrown.

"Maybe you should go upstairs, Kenya," Sheila said.

Kenya was only too glad to take a hiatus from the gloomy meetings of the MOVE days. For a string of Saturday nights, she stayed in her room and read a book called *The Little Princess*, in which a very rich girl in England became an orphan and could stay at her boarding school only by becoming a servant. She had to clean up after girls who used to be her friends, and they were not very gracious about it.

But as the fire receded into the past, things returned to normal (even for the little girl in *The Little Princess*, who ended the book rich again). Johnbrown, who had stopped pouring libations to Julian Carlton, began mentioning him again.

"For Julian Carlton," he said, "and the spirit of true sacrifice."

("Mmm," said Alfred.)

Kenya hadn't thought much more about the butler than

she had Fred Hampton or Charles Drew. But one night she woke with a start to the sight of a man on the chair at the foot of her bed. In the streetlight, which seemed unusually bright, she could see his face glistening with sweat. Then she saw the ax on his lap. She tried to scream; she woke up whispering.

Around the time she had the dream, Kenya came down to breakfast to find her parents looking at her with wide, shifting eyes.

"Babe, do you remember last night?" her mother asked.

Kenya frowned.

Her father said, "You don't remember?"

"What?" Kenya asked, becoming worried.

Whenever something serious happened, they spoke in tandem. It had been like that when Harriet Tubman the cat needed a four-hundred-dollar operation and therefore had to be put to sleep. ("Harriet is very sick," said her mother. "She needs more than we can give," said her father.)

It seemed that Johnbrown and Sheila had been jolted awake to the sound of music around three o'clock in the morning, which at first they thought was coming from the house next door. But Mrs. Osgood, who enjoyed loud music with jug wine, played only gospel. The sound, clearly coming from their own house, was the Funkadelics. The disc jockey was Kenya, who had stood in front of the record player downstairs, staring at the wall above. Kenya could not remember any of it, but now she felt she could hear a nightmarish echo of George Clinton singing.

Because it was sleepwalking, it was hard to say when it had started, but once her parents told her about it, Kenya tried to control it. She couldn't be sure if she was successful or not. She never woke up outside of her bed, but she would sometimes have odd memories of the cold of the refrigerator, or note that the soles of her feet were especially dirty. Sometimes she tried to get up before her parents to make sure she hadn't been downstairs in the night and left the television on, or the basement door open. Kenya wondered if she ever played music again and why she had chosen the Parliament Funkadelic record, whose insane and intricate album cover art she had often studied. *Here's a chance to dance our way, out of our constrictions,* sang George Clinton.

In the fifth grade, Duvall, who had been in Kenya's class since kindergarten, was moved down to Special Ed in the basement. Sometimes Kenya saw him as their lines passed on the way to lunch or recess. It seemed he was popular in his new class, and he was often flanked by admiring classmates as he led the charge against a sad, rotund boy everyone called Jiggles. Kenya tried to put Duvall and anything to do with him in a box in her mind and seal it up tight. Thinking about him made her feel bad, like the vile taste of scrapple in her mouth.

Fifth grade was also the first year Kenya remembered Sheila going on housekeeping strikes, which occurred if Johnbrown was too busy working on The Key to keep up with his negligible household duties. When this happened, Alfred and Yaya would host Seven Days meetings. Then Kenya got to know their son, Commodore, a thin-faced boy in her year at school who made everything he said sound like a joke. For no reason, he called her "Ooga Booga" as soon as their parents left them in the den, where they played Uno. As stupid and luck-based as Uno was, Commodore nearly always lost, because he got bored or distracted, or wanted to change the rules. Then he would forget he changed the rules.

"Commodore, you're not even trying," Kenya said. He had laid a green four card on a blue seven.

"Aren't we doing odd numbers primary colors?"

Sighing, Kenya took the green four and put it next to the blue seven.

"You got me there, Ooga Booga." Commodore laughed.

Kenya did not "like" Commodore, something her parents teased her about. He was too goofy. And he certainly did not "like" her. But they were friends. One of the first things she'd done when they met was to answer to "Ooga Booga" without getting upset. She was proud of herself for that.

She also liked that Commodore's favorite show was *The Incredible Hulk*. It was hers, too, though it was kind of sad. She felt sorry for David Banner, who ended each episode walking along the highway in what looked like searing heat. He had to leave every town he came to—even if he fell in love with someone there. But how thrilling to lose control and demolish a person! Kenya particularly remembered one episode where a crazy man chased David Banner as if he were hunting an animal. The man left taunting tape-recorded messages along a trail. When the Hulk finally materialized eight minutes before the show ended, Kenya almost burst into relieved tears. When she asked Commodore if he'd seen that one, he started laughing.

"What?" said Kenya, getting angry.

"I didn't really see it," he said, "because I was hiding be-hind my hands."

She just looked at him.

"What? That mess was scary!"

That year, Cindalou, whom Kenya noticed growing fatter and quieter, introduced a woman named Marjorie to the Seven Days. Marjorie and Cindalou had gone to high school together down South and had recently run into each other downtown. Marjorie had come following a man who had left her for a white woman who made her living as an artist's model.

Marjorie's dark brown pinched face reminded Kenya of a gerbil. She never wore pants, and, unlike any of the other women in the Seven Days, she straightened her hair.

"So y'all are not doing anything illegal?" Marjorie asked at her first meeting.

"No, ma'am," said Johnbrown. "Unless getting on white people's nerves while trying to help black people is illegal. Well, I guess in some states . . ."

"So nothing illegal, right?"

"Correct." Reassured that she would not be arrested for having truck with folks who didn't revere the flag or straighten their hair, Marjorie unveiled her idea.

Having just seen *Bush Mama* at a film festival, she wanted to stand outside of Planned Parenthood encouraging black women not to kill their babies. She said she could use the mimeograph in the teachers' lounge where she worked to print up flyers on her break. After Marjorie's first meeting, Sheila turned to Johnbrown and said, "I can't believe your informant radar isn't going off."

Kenya's father laughed. "The FBI wouldn't send somebody *that* obvious."

Robert stopped by later that week looking for Johnbrown. While he and Kenya's mother drank beer and Kenya drank apple juice, Sheila said the same thing about Marjorie being an informant.

He didn't laugh. "I seriously doubt that. But I was thinking about something. Maybe JB doesn't need to bring up that gun business for a while," he said. "Also, where does he keep the thing? Or, maybe more important, the papers for it."

"What does that have to do with anything?"

"I just think if we're going to have folk we don't really know hanging around . . ."

"Why would Marjorie be down in our basement?" Sheila asked.

"I don't know," he said. "I don't know, okay? But what if he starts talking about guns and his whole 'burn it all down' thing in front of her?" His voice moved comically higher as he said the phrase *burn it all down*.

"Robert, are you making fun of Johnbrown?" Sheila asked.

He looked thoughtful. "Maybe a little."

That night, and more and more, it seemed, Johnbrown stayed away in the evenings, citing trips to the main library and important meetings about The Key. One morning, Kenya was knocked out of sleep by her parents' furious voices.

". . . just fell asleep there!" she heard her father screech.

"You just fell asleep in the library? What are you, a bum? Do you need someplace to sleep?"

"Look, you know how hard I've been working. I was just resting my eyes for one—"

"So you *slept* there!"

"So what if I did?"

The morning after another one of these fights, Sheila had that concerned look on her face again. "Kenya, I found you in the kitchen last night, with the refrigerator open," she said. "Do you—?"

"No," Kenya said. "I don't remember. I don't remember!" She loathed the idea that people were talking to her while she was asleep.

"Calm down," said Sheila.

"I can't! And I can't sleep with all of this fighting!"

Just then Johnbrown appeared in the kitchen, rubbing his eyes. "What's all this yelling about?"

Kenya saw her mother look coldly at her father, her lips tight. Her father stared back.

"What?" he barked.

Kenya burst into tears.

One warm afternoon toward the end of fifth grade, Kenya's father arrived to pick her up from school. Outside on the steps, he crushed her to him in a way that embarrassed her. She heard a showy laugh nearby and didn't have to look up to know that it came from L'Tisha Simmons. She knew L'Tisha was probably not laughing at her father. After all, when L'Tisha's mother picked her up, they acted as if they'd been sold away from each other that morning. But it didn't matter what L'Tisha was laughing at; it just hurt that she was laughing. Kenya went stiff in her father's arms.

"Hey, Monkey," said Johnbrown.

"Hi, Baba," Kenya said in a low voice.

"Let me get that for you," he said now, taking her backpack. He fake-stumbled. "Don't they use books anymore?"

"Those *are* my books."

"These feel like *bricks*," he said. "Are you taking up masonry?" Then he worked up a wan smile that Kenya knew as one pasted atop a bleak mood. Her mother referred to it irritably as his "brave" smile.

"What's wrong?" asked Kenya.

"Don't worry about me," he said. "I don't want you worrying about me."

"Okay, Baba."

"That was a very worried-sounding 'Okay, Baba.'"

"That's all I got," Kenya said.

Johnbrown shook his head and laughed. "Oh, that's all you got, huh?" Then his face began drooping again.

Kenya wasn't so much worried for her father as she was for herself. She did not want to watch her parents' act that night: Johnbrown dragging his face on the floor, Sheila feigning sympathy, then moving into cold rage. Once when Kenya had asked, "Why do you hate Baba?" her mother had responded with an open-handed slap. It was not heavy, but so surprising that it made Kenya, who was six at the time, explode into tears. It was the only time either one of them had hit her.

"Feel like going to see your mom at her job?" he asked now. "Or do you have too much homework?"

Kenya loved being on Fortieth Street, near the Penn campus. She loved the trees and the busyness of it, the food trucks, the jewelry vendors, Marty's Discount, where she sometimes got small toys or a soda, the students playing Frisbee on the lawn behind her mother's library. Though it was nothing like her block, all black and fairly quiet, with its aluminum-sided fronts, and nearly a half mile away, she liked to think of it as part of her neighborhood. Sometimes it was fun to walk there with her father when he was in the mood to chatter about his school days or the characters he met painting houses. But heading down there from school and then walking back up to Irving Street could take a long time that would feel even longer on a warm day. It seemed breezier and calmer down by the library, brighter and sourer as they walked deeper into West Philly, especially on days when Johnbrown was silent.

But then Kenya imagined herself trapped in the house, crouched over long division. She opted for the image of her mother in her bright, silken weekday clothes, using her smooth work voice.

When they reached the second floor of the library, Sheila's boss was at her mom's desk. She beamed at Johnbrown's approach.

"Heya, Susan," he said, with an expression that Kenya couldn't read.

"What a nice surprise. Hi there, Kenya!"

Susan Zabriskie's body was a slapdash arrangement of lumps that Kenya found confusing. She had a gold tooth, floppy black hair with gray strands, and green eyes, which became extremely bright when she shined them on Johnbrown. Sheila sometimes teased Johnbrown about her boss's obvious regard for him. ("Aren't you the lady-killer?" she would say. "I'm about to be," he'd answer, mock-waving his fist.)

"Hello, Mrs. Zabriskie," Kenya said, remembering too late what the woman always said when Kenya called her "Mrs."

"It's *Miz*," said Susan Zabriskie. "Don't marry me off yet!" She blushed and Johnbrown made a noise headed for, but not quite arriving at, a laugh. Then he cleared his throat.

"Sheila went home early," sang Ms. Zabriskie. "She wasn't feeling well."

"Is that right?" asked Johnbrown.

"I'm afraid so," said the boss with a nonsensical laugh.

Kenya found herself looking at her father out of the corner of her eye, for the first time wondering what Susan Zabriskie saw. He was not sloppy or decrepit. He wasn't much more either, just a slight man in clean clothes, with somewhat sickly-looking skin. The only thing distinctive about him was his beaked nose, of which Kenya's was a less severe version, that and the fact that due to a peculiarity of his voice, he was sometimes mistaken for a girl on the phone. The question had always been how he'd snared her mother, so stylish and confident.

The boss continued, "Oh, I'm sure it's nothing serious. She said she had a bad headache. Say, Kenya, do you need something to read? Or one of the new filmstrips? Have you watched *Really Rosie*?"

Kenya thought about Pierre-I-don't-care in the lion's mouth and was about to ask to see it again when her father spoke.

"We'd better go check on her mother," Johnbrown said.

After chatting briefly about his day (more breakthroughs in The Key, all reported with a kind of fake cheer), Kenya and her father walked home in the boring and unsettling silence that she had anticipated. She wouldn't ask him again what was wrong or anything else; it was too tedious. When Sheila was angry she let you know and she let you know why. The atmosphere around

Johnbrown was a mist that might evaporate or turn into a rainstorm. It was as mysterious—and as bothersome—as bad weather.

Kenya tried to lose herself in other parts of the walk by studying West Philadelphia. She gazed without comprehension at the large, neat houses near the campus painted with Greek symbols, and wondered why the young white men sat shirtless on the porches. She and her father passed the Acme supermarket, where Kenya had spent many dreary hours, the stuffy Laundromat they frequented before Sheila defied Johnbrown and bought a washer-dryer on credit. They passed the delicious Koch's Deli, where Kenya's parents agreed they would never go again. After an altercation with a black customer who had left the store, the cashier had hissed to the guy making sandwiches, "He doesn't know how it is! I could get him *lynched!*" Johnbrown never stopped regretting that all he'd done was walk out, claiming that he had been afraid of what he might do.

On days like this, Kenya noticed every pile of dog crap, every bit of trash, abandoned Hug bottles, newspaper sections. She wondered why her family couldn't live closer to the campus, where the streets were orderly and cooler. Of course she knew—money and race—but still. These thoughts and her father's droopy and ominous silence made her angry. His slow shuffle reminded her of Aslan moving slowly with Susan and Lucy to the stone table, where he allowed himself to be killed. But Aslan had made a deal with the White Witch to nobly sacrifice himself for the traitor Edmund. If Johnbrown was sacrificing himself, what was it for?

• • •

The house was in chaos. Papers and envelopes covered the floor; winter coats from the downstairs closet were piled on the couch. Nearly half of the books seemed to be missing from the shelves. Kenya tasted terror.

Her father stood behind her gripping her shoulder. He said her name in an alarmed way, as if he was about to give her an order. Kenya wondered if he had time to get his gun.

But then something changed.

"Oh, *shit*," he said, moving Kenya aside and bounding up the stairs. "Sheila!" he called. "Sheila!"

Kenya followed him. They both stood at the top of the stairs, where they could see Kenya's mother in her room, which looked hurricane-tossed. Sheila, who had been known to spend hours folding underwear to pack for trips to the Jersey Shore, was throwing things into her suitcase.

"Sheila?" said Johnbrown again.

She did not stop what she was doing. "What the fuck do you want?"

Kenya knew they had forgotten her. In a flash she was looking at the closed door of her parents' bedroom. She heard the lock click.

"What is going on?" Johnbrown asked. "What—"

"You know what the fuck is going on!" Sheila screamed, her voice hoarse, as if she had spent the day screaming.

Kenya stood in the hallway picturing different ways to get into that room. She imagined banging on the door. She thought of falling down the stairs, but she knew she couldn't do it loudly enough without seriously hurting herself. She imagined screaming her voice raw. Then it dawned on her that it didn't matter. She could hear everything they said, though her father was speaking in a low voice. It was all wrong. Usually Johnbrown was the one screaming, and Sheila was the one you could barely hear. Kenya felt the floor tipping at angles and fell in a slump against the door.

"I thought you didn't even *like* that bitch! 'She's not *my* cup of tea,' you said! Remember when you said *that* shit? I should have known: you don't even *say* that! You don't even drink *tea*!"

"Sheila, it's not—"

"Not what? It's not what I think?"

"Let me talk, please. Let me—"

"Explain? Apologize? What the *fuck* is the point of that?"

"I was going to talk to you about this today. I swear, baby, I was going to talk to you about this today."

"How could—?"

"Sheila, Sheila, it's not what I wanted. You know it's not what I wanted, but I think we can work this—ouch! Stop— now!"

They had never fought with their hands. Kenya stood up and banged on the door.

"Mom! Baba! Baba!" she yelled. No one answered her. She heard only an occasional curse, scuffling, and a slap. A dull thud. She slid down the door and sat on the creaking wood floor. She wanted to go somewhere else in the house and ignore them, or even walk out the front door. That would show both of them—if they ever came out of that room.

Their muffled voices started up again and she covered her

ears and hummed. Then she started singing all of the songs she knew by heart; songs she liked ("My Cherie Amour") and songs she hated ("Ain't No Stoppin' Us Now," to which the fifth grade had to perform a humiliating dance on May Day), songs that made no sense (like *Here's my chance to dance my way, out of my constrictions*). She was trying to sing a solo fugue when the door whipped open and she fell backward.

"Kenya!" her mother yelped, and then abruptly leaned down, pulling Kenya up into her arms. Her eyes were ringed with black. Kenya hadn't known she wore eye makeup. It made her cry. "Shhhhh," Sheila said. "Shhhhhhhh. It's okay. I'm going to make dinner."

"Hi, Monkey," her father said. He still stood in the room, amid ruins.

"Are you going to get a divorce?" Kenya mumbled into her mother's chest. She couldn't believe she was asking this, that this was happening. She remembered how confident she'd been the year before when she'd comforted Charlena, how sure she'd been that Charlena's family would fall apart, and that hers would stay together.

"I'm sorry you heard all of that, Kenya. We're all going to sit down and have dinner and talk," said Sheila.

Johnbrown and Sheila moved stiffly about the downstairs as if there was some danger of their touching. Kenya stood staring out of the window like TV characters did when they were thinking about something weighty. But all she could see were the boards on the windows. Sheila had gone from suggesting dinner in a calm voice to slamming pots in the kitchen, as if she'd just remembered reality. Johnbrown came over to Kenya and smoothed her cornrows.

"You're my life," he said.

But apparently she wasn't.

It seemed that Johnbrown Curtis and Cindalou Matthews had fallen in love, and that Cindalou Matthews was carrying Johnbrown Curtis's baby, Kenya's brother or sister. At that Sheila snorted, "Half," as they sat at the table, picking over spaghetti.

"Don't be like that, Sheila," said Johnbrown. "We're not like that. We're not like my mother." It seemed crazy to Kenya that Johnbrown was still talking. She nearly emptied the canister of powdery Parmesan cheese onto her plate, stopping only when her mother said her name sharply.

"So *are* you going to get a divorce?" Kenya asked again.

Her parents looked at each other. Johnbrown cleared his throat.

"Well, now is as good a time as any to speak to you both about something I wanted to ask."

If Kenya had been older, she would have seen her mother's eyes fill with anticipation and the hope that whatever Johnbrown offered would save them all. As it was, all Kenya saw was a withering glare. Not that it mattered, given what her father said next.

"With your permission, Sheila and Kenya, I'd like for Cindalou and the baby to move in here. I'd like for us all to be a family."

"What did you say?" Sheila asked. She dabbed at her mouth with a napkin and looked genuinely as if she hadn't heard, as if she was asking for a small clarification: *Did you say "cream or sugar"? Lemonade? You want me to pass the lemonade?*

"Well, Cindalou and I have been going to some events at the Yoruba temple and—"

"Oh, you actually go *out*? Of the house? Glad to hear *that*."

"And I don't think the temple is for me. I mean, organized religion is organized religion, but some of the families, in the traditional African—"

"Get back to the point. So you want to move that bitch and her bastard up in here? Where I pay the mortgage? I'm not understanding what this has to do with the temple. Because from what I know about traditional West African polygamy (Lord Jesus have mercy!), the man supports the family. No, brother. *I* make the money." And here she laughed. "What you proposing is pimping and—"

"Sheila," Johnbrown said.

"—I AM NOT A WHORE!"

Kenya was tired of crying. Her head hurt. She was thirsty but the thought of apple juice on her tongue made her nearly hysterical. Her mother looked at her across the table, her purple skin and wide brown eyes in a gorgeous blaze.

"No, Kenya," she said, lowering the volume and sweetening her voice with a flourish, "your father and I are not *getting* a divorce because we never *got* married."

"Sheila!" Johnbrown yelled.

"Stop saying my name."

Kenya felt sure that she'd never been more miserable. Then, as if to make herself feel worse, to see how much she could stand, she fell again into the memory of Charlena and the girl's fear about her parents breaking up. Kenya remembered how smugly secure she'd felt about Johnbrown and

Sheila's marriage. *Marriage!* Now Charlena's mom was pregnant and their family was moving to a bigger house. Charlena might even have to transfer schools. Frankly, Kenya was more broken up about that than Charlena was. Now it was Kenya who sometimes proposed playing *Star Wars*, and a little desperately at that.

"But you—" Kenya tried again with her parents.

"We thought it would confuse you. Also, I don't know that we ever agreed on the whole setup. See, your father, this principled man here, doesn't believe in marriage. He didn't see why the government had to be involved in our family life. He didn't need a piece of paper to be committed to us, he said. But maybe, you know if I ever speak to that bitch Cindalou again, I should tell her she needs to *get that paper.*"

Johnbrown rubbed at his temples, staring down at his plate. "This wasn't what I wanted at all. This wasn't the way to go about this at all."

"Go about what? Is there a way to go about cheating on your wife with her girlfriend? Oh no, you're probably talking about some bullshit like the right way to propose half-assed polygamy to your family. Maybe there's a strategy of some sort, or some literature I could have brought from *my job!* The one I keep to support this *family.*"

Something, Kenya wasn't sure what, switched over and her parents assumed their normal fighting positions.

Johnbrown screeched at Sheila that her problem was that she wouldn't let a man be himself.

Sheila asked calmly what Johnbrown thought a man was and how he thought the definition applied to him.

Johnbrown said this was exactly the kind of conversation

he never had with Cindalou. Abruptly, Sheila said, "I see your mother every year. She gives us money."

Johnbrown clenched his fists. "I need to go," he said. "I just need to get out of here, because otherwise—"

"So GO!"

But he didn't, not just yet. The three of them sat trapped, not eating their cold spaghetti in the dim dining room. By now it was probably night outside, but Kenya couldn't tell.

Then, after an eternity, with a final pleading look at Sheila, Johnbrown got up and left. No one ever found out where he went, because of what happened when he returned, what happened with a sleepwalking Kenya and his lawfully registered gun.

The Little Princess

Sometimes Kenya thought that if the world before the walk she took with her father could be real, then the world on the other side could not be. Sheila had been shot. It was years before Kenya could say in her mind *I shot my mother in the shoulder.* Whether she'd been asleep or not, it made her want to die.

That late-spring night was a blur that reminded Kenya of a sickening amusement park ride. Johnbrown, who did not have a license, driving them crazily to the hospital; Sheila cursing, sobbing, and bleeding; Johnbrown ordering Kenya to stay quiet at the hospital when they asked what happened. He would take the blame for the shooting, he said. Kenya should not worry. He would take the blame, he kept repeating. The last image of her father Kenya had for a long time was him kneeling, as if praying, as he dripped tears on her mother's hospital bed.

After it became clear that Sheila would be okay, Johnbrown had fled the hospital, off with Cindalou, her mother guessed, to who knows where. But to Kenya it felt like she and her mother were the ones who had disappeared, going to stay at Grandmama's home. Kenya now noticed that the air there was always damp and the house contained odd things, like an extensive collection of old used toothbrushes and all of her dead husband's shoes.

In Johnbrown's absence, it was Sheila who mustered the "brave" smiles. Also, even after she healed and stopped taking pain pills she often stared into the distance, reminding Kenya of Brother Camden and his loose eye. It occurred to Kenya sometime after everything happened that she wouldn't even mind seeing Brother Camden now.

On the other hand, the thought of Cindalou and her dumb fruity smell made Kenya's stomach lurch. One sweltering afternoon, Kenya walked past the room where her mother slept and heard ragged crying. Until then, her mother hadn't cried, or at least Kenya hadn't heard it. Now the sounds she made seemed to hurt. Kenya went into her own room, with its ugly series of Harlequin pictures and its scratchy afghan, made by Grandmama's mother. She took out a notebook and pen and wrote: CINDALOU MATTHEWS.

Then she went into the backyard by the ugly pink rosebush, made sure no one was watching, took out one of Grandmama's cheap lighters, and burned the paper, watching it blacken and curl.

Just before the school year started, Sheila and Kenya moved into a place of their own in the town right next to Grandmama's. Sheila did the house hunting on her own, so by the time Kenya laid eyes on the large apartment building of yellow-brown brick, it was her home. A well-maintained sign that reminded Kenya of fifties sitcom credits advertised it in cursive as the *Ardmore Arms*. At the desk in the entryway, which smelled of bad breath, there was a fat white guard, who watched Sheila struggle with a box so she could sign in. He greeted her only when she finally said a starched "Hello." This was how they would interact until Kenya and Sheila moved out nearly a year later.

The apartment, with its yellowed-ivory walls and beige carpets, was the kind of place that Kenya had heard Sheila call "charmless" in the past. "Here we are," Sheila said in a flat voice the first time they entered. Kenya recalled books she'd read where families had to move and mothers and fathers pleaded with reluctant children to admire the new backyard swing or their brand-new blue bedroom. Sheila said nothing of the sort; she never asked whether Kenya liked it or not. So Kenya never mentioned how intrigued she was by the sensation of wall-to-wall carpeting underfoot, or how much she enjoyed having boardless windows. At a certain time of day, the apartment, including her chalk-yellow bedroom, would flood with light and things would seem okay. In the beginning, at least.

While Grandmama's initial plan had been to send Kenya to the best local public school, she also insisted that Kenya take the test for the fancy private one down the road. So before she even set foot in the local junior high, Kenya was accepted to the Barrett School for Girls, with a decent scholarship. This was all provided she would repeat fifth grade, as was standard for all entrants from the city school system.

Completely unmoved by Kenya's indignation about being held back, Grandmama was insistent. "Of course you'll go there! My mother used to wash the floors and clean the bathrooms for those filthy—*little girls.*" Grandmama's parents had been of the generation that was middle class on the weekends, at their churches and social clubs, but cleaned floors and swallowed bitterness during the week. "Now you're going there," she said, coughing, which she sometimes did until her eyes watered, and clapping her hands. *"You'll show them."*

"How to become a filthy little girl?" Kenya asked.

"What a little colored girl can do!"

While Grandmama plotted her revenge, Sheila offered up a faint smile. She didn't even try to catch Kenya's eye the way she used to when Grandmama said *colored*. When Kenya whined about repeating the grade, Sheila shrugged.

"Maybe starting last year all over again is not such a bad idea," she said.

Kenya could not argue with that.

At one end, the Barrett School for Girls looked like a castle, with its stone walls, decorative roofs, impossibly high ceilings, and ancient-looking tapestries. At the other, it was low and sleek, like something in one of the architecture magazines Kenya's father had collected during a brief phase. In fact, whatever wasn't old at the school seemed extremely new. The white desks reminded Kenya of spaceships, and many of the rooms had track lighting.

The cafeteria was called a dining room. There you could eat roast chicken for lunch, served up by black women—the only black adults in the building besides the cleaning ladies. As they spooned mashed potatoes onto her plate, they beamed Kenya smiles she was too embarrassed to return. She wondered if they traded smiles with the smattering of other black girls who went to Barrett (twelve by her count the first week).

She could not imagine Lolly Lewis, the only other black girl in her grade, who lived in Wynnewood and had gone to Barrett since kindergarten, joining in this conspiracy of greeting.

Each day at Barrett was a new sensory experience for Kenya: chilly stone hallways; clammy modeling clay; picking impossibly sticky long hairs off her schoolbag; a school uniform of scratchy bloomers with a navy-blue dress called a tunic or a gray skirt called a kilt; a rubbery-tasting mouthguard for field hockey; the sound of hand bells; *what shall we do with a drunken sailor*; the distinct sneaker-fart funk of the school bus; a gym teacher with a British accent; dreidl (*dreidl, dreidl*); cupcakes for Trinity Howell's birthday, cupcakes for Katherine Stein's birthday, cupcakes for Sengu Gupta's birthday; body on fire with cold as Kenya finally, after two weeks of increasingly irritable cajoling from Mrs. Winston, forced herself into the pool in gym class.

Once Kenya was underwater, she tried to stay as long as she could. The murky echoes, soft shapes, and slow movement suited her. Everyone at Barrett was *so nice*. The school was *so nice*. Yet she did not want to come back up to the surface.

Being black on the Main Line was *no fuckin' picnic*, her father had said.

Kenya was careful never to say to these new girls that her parents were "divorced," but she led them to believe this was the case. Divorce, so shocking to her before, was almost fashionable at Barrett. Cynthia Malder and Kristin Shoenbaum were children of divorce. Tuff Wieder and Sharon McCall were children of long-term separation. Mothers were starting interior design businesses and dating old men. Fathers were buying sports cars and dating young secretaries. All Kenya said was that her parents were "not together," and that she didn't talk to her father very much. No, she didn't go live with him and a bitchy stepmother in the summer. No, they didn't go on vacation.

The fifth graders who attended the Barrett School for Girls had heard a lot of crazy things about the city. They'd heard that kids their age carried knives to school, and that everyone was on welfare. They'd heard that being on the street after dark was a sure way to get mugged. They'd never heard the one about the family where the father was cheating on the mother, the father-not-husband because they were never married, the one where the father suggested that they all live together in a polygamous arrangement. They didn't know the one that ended with the sleepwalking daughter shooting the mother with the father's gun; they didn't know the one that began when the father, trying to keep the daughter out of foster care, said he would take the blame—then disappeared into America with his pregnant girlfriend. Kenya wasn't going to tell them any of those.

Sheila said little to Kenya about their new lives. In the void, as Kenya learned to sing in French and play lacrosse, she kept hearing Johnbrown's voice. The "shame of being alive" *was* in fact the shame of being black and having a mere ten minutes to untangle your hair in the locker room after swimming. And some days she heard his voice saying: "Meanwhile, some kids in West Philly don't have books. Shit don't make sense."

Back in her other life Kenya's parents had even argued over whether they should allow Kenya to participate in the Mentally Gifted program at Lea School. The principal had been a parchment-colored snob who was so excited about the twenty white students who went there that all of them, even an excitable boy named Benjamin, whose knuckles practically dragged on the floor, were in MG. Johnbrown, who had originally talked about homeschooling her until it became clear that he would have to be the teacher, thought MG would make Kenya "an elitist."

"You're being a fanatic," Sheila had said. "But I'm not drinking your Kool-Aid. It's not like we're talking about private school."

"And we never would, Sheila, we never would."

"Well, with only one of us working, we could never afford it."

"Oh, is that why? Because I didn't know that was the reason. I thought the reason was we were raising a black child who wouldn't hate herself any more than this *sick* society already wants her to."

"Don't you dare give me one of your speeches, Johnbrown."

Sheila's winning the battle over Mentally Gifted meant mainly that Kenya got to go to movies and plays where the characters had British accents. ("Satisfied?" her father asked her mother, rolling his eyes when Kenya missed an entire day of school to go to a local production of *A Christmas Carol*.)

"How is the Barrett School for Girls?" her mother would ask now, every evening at their sad dinners at the kitchen counter in the Ardmore Arms. Sheila cooked on the same schedule as before, but now everything was drier. She had started going to Weight Watchers, which surprised Kenya, who'd never thought about her mother's weight.

Most nights Kenya said that school was "fine," which, she supposed, it was. But one night, struggling to swallow baked ziti without enough sauce, she said, "Remember that fight you and Baba had about private school? He never wanted me to go."

"Well, I didn't either."

Kenya blurted, "What do you think he'd say if he knew about Barrett?"

"He wouldn't care," Sheila said in a brassy voice.

Kenya felt the hit in her chest.

"I shouldn't put it that way," said her mother, more softly. "The truth is he's got his own problems."

What Kenya knew was that Johnbrown was doing okay somewhere in America. A few months after she and her mother moved into the Ardmore Arms, the first postcard arrived. Kenya had looked without seeing it, an ugly picture of St. Louis, which she put in the mail pile. Sheila had an old library school friend who lived in San Francisco and traveled a lot. No matter where she went, Houston, Bermuda, or Mexico, she sent a faded-looking postcard. That afternoon, Kenya looked up to see her mother in the doorway of Kenya's room, holding this one.

"Your father sent this," she said.

"I thought it was Aunt Sandy."

"Nope."

The postcard was written in block letters. *Thinking of you every day*, it said. *Every day, thinking of you. All my love. B.B.*

"How do you know this is from him?" Kenya asked.

Sheila wrinkled her nose at Kenya's unmade bed and started making it up. She spoke as she moved. "We used to talk sometimes at Seven Days meetings about if one of us had to run."

"Run from what?" If they'd had this conversation more than once, she hadn't heard it.

"It was just talk as far as we were concerned. But you know back in the day a lot of movement people wound up on the wrong side of the law. Anyway, sometimes those people would run because they knew they wouldn't get a fair trial. And if they had to leave family behind, they would send cards sometimes, but not from anyplace they were currently."

"So all this says is he's not in St. Louis."

"It says more than that."

Kenya rolled her eyes. "You mean it says he loves me?"

"Well, it does," Sheila said.

"Mom, how long is this going to go on? I mean, what would happen if he got caught?"

Sheila looked around Kenya's room, furnished with the small child's desk they'd borrowed from Grandmama and the tall shelf of books of which Kenya was proud. There was a dresser, a couple of orange crates full of board games brought from the city, and that was basically it. Kenya hadn't decorated the ugly yellow walls, feeling too angry at the Black History Month calendar pictures and UNICEF posters of the world's brown children that her mother had hung in her old room back in the city, but not knowing where to go next.

Instead of answering, Sheila said, "You would think you would go crazy in here with nothing on the walls."

"Mom!"

"I don't know what would happen, okay? There's a warrant out for his arrest for . . . what happened."

Kenya looked down, but the world kept spinning and her mother kept talking. "I told them I wouldn't testify against him, but he claims the prosecutor is out to get him."

"Is he?"

"I don't know. But the other thing is . . ." And here she managed to roll her eyes, even as they filled with water. "There's stuff I didn't know about."

"What?"

Sheila sighed. "Well, I guess your father and Cindalou were going around vandalizing police stations? So your father's on probation and he already spent a night in jail."

Kenya remembered when she'd awoken to the sound of her parents arguing about where her father had spent the night. He claimed he'd fallen asleep in the library. Maybe he'd been in jail. Or, she thought, feeling queasy, making a baby with Cindalou.

"What's going to happen?" she asked.

"I really don't know," Sheila said, her face wet with unacknowledged tears. Then, as if she absolutely couldn't stand up anymore, she sat down on Kenya's bed.

It was not the tears but the sitting that did it. Kenya found that when she went to ask her mother more questions, her mouth would not move. *How could you not know all of this? Is Baba a crazy person?*

"Okay," said Kenya. "Okay."

Shortly after that conversation, Kenya realized she'd squandered what might have been her last chance to ask about what had happened to their family. The subjects of Johnbrown, Cindalou, and even the Seven Days had been sealed up underground, like the man in the Edgar Allan Poe story she had read at school.

One subject that didn't need to be closed, as it had never been opened, was how Kenya, sleeping, came to hold a loaded gun, and why she chose to aim it at her mother. The one thing Kenya felt sure of was that she had not had to unearth the gun from its hiding place in the basement. One of her parents had taken it out. She never found out which one it was. She could easily imagine Sheila going for it in a moment of indignant rage, or Johnbrown moving it to keep it from Sheila's hands. Or maybe it was the desperate Johnbrown trying finally to win a fight.

When Kenya asked herself, of all things, why, even sleeping, she would shoot her mother, no answer suggested itself. Whenever she found herself pondering this question, she felt that a cord had snapped and she was flying away from her body.

That December, Sheila and Kenya did not have to make a special secret trip to Bryn Mawr to see Grandmama. Instead they were invited to Christmas dinner at her house. "Nothing fancy," she had promised.

Knowing Grandmama, like attending Barrett, was a constant education for Kenya about the well-to-do. For instance, while she dreamed, in spite of Grandmama's warning, that the house would be decked out with scarlet ribbons and softly glowing white candles, there was only a squat businesslike tree hung with a few pink balls and an ugly clay ornament that Kenya had made at Barrett. At the top sat a black angel with a white chip in its cheek.

"When your father was young," Grandmama said as they sat at the dining room table, "we would all go with the man who worked for us to chop down a tree. I thought it was splendid fun. But oh, John would moan and groan about the weather."

"He never did like the cold," Sheila said with a distant look.

"Kenya, we'll have to take you to the Christmas farm one day to pick out a real tree," said Grandmama. "You seem like you might be made of some pretty sturdy fiber."

More education: sometimes for Christmas the upper classes served slices of turkey and pale stuffing out of Acme supermarket cartons, and gifted ill-fitting sweaters that smelled distinctly like basement. All of this made Kenya feel she had not been cheated by Kwanzaa after all. But then again, Kwanzaa dinner back on Irving Street was an altogether different beast from the one she now shared with her mother on Umoja at the Ardmore Arms. Kenya had never enjoyed listening to her father talk about the stifling confines of the slave hold while supposedly enjoying a holiday. But now she longed to hear anyone talk with interest about anything at all as she pushed around her mother's brandied chicken, which had been more edible in the pre–Weight Watchers days.

Though it seemed like it would have been Johnbrown's idea, Sheila had been the one to push for Kwanzaa. Johnbrown thought Karenga was a huckster who would one day become rich from something called "licensing." He often brought up the fact that Kwanzaa was an American creation, rather than an African tradition. "It's a Hanukkah rip," he had once said, "and that's barely a real holiday to start with."

"So why do we do it?" Kenya had asked.

"It's not always about complaining and tearing everything down," Sheila said firmly. "People need celebrations."

The word *celebration* would not have come to anyone's mind observing Kenya and her mother during the seven nights of their first holiday in the suburbs. At one time Kenya had viewed the length of Kwanzaa as an advantage over Christmas, which was one lousy day that peaked well before noon. But now, Kenya dreaded each night of Kwanzaa in the Ardmore Arms, where she would face her mother at the kitchen table, making promises like being extra kind to the girls in Daughters of Isis, the black students' group, and working harder on her math homework. On the second night they hosted Grandmama, who kept saying how interesting it all was and insisted on trying to pronounce the pertinent Swahili words.

"You know, Kiswahili is not a real language," she announced, clearing her throat, after a botched attempt to say *Kujichagulia*. "It's a mishmash of other languages."

"Well, it's a trading language," Sheila said without commitment. Kenya noticed that her mother rarely disagreed with Grandmama.

That night, after Grandmama left, Sheila mysteriously produced a can of beer, which she sipped as she cornrowed Kenya's hair. They watched *It's a Wonderful Life* without really watching, and Kenya remembered her father's running commentary about "fantasy capitalism." She recalled that the Seven Days once bitterly debated Christmas and whether it was "categorically antirevolutionary," as her father put it, which especially angered Earl. As if reading her mind, Sheila said, "They knew."

"Who knew what?"

"All of them knew about your father and Cindalou."

Kenya twisted around to look at her mother's face. "You mean the Days?"

"Yeah, the *Seven Days*," snorted her mother.

"Did someone tell you that?"

"They didn't have to. How could they not know? And if I know your father, he was building his case to them."

"Ow," Kenya said. Her mother's braiding became unpredictable when she grew agitated.

"I know that didn't hurt," Sheila said.

Kenya didn't contradict her.

"Oh fuck this. It's making my teeth hurt," her mother said, indicating the television with her head. She worked the remote control until she landed on an old episode of *Star Trek*.

"Mom," said Kenya, "wouldn't someone have told you? Yaya?"

"You would think," she said in an acid voice. "But I guess they didn't want to break up their precious group."

"You were part of it, too."

"Not like them, Kenya. I mean, yeah, I was part of it. And I believed in it. But not like your father."

Kenya did not ask her mother to elaborate, but she continued talking anyway. "I'm going to level with you. You know I grew up in the projects. It wasn't bad when I was little. It was just a decent place you lived with a bunch of other black people who worked hard, but it fell apart when the drugs and guns came in. Folks started going to jail, getting strung out, getting dead. The way I figured it, not getting pregnant, going to college, having a decent job, and taking care of my family was doing something for the community." Sheila had taken her hands out of Kenya's hair to make a mock-grandiose gesture when she said *community*. Then she turned Kenya back around roughly and continued to cornrow.

"On the other hand, people like your father, or even Yaya and Robert, they grew up with daddies and all of that. They had a little bit more to prove, especially your father. He liked to tell a lot of stories, but did he ever tell you the one about when he used to run with some Panthers and a bunch of them got picked up by some white cops?"

Kenya shook her head no.

"Keep your head still. Yeah, well, everybody got slammed against some brick wall. They were all about to get hauled downtown and strip-searched, and your father pulled out a little card his mother had snuck into his wallet and gave it to them. So he got to go home without a hair out of place."

"Okay," said Kenya.

Sheila laughed. "I mean shit, I was the community. 'Course, I wasn't a backwoods charity case like some people."

Cindalou.

"Uhura," Sheila said, now talking about the black woman in an aerodynamic minidress on the television. "You know she wanted to quit this show and Martin Luther King called her and asked her not to? Because she was a role model? Like Martin Luther King didn't have anything better to do that day?"

The summer before Kenya's second year at Barrett, Grandmama died of lung cancer. Kenya had grown used to her cough and didn't think it was unusual that Grandmama often excused herself for several minutes of hacking in the bathroom. Kenya had also gotten used to finding the occasional tissue delicately spotted with blood around Grandmama's house.

"You need to get that cough checked out, Eveline," her mother would say gently.

"For what?" Grandmama would ask drily. "For them to tell me it's a cough?"

At Barrett, Kenya's science class had been subjected to a terrifying weeklong unit on smoking. Phyllis Fagin had run weeping out of class and tried to win an audience at lunch wailing that her dad smoked cigars, which was even worse! It was true that Phyllis was, as the other girls said, a "drama queen," but maybe Kenya might have cried, too, if she'd thought something like cancer could happen in her family. Family such as it was.

When she died, Grandmama's few remaining friends were dreaming away their days in nursing homes, which she called "the poppy fields." Her funeral was a small cemetery affair on a muggy July morning, attended by Sheila, Kenya, a few neighbors, and Grandmama's oldest sentient friend, a black dentist. Kenya had met the large, slow-moving, and deep-voiced Dr. Walton before. Grandmama had spoken proudly of his accomplishments as the only black dentist on the Main Line, but bitterly of what she characterized as his eagerness to get his hands into the mouths of white people.

The service was presided over by the young minister of the Episcopalian church Grandmama had long since stopped attending. He kept mispronouncing her name, evidently confusing it with the name of the wicked witch in *The Wiz*.

Kenya couldn't cry. She did not feel the acute sting of sadness so much as a heavy, damp feeling. For days after the funeral, she tried to snap herself out of the strange spell cast by Grandmama's death. One night, unable to sleep, she charged out of her room and into the living room, where Sheila sat watching a police show that she repeatedly denounced as racist but never missed.

"Kenya?" Sheila said in an alarmed voice.

"I'm awake!"

"Of course."

"You thought I was sleepwalking," said Kenya accusingly. Sheila rolled her eyes. "What are you doing up?"

"I'm sorry," said Kenya.

"Sorry—?"

"I'm sorry I shot you!"

"What?"

"I'm sorry. Everything is my fault. It's because of that. But I didn't mean to do it. I didn't mean—I don't remember—"

"Come here," said Sheila.

Kenya cried then while Sheila stroked her head and told her it wasn't her fault. Kenya had been sleeping, Sheila said; who knows what happened, everyone was fine, her shoulder had healed quickly, it didn't matter.

After her tears had dried, Kenya pulled out of her mother's arms to face her. "I know you say it wasn't my fault. But do you forgive me?"

Sheila's face grew strange. Not angry, but as if she was trying not to say something. "I forgive you," she said.

Kenya nodded.

"I'm okay, Kenya," Sheila said, turning to stare straight

ahead at the television, "but it hurts too much to think about it. Can you understand that?"

"Yes," Kenya said in a whisper, tears gathering again in her throat.

"No more crying," her mother said. "There's been enough crying."

Kenya thought of the one time she'd heard her mother secretly sobbing. She thought of her father dripping snot and tears over her mother in the hospital. There had not actually been a lot of crying, she thought. But perhaps her mother was right that more would not help.

A few months after Grandmama's death, Kenya watched Alma Lewis, the mother of her one black classmate, sweep through Grandmama's house with Sheila at her heels.

"Estate sale, hun," Alma Lewis said, touching a yellow porcelain lamp. "Darling, please, county dump," she said, touching a chipped glass table.

Sheila protectively caressed the coral-pink silk sofa where Kenya sat curled up with her English homework. "You don't think just take the plastic cover off? Vintage?"

"Repeat after me," said Mrs. Lewis. "E-state sale. I think she'll get it after a while, don't you, Kenya?"

Kenya nodded.

Grandmama had left most of her money to a medical charity in Africa. To Kenya explicitly, she left a modest amount to continue helping pay for Barrett, which Kenya didn't know she had been doing already. To Sheila she left the house and a tidy sum for upkeep and taxes. She and her mother would be moving into the house.

Kenya remembered back when they lived in the city, driving back from those secret visits when Sheila spoke derisively of Grandmama's house with its six bedrooms and four bathrooms. "Shit don't make no sense," she'd say. "My foster sister and I slept in one bedroom! My mother slept on the couch. That woman has one grown-ass child who doesn't even speak to her. What she need six bedrooms for?"

Now Sheila seemed to like the idea of multiple bathrooms and to enjoy calling the downstairs toilet a "powder room." Kenya wondered if her mother had actually changed, or if this was just life without her father's ideas about what was right and wrong. Maybe it was only inevitable that a girl from the projects might like to have a powder room.

What did not seem at all inevitable, and gave Kenya a sensation close to fear, was that Sheila could enjoy the company of someone like Alma Lewis, a thick-figured, brown-skinned woman who wore noticeably pale face powder. Alma's curious accent combined the way uneducated white people in Philadelphia spoke with the sharp inflections of Mrs. Winston, the British gym teacher: like white people from scary racist neighborhoods, she said "hun"; like Mrs. Winston, she said "darling." Now Kenya suppressed a cough as the scent of Mrs. Lewis's Giorgio cologne filled the house. As popular as it was among Main Line mothers, it smelled to Kenya like burnt pastries.

Mrs. Lewis spoke to her again. "Wouldn't you like some brand-new furniture, Kenya?" she asked as her manicured and bejeweled hand rested—threateningly, Kenya thought—on Grandmama's dish of blue peppermints.

"I guess," Kenya said, wondering for a split second if Alma Lewis was planning to buy these new things for them.

"And when you get the place all fixed up, you can finally have a party."

"Why couldn't I have a party before?" Kenya asked.

"Want to take a look upstairs, Alma?" asked Sheila.

Kenya tried to focus on her homework. But even when the women toured upstairs, phrases like "recessed lighting" and "wainscoting" and "good bones" came shooting out of Sheila's mouth and ricocheted about the house.

"Alma, don't forget to give me your decorator's number," Sheila was saying as they came back down.

"Of *course*, darling," sang Alma. "Lars is like family to us, so please mention my name. My husband hates to see him coming. He knows it's just going to be more money getting up and walking out the door." She laughed. Sheila tried.

"How *does* somebody black get to be so *phony*?" Sheila asked Kenya as they watched Mrs. Lewis get into her Jaguar from the tall windows of their new-old house.

"Her daughter's even worse," said Kenya.

Before she knew anything, Kenya had tried to make friends with Grace Lewis, who was called Lolly for some unknown reason. Lolly wasn't especially nice to Kenya but was too nice to tell her to go somewhere with herself, and so the friendship had stuck. Lolly's best friend was Phyllis Fagin. Though as far as Kenya could see, Phyllis Fagin, who had shiny black hair and dark green eyes, was the prettiest girl in their class, she was universally regarded as a spaz. It was unclear what had drawn Lolly and Phyllis together, but Kenya noticed that Lolly seemed to actively enjoy betraying her friend. On more than one occasion, Kenya was nearby when someone said something nasty about Phyllis that was flattering to Lolly, like "I don't know how you can hang out with her." When this happened, Lolly would respond with a secret about Phyllis—she used baking soda instead of toothpaste, for instance, or that her mother made some of her clothes.

As for herself, Kenya was not grateful for Lolly's polite friendship, because the girl was nearly insufferable. Often she screamed "Oh my God," flecking white spit everywhere; she still believed militantly in the tooth fairy, the Easter Bunny, and Santa Claus. (In music the class learned to sing spirituals. The teacher, Miss Clyburn, the first adult Kenya had seen with braces, asked, "Does anyone know why Afro-Americans came to this country from Africa?")

"I don't know, Kenya. Maybe we shouldn't be so harsh," Sheila was saying.

(In music class, Lolly Lewis raised her hand. "For a better life?")

"Maybe we should be harsher," Kenya said.

But Sheila was already walking toward the back of the house. "Finish your homework, all right? Might be a while before we get back to the apartment."

Kenya was not excited about the move to Grandmama's house. It was true that she would have been embarrassed to have company from Barrett at the Ardmore Arms. She'd soured on the place once she discovered that no one—but no one—lived in an apartment. Some families did, of course, own apartments in Florida or Manhattan, or even apartment buildings in Philadelphia. From her research at other Barrett girls' houses, she'd discovered that everything at the Ardmore Arms was old, but not in a grand way. Still, something in Kenya rebelled at the idea of taking possession of Grandmama's large house, the house where her father had learned that *being black was no fuckin' picnic*. And she had the sense that because of her mother's passion for moving on, they were getting further away from where they could be found.

Despite her distaste for Lolly, and the fact that Phyllis Fagin had little to recommend her, Kenya became their third wheel. Zaineb Husain, a small, pointy-looking girl who had recently transferred to Barrett from a public school in the suburbs, eventually joined them. Kenya felt cheered when she discovered that, like her, Zaineb had to repeat a grade. She also found it endearing that in contrast to the excitable Lolly and hand-wringing Phyllis, Zaineb always seemed tired. By Kenya's second year at Barrett, the four of them had calcified into a clique.

It was clear to Kenya that what drew them together was not laughing, fun, or a shared passion, but seating charts, laziness, and the desire to move in a group. Just about every Barrett student from kindergarten up aspired toward numbers. Kenya couldn't quite understand the fear of being alone there. There was no L'Tisha Simmons or Mrs. Prescott to publicly humiliate you, as there had been at Lea. And yet at Barrett, walking the halls or waiting for the school bus alone seemed unimaginable. Only Dorrie Futter, who vocally expressed her love of science and had a pet tarantula, shrugged with indifference when she had to partner up with the teacher, and preferred to eat her lunch by herself. She sat nearby but not with Kenya's group. Kenya sometimes wondered what she thought of their conversations, or if she was even listening as she wolfed down her food so she could read the books of Piers Anthony and chew on her hair.

"Mr. Stauffer is, like, so nice," Phyllis was saying now, as if it wasn't clear to everyone that she had a crush on the burly, red-nosed history teacher.

"He's not *that* nice," said Zaineb. "He only gave me a B-plus on the paper."

"I wonder if he's married," said Phyllis.

"He's, like, thirty! Who cares?" said Lolly, which reminded Kenya that she'd overheard her in the locker room telling Lizzie Canwell that Phyllis was in love with Mr. Stauffer.

"He doesn't wear a ring," said Kenya, though she knew from her father and mother, who had both worn gold bands, that wearing rings didn't mean much.

"Oh my God, Kenya, you're right!" said Phyllis.

"So what, Phyllis? Are you going to marry him?" asked Zaineb, pushing up her glasses.

"God, Zaineb!" Phyllis yelled.

"Maybe he dates one of the other teachers," said Kenya. Sometimes she participated in these conversations like the others. Other times she half listened while caught up in her own thoughts and daydreams. In particular she daydreamed about having an actual best friend: someone who would laugh at her jokes and sit intently on the opposite of a long gossipy phone call, saying "Oooooooh!"; someone who also liked the minor-key songs on the radio—"What Is Love" by Howard

Jones and the mournful "If You Were Here" by the Thompson Twins. She thought of a McDonald's commercial she'd seen featuring two white girls who laughed and whispered together, jumped in the rain with matching raincoats, and then ate cheeseburgers, alternating bites with sips of milkshake. The commercial had pierced her with yearning.

"So your birthday falls on a Saturday this year, Kenya," Sheila announced, a month before Kenya was to turn thirteen.

"That's nice," said Kenya. The winter holidays had just ended, and while Kenya didn't particularly enjoy lonely Kwanzaas with her mother, she had enjoyed staying home from Barrett. "I won't have to go to school on my birthday this year."

"Well, no, but I meant maybe you might want to have, you know, a party. You could invite Grace Lewis and the other Daughters of Isis."

"Uh-huh," Kenya answered. She didn't mention that Lolly was not really part of Daughters of Isis. Only two or so meetings per year brought the Daughters of Isis together, at events that were mostly for their parents. When they ran into one another in the high-ceilinged halls of Barrett, they would make sure no one white was looking before they mumbled hello. A couple of them were nice. There was Sarabeth in the Upper School, who enjoyed regaling younger girls with stories about the boys she'd gone with, including the one who liked to put his penis on her stomach. There was China, who always talked about Prince, who would recount the plot of *Purple Rain* if you gave her even a second. Her favorite scene involved Prince luring Apollonia into a cold lake. "Prince totally has a great sense of humor," she would say. "That's what makes him my type." (Kenya could sense the tragedy in China, dark-skinned, tall for her age, and heavy of hip, fantasizing about a romance with the fey and creamy Prince. But she would not understand the extent of the tragedy until the monstrous-black-mammy dream sequence in *Under the Cherry Moon*.)

"Well, who do *you* want to invite?" Sheila persisted. "Besides Grace Lewis."

"It's Lolly."

"What's Lolly?"

"They call Grace Lolly," Kenya said, her voice teetering on the edge of snotty. Then she became outright reckless. "I've been telling you that for two years. Anyway, you just want to show off the house to her mother."

"First of all, Alma refers to her as Grace. And second of all, who do you think you're talking to?" Sheila asked. "I know how those white girls talk to their mothers." (She knew because Kenya had told her about it with amazement: "*Mo-om, you're so stupid!*") "Start talking to me like that and you'll be lucky to have a birthday, let alone a party."

"Fine, then. Let's not have a party," Kenya said.

Sheila's face crumpled. "You really don't want a party?"

A few days later at lunch Kenya reluctantly invited her friends.

"Oh my God, awesome!" said Phyllis. "Can we get beer?"

Lolly seemed nervous. "Who are you gonna invite? I mean, besides us."

"I don't know," said Kenya. "It's my mom's idea."

"My mom loves throwing birthday parties," Lolly said.

"I know," said Kenya.

"So who *are* you going to invite?" Zaineb asked.

"Guys, don't talk so loud," said Phyllis, gesturing toward Dorrie Futter with her head. But Kenya vaguely wondered what it would be like to have Dorrie Futter at her house. She had even tried unsuccessfully to talk to her a few times, but the truth was that Dorrie Futter was not especially friendly.

The more Lolly, Phyllis, and Zaineb discussed it, the more miserable Kenya began to feel about the whole thing. Though much had changed in her life, she and her mother still didn't eat pork, so she wouldn't be allowed to order pepperoni on any of the pizzas; they'd be stuck with plain old cheese and then some disgusting slices clotted with dry vegetables. Kenya didn't know what her guests would do for fun. She didn't have cable television and the VCR worked only half of the time. At Lizzie Canwell's sleepover, when someone suggested board games, the other girls called her a baby. Instead they played Truth or Dare, which mostly involved doing things to Lizzie's brother, who was hiding in his room. Also lately everyone had been playing the choking game, where someone propped you up from behind while you held your breath until you fainted in her arms. If Sheila so much as got a whiff of that entertainment, Kenya knew that her guests would be stuck with her mother for the entire party.

"I guess I'll invite Lizzie, since she invited me to hers," she said.

"Oh," said Lolly, her face falling. "Do you think she'll come?"

Kenya knew that Lolly, who aspired to a friendship with

Lizzie that would propel her out of their clique and into Lizzie's, would be embarrassed to be at Kenya's sleepover, even if Lizzie herself was there. And this was exactly the kind of wearying mess that made throwing a party seem like something you should do only if you absolutely did not want to have fun.

But the train was on the track. Sheila researched piñatas at the library, even though Kenya felt she was way too old for a piñata. Every night as they watched TV after dinner, they soaked newspaper in a slimy glue concoction and pasted it on the balloon core. Then, a week before the party, a blizzard appeared in the forecast.

"Why couldn't you have had me in the summer?" Kenya asked.

"You should be grateful I had you at all," quipped Sheila.

The weatherman tripped over his words in excitement, wielding his pointer with extra zeal. It was as if he was also planning a party for Saturday but could have his only in blizzard conditions. Seven to ten inches, maybe a foot! It would be heavier to the west of the city, he said, which is exactly where Kenya and her mother now lived. Maybe if they still lived in West Philadelphia she wouldn't have had to worry. But then again, if she lived there, no one from Barrett would come to her party. That's what had happened to China, who lived not far from Kenya's old house. The week after, China's mother had let her stay home for two days, nursing humiliation. When Kenya told Sheila about it, Sheila made it clear that she thought China was a big baby and her mother was, too.

"Whatever happens happens." Sheila shrugged, glancing sadly at the piñata, a tumorous rainbow-colored lump filled with Tootsie Rolls, though Kenya hated Tootsie Rolls. She could not bring herself to request a higher grade of candy. You could never tell with Sheila these days. One moment she was admiring someone's "champagne-colored" Jaguar, and later that same day she was mocking Kenya for "talking like those girls."

The Friday before the party, Zaineb told Kenya at lunch that she might have to cross-country ski to her party. "My mother is too scared to drive in the snow. She's a class-A moron."

"Mine is, too," said Phyllis Fagin. "She barely drives in the rain. I'm like, 'Mom, duh, it's just a little water. You won't *melt*.'"

Zaineb glared at Phyllis. "Shut up, Phyllis," she said.

"You shut up, Zaineb," said Lolly. As they told one another to shut up in a round, Kenya imagined them at her grandmother's house having the same conversation over vegetarian pizza options and cake. She'd invited a haphazard group of fifteen girls, nearly half of the class, but she knew she could count on only a few people to show up. This lunch table crowd would probably be it.

Kenya woke up on Saturday to a grim parody of the TV shows and books in which children got out of bed, raced to the window, saw snow, and celebrated. Now Kenya and Sheila had switched places; Kenya suddenly hopeful and "Maybe it won't be so bad," and Sheila murmuring "We'll see" with a pained expression. But the snow wasn't just falling; it was blowing in the gray darkness with mute violence. Kenya sat in front of the television in her pajamas, glued to dispatches from Ukee Washington, the black weekend weatherman, whose voice was so reasonable she thought any minute he would call the whole thing off.

Zaineb called to say there was "a ninety percent chance of a foot of snow and a zero percent chance that I'll make the party." Then Kenya listened as Sheila took a similar call from Alma Lewis. It seemed from the one side of the conversation Kenya heard that Alma had used the occasion to crow about Lolly's July birth and to reminisce about the wonderful pool parties she'd thrown over the years. Phyllis Fagin called and took forever to state the obvious, while bringing Kenya up to date on area historical records of snowfall and *like, oh my G*—

"Phyllis," Kenya said while Phyllis was still screeching, "Lolly said your underarms look like the Thing."

"What?"

"Nothing," said Kenya.

"Oh my God, what did you just say?"

"My mom has to use the phone. It's a snow-related emergency."

Kenya didn't realize she had fallen asleep until she woke up to the dreary Saturday-TV buzz of neglected sports (figure skating in this case) and her mother standing over her.

"Kenya, I have to pick up your cake."

"What?"

"Well, it's ready and I put a deposit on it. I paid good money."

"But they said it's really dangerous to drive. Is the bakery even open?"

"Yes, but not for long. I have to go. You'll be fine here."

"Not if you get killed in this blizzard!"

"Shut up, Kenya," Sheila snapped; she sometimes thought that when people said things like that it would make them happen. "Look, I have to go before it gets worse. There's deli turkey and bread and Ellio's pizza. And the chips . . ."

"You can't just leave me here!" yelled Kenya. It was the mention of Ellio's that did it. Kenya imagined herself chewing the cardboard crust with its promise of a bitter aftertaste and eating the sauce, which came off in shards. The disappointment that had been floating in the air since Kenya had woken up to the metal-colored sky finally settled on her chest. There would be no party. But most galling of all was that she hadn't even cared before. When had she started caring about the party?

"I'm so sorry," her mother said, actually looking sorry. "We can have it next weekend. We can even freeze the cake."

She was still talking about that fucking cake!

"You're still *going*? I mean, how much money is it, anyway?"

"Don't talk to me like that. I know you're upset, but you're not one of your little friends and neither am I."

"Don't I know it?" Kenya said, not quietly enough. For a moment, she thought her mother might smack her.

But Sheila was on her way out of the door. "Be dressed by the time I get back," she said. "You're starting to smell like a cheesesteak on my new sofa."

Kenya watched the door close. Though her mother had not, in fact, hit her, her eyes watered and her cheek stung anyway.

In the three hours that passed before Kenya's mother reappeared triumphant with snow-coated hair and eyelashes, the cake, a real pizza, and a story about a man who'd helped her out of a snowdrift, a lot happened, most of it in Kenya's head.

She stayed where she was for a while, stinking up the new purple couch, and entertained the thought of downing a bottle of aspirin. She imagined her mother in the front pew of an imaginary church, weeping about how she'd abandoned Kenya in a historically significant blizzard to hold on to a measly deposit for a cake, and even before that, forced her to have this party, and even before that, yanked her out of the city and into this surrealness.

There was the problem of Johnbrown. She wondered how Sheila could get in touch with him if Kenya killed herself. There had to be a way, because otherwise it meant Johnbrown didn't care enough about her to be reachable in case she died. Also distressing was the thought of Barrett's reaction to her suicide. Her funeral would be crowded with hysterical white girls pretending she'd been their best friend, and their parents, who would suspect that her being black was the reason she'd killed herself, which would be only partly true. Phyllis Fagin would put on a show of crying the hardest. Alma Lewis would manage to work superiority into her condolences.

But maybe, Kenya thought, she could take enough pills to generate a hospital scene but not enough to kill herself. Her mother would feel sorry for all of the same things, but now she could promise to make it better. She would also exhaust all means to get in touch with her father, who would show up at her hospital bed, just so Kenya could spurn him.

"You did this," she would say. He would cry, like he did that night, choking and dripping all the way to University Hospital, and Kenya would hate him even more. The whole thing would be like the hospital scenes she'd seen countless times on her mother's VCR recordings of *The Young and the*

Restless, which Sheila now watched openly. She imagined that most Barrett girls would avoid the hospital but that she could at least count on Zaineb to visit and apologize for her "zero percent" crack.

Then Kenya remembered a recent story on the evening news about a young man who had tried to commit suicide. He had been found too soon—and yet not soon enough. Now he traveled about in a wheelchair pushed by his elderly mother and had to work extremely hard to pull his tongue into his mouth to form words. One of his eyes was permanently shut, making him look like the cat in the *Bloom County* comic strip. He went around the state lecturing about why you shouldn't commit suicide. The news showed footage of him on a stage in a school auditorium. "You might miss," he garbled.

Kenya thought briefly about destroying her grandmother's house as redecorated by her mother and the nutty Lars, tearing lacy curtains, puncturing throw pillows with geometric designs. But she would sooner chance suicide. Finally she pictured herself lying on the couch, still in her pajamas when her mother came home, not so much defiant as paralyzed with grief and despair. But she knew she couldn't even do that. The only option was to get up.

After she was showered and dressed, she put in a tape she'd made of the nightly countdown on Hot 98 and listened to "Owner of a Lonely Heart" over and over again, thinking that it sounded like being trapped in a snowstorm. Then she remembered the blank purple book that smelled like perfume that she'd bought at the card and candy store. The girls in the novels she read kept diaries, journals, or important notebooks a la *Harriet the Spy*. Kenya had never felt like writing in hers, because she didn't know where to start. She pulled her journal out of her desk drawer and stared at a blank page for several minutes. After rewinding back to the beginning of the song again, she wrote the date and the song's title, and then underlined it with a flourish. She closed the journal and hid it in her underwear drawer.

She ate chips, half a family-size bag of cheese curls, and two and a half slices of the crappy pizza, which she was too impatient to heat all the way through. When the urge to vomit passed, she got the piñata off of the dining room table and took out the plastic bat they'd bought to hit it with. She put the lumpy thing in the middle of the living room floor, pushed the glass coffee table away from it, and slammed it. Then she hit it again. To make sure it stayed steady, she put a foot on it and hit it again and again. Each time she made contact, it felt as if the thing was gathering strength against her. Apparently, she and her mother had fortified it with gluey paper to the point of indestructibility. So when Sheila returned, Kenya was back on the couch watching TV and the piñata was back on the dining room table, completely intact.

A week later, Mr. Jaffrey ("call me Teddy") finally breached the piñata. Then he grinned proudly at Kenya.

"How 'bout that?"

He had used an actual wooden bat—he just happened to have one in his car—to make a dent, and then a hammer to finish the job, making one small hole. Teddy Jaffrey was the man who had pushed Sheila's car out of the snow on the disastrous afternoon of Kenya's party. After Kenya voted down the idea of rescheduling the party and the two of them made it official by giddily making their way though most of the cake, Sheila invited him over for dinner the following Saturday to thank him for his help.

Teddy lived with his parents nearby on one of the cramped-looking blocks traditionally occupied by the black servants of the Main Line.

"Do you think he knew Baba?" Kenya asked as Sheila set the table hours before he arrived. She did not pause her movements to answer.

"No."

"But they're both from Bryn Mawr. I mean, how many black—"

Sheila spoke in a low voice, as if she could not both talk clearly and fold napkins. It sounded as if she said the man was ten years younger than "your father." Then something hit Kenya.

"Are you going to date this guy?" asked Kenya. The divorced mothers at Barrett did not date. A couple of the girls had step-fathers, but there was no talk of how that had happened. It was almost as if those marriages were arranged.

"Who said anything about a date?" said Sheila, who, Kenya noticed, was cooking spaghetti instead of Saturday night's usual turkey franks. She was also forming actual meatballs instead of just crumbling beef into sauce like she usually did for Wednesday's dinner.

"Well, a man is coming over. Did you say he was ten years younger than you?"

"Look, I don't know if he's single," said Sheila. "And how 'bout you stay out of grown folks' business?"

"I'm trying to. But you're bringing home dates. Wait, is he old enough to date?"

"I'm going to hurt you, Kenya," Sheila said lightly.

Kenya became sure that the evening was a kind of a date when Mr. Jaffrey stepped into the house. She considered her father's pale complexion, his wiry build, and the fact that he was never what anyone would call tall, barely emerging above Sheila. This man stood at least two heads above her mother, his complexion favored the birthday cake icing, and he looked able to toss a heavy box with one hand. He did not look like Billy Dee Williams, and certainly did not have Billy Dee Williams's suspicious hair texture. Yet he made Kenya think of Billy Dee Williams as he stood in the foyer holding pink flowers that seemed anxious to die.

"Hello, Mr. Jaffrey," Sheila said. "These are lovely!" She flitted around, taking his caramel-colored coat, which looked heavy and expensive to Kenya. She thought of a trip she'd taken to the Second Mile Thrift Store with her father. There he'd bought what became his favorite tweed jacket, despite its having one torn cuff and a missing button. Her mother had often threatened to burn it. ("But then I'll be cold," Johnbrown would say. "I mean, when the fire goes out.")

"Hello, Mrs. Price," Teddy Jaffrey said, confusing Kenya. She wondered if her mother was using a fake name. Were they also on the run? Then she remembered that her mother had gone back to using her maiden name. Curtis had been her fake name.

"That's *Miz*, okay?"

Mr. Jaffrey laughed. "Roger that," he said. "And who is this young woman?"

"This is Kenya," Sheila said, smiling more than Kenya thought she would have.

"Kenya," he said, extending his hand. "It is *great* to meet you."

"Hello," said Kenya.

"And though your mother may call me Mr. Jaffrey for her own mysterious reasons, I think Teddy will do just fine for us."

"Okay," Kenya said. She certainly wouldn't call him Teddy and hoped he wouldn't become "Uncle" Teddy. China, whose father had died of a heart attack when she was small, had an "Uncle" DeWitt, an older man; she sometimes encountered his teeth floating in a glass in the bathroom.

"I have home training, right?" Teddy Jaffrey was saying. "So usually when I'm invited to someone's home for dinner, I like to be civilized, sit down, catch up. But something smells *very* good in here. I might need to eat that *very* soon."

Sheila laughed. "Well, since this dinner is to thank you for saving my you-know-what, you can have it when you want it." Then she led them into the dining room, where the table was set for the first time with Grandmama's dishes.

Later it would become difficult for Kenya to remember the first dinner they'd had with Teddy Jaffrey, because before long he was there more nights than not and each of these nights was the same. It was like watching badminton, sitting at the table as he and her mother batted the birdie of their chatter toward each other. Sheila talked about her desire to stop commuting into Philadelphia and transfer to one of the nearby, suburban libraries. Teddy, who was getting his real estate license, talked about housing prices in the different towns—Paoli, Haverford, Devon—and wondered aloud if these white folks would buy a home from a black man. The game fell apart every so often when someone tried to lob the birdie at Kenya. It was difficult, Kenya thought, for her mother to flirt with this man and talk to her daughter at the same time, because Sheila had to keep a smile in her voice when she said things like "Kenya, you might have to go out and get a little job to pay for the Winter Ski Trip. I'm not made of money like these girls' parents."

As awkward as it was for Sheila to be Kenya's mother in front of Teddy Jaffrey, at least Sheila knew what to say. Kenya, on the other hand, found it challenging to talk to him. She wasn't at all sure how to answer questions like "Do you know how proud it makes me to hear of a young lady like yourself going to Barrett?" or how to respond when he extended an imaginary microphone and said, "Tell us, Kenya, what is it like to have a five-star chef for a mother?" Even saying hello to him was fraught, because she never knew when he was going to try to give her a complicated soul handshake and then say, "I bet they don't teach that at the Barrett School for Girls." Kenya began to long for the lonely, calm dinners on chipped dishes she'd shared with only her mother, which had now become a rarity.

Teddy was a dork. But that wasn't the thing that had bothered Kenya since she first saw him. The sense of an unsolved mystery about him nagged at her until her mother engineered a sleepover at China's house one Friday evening, despite bitter complaints from Kenya. So it was a long night of eating cheese curls (which she hadn't touched since her birthday a month and a half ago), putting white cream on their faces, which China insisted ladies did at night, and listening yet again to the plot highlights of *Purple Rain*.

The next morning, when Sheila and (surprise!) Teddy Jaffrey came for Kenya, China pinched her arm hard and whispered hot in her ear, "Oh my God, he is, like, so gorgeous!"

Then Kenya realized it was this that had been bothering her like a small stone in her shoe: Teddy Jaffrey's gorgeousness. Because though her mother's face, with its lush eyebrows, bright eyes, and gapped front teeth, had always made something soar in Kenya, she knew that Sheila was not what most people called beautiful. It made her wonder what Teddy wanted from them.

One spring afternoon, not long after the sleepover at China's, Kenya sat in her room with the door open, struggling with algebra. She thought about the old days when she would ask her father for help. Back then her mother was often at work or in purposeful motion at home, but Johnbrown couldn't stay focused on the task long without tumbling into a tirade about the American education system or the great mathematicians of ancient Kush. Finally her mother, who had adored math in school, would appear or pause what she was doing to save the day. Kenya thought of that now, musing that her mother wouldn't be home for at least an hour and a half. Her mind jumping to the occasional mouse problem they had, she yelped in terror when she saw movement out of the corner of her eye.

"It's just me," her mother called.

"You scared me! Why aren't you at work?" Kenya yelled back.

"I had an appointment."

"Are you okay?"

"Kenya, can I have a minute?"

Kenya heard the bathroom door click shut. A terrifying thought flew into her head and she closed her eyes to entertain it. Her mother had left work early to see a doctor, and had run home to the bathroom, where she was undoubtedly crying because she was fatally ill.

Her mother was dying!

After an agonizing interval, which the clock claimed was less than two minutes, Sheila appeared in the doorway of Kenya's bedroom. Kenya noted her expression first. It was embarrassed, pleased, defensive, a mess. Then she saw that her mother's hair now framed her face in smooth, though limp, curls.

The hair was pretty enough, but it belonged somewhere else, like on Mrs. Huxtable or on a doll.

"Time for a change," Sheila said, reaching up self-consciously.

"That's a change."

"It doesn't look so bad, does it?"

"No," Kenya said. "No, Mom."

They looked at each other in silence. There was no way, Kenya thought, to ask the questions she wanted to ask. Unconsciously, she fingered her own hair, still in rather girlish cornrows done by her mother.

"I'm going to start dinner," Sheila said. "Teddy is coming tonight."

After watching her mother walk away, Kenya pulled her purple book out of its hiding place in her underwear drawer. *My mom got a perm*, she wrote. She thought back to a few moments ago, when she thought her mother was dying, and imagined her in a coffin, doll's hair framing her face.

Like everything else around them, her mother was changing. Kenya had intuited that she shouldn't say anything negative—not about Sheila's alliance with Alma Lewis (which continued though Sheila frequently mocked her), nor about the hours and money spent on Lars the decorator, who painted the powder room black and pouted when Sheila wouldn't approve a mini-chandelier in there. Now, most solidly with the perm, Kenya knew to keep her feelings about the rate and dramatic quality of these changes to herself.

She felt all of this even more painfully a few weeks later when Sheila asked her how she felt about Teddy Jaffrey moving in with them.

"I guess it would be okay," Kenya said. Given everything that had happened, and the fact that he seemed nice enough, Kenya couldn't think of an honorable reason to object. She had heard her mother saying on the phone to Alma Lewis that Teddy was an incredible second chance. He was almost too good to be true, she said. And perhaps Alma Lewis had said something about him still living with his parents, because Sheila came back with "Like I said, *almost* too good to be true."

The night that Sheila told Kenya about Teddy Jaffrey moving in, she didn't say it, but he was clearly on his way over. She had set the table with the nice dishes and had reapplied lipstick. Kenya stood in her mother's doorway while Sheila sat at her dressing table, propping up curls with a few touches of the hot iron. Kenya sneezed at the smell of singed hair that quickly filled the room.

"Do you think you'll marry him?" asked Kenya.

"We'll just see how this goes first," her mother said. It sounded like a threat.

The next morning Kenya woke up from a too-vivid dream of having been down in the basement of the house—a too-vivid dream and extremely dusty feet. She didn't tell Sheila.

"So, young lady," Teddy Jaffrey was asking at dinner, "tell me about your boyfriend."

Kenya tried to read his expression. Was he making fun of her? Genuinely interested? Was this part of his Uncle Teddy act? She glanced at her mother, but incredibly, Sheila looked as if she was eagerly awaiting the answer.

"I don't have a boyfriend," Kenya said, trying to sound neutral.

Boys had been in the air for a while but had only really shown up just as the Teddy Jaffrey era was beginning. It had started gingerly with the sixth-grade mixer, and now, near the end of seventh grade, people were murmuring their names: Phil McCartney, John Jessup, David Beloff, Matt Smith. They went to Haverford, Episcopal Academy, and Friends. They did not go to the Catholic school across the street from Barrett, which was for mallchicks and guidos. Phil was a joker, John was his best friend, David was so cute, and Matt was *so nice*. Kenya imagined them as trading cards. And there were less-mentioned others. One day at lunch Phyllis Fagin said, "Oh my God, Kenya, I was at a thing at my cousin's house and I met a guy you would love."

"Who?" Kenya asked. Years later, it would seem so absurdly,

stabbingly obvious where this was going that Kenya would want to go back in time to that conversation and punch herself in the face.

"He's really nice," Phyllis said.

"How does he know your cousin?"

"He goes to Germantown Friends." Kenya's mother would have preferred her to go to Germantown Friends. Though far from where Kenya had grown up, it was in the city, and not as stuck-up as Barrett. But they'd offered a measly scholarship. Later Kenya found out that Grandmama had stipulated that she would only help Sheila pay for Barrett. Perhaps if Grandmama's mother had cleaned Germantown Friends, it would have gone differently.

"He's so cool," Phyllis continued.

"So why don't *you* like him?" Zaineb asked. "If he's so cool."

"I just really think Kenya would like him," said Phyllis.

"What's his name?" said Kenya.

"Tyrell Smith," said Phyllis.

"Ew," said Lolly, "what kind of name is Ty-*rell?*"

It turned out that Phyllis barely knew Tyrell Smith; he didn't seem to remember her a week later when they ran into each other at a mixer at Episcopal. The music was loud and the conversation confusing. He walked off distractedly in the middle of being introduced to Kenya.

"You thought I would like him?" she asked Phyllis. Tyrell Smith's forehead was a map of acne scars, and he was over-dressed for the dance, in a pressed paisley shirt and creased pants.

"He looked better when I met him," said Phyllis ruefully.

"He's a total dog!" said Lolly.

Kenya stood there in the blare of the unfamiliar gym, where she, Tyrell, and Lolly were the only three black people. She looked around at her classmates, who had smeared themselves with makeup in the bathroom. Ever since the night she'd woken up shooting her mother, she had moments where she had to reassure herself that yes, she was in this room, in this body, on this earth. No, she wasn't part of someone's dream. In the months after she and her mother moved out of the city, she sometimes spent whole days reminding herself that she was here. It happened less now, but every so often, she had to go over the whole thing in her head again.

"I don't know," said Phyllis, "he reminded me of Kenya for some reason."

Zaineb began laughing. "I wonder why!"

"What—could—it—have—been?" Kenya said between fake giggles.

"I have no idea!" said Zaineb.

"You guys are so obnoxious," said Phyllis. "I was just trying to be nice."

Lolly stared off into the air. Kenya wondered if Lolly sometimes went to the same place she herself went, the place that was nowhere at all.

Phyllis wasn't the only one who tried to help Kenya with her love life. After boys appeared, it became a semiregular occurrence: someone Kenya was friendly with, or even someone she didn't talk to that much, would tell her about Barry Jackson/LeVaughn Smith/Charles Williams III and a boy named Allmon, whose name sounded faintly familiar. *Allmon, Allmon, Allmon,* she said to herself, trying to place it.

Sometimes when people kissed on television or in a movie,

or when a man looked at a woman a certain way, Kenya got a warm, ticklish feeling in the center of her body. Sometimes she poked and plucked at herself in the dark, then got up and scrubbed her hand raw like Lady Macbeth, whom she'd gotten to play in the seventh-grade English drama project. But getting a boy involved seemed as possible as China taking Prince to the prom. Most of the boys around were white, and everyone around Kenya conspired to keep her and white boys apart. There was her mother, with the long-standing, unstated "no white boys" edict, and the memory of her father's theories about slave masters and slave women. There were the girls at school, frantically suggesting Barry Jackson/LeVaughn Smith/Charles Williams III. But the biggest barrier to romance with the John Jessups, David Beloffs, and Matt Smiths of the world was the white boys themselves, who looked straight through Kenya.

At one mixer, Phil McCartney, popular in spite of always wearing Hawaiian shirts and being perpetually sweaty, bopped over to her. Kenya was dancing to "Word Up" with the other girls, and it was unclear if he was actually moving next to her or dancing with Phyllis. Unlike most of the girls, Phyllis had actual cleavage, which you could see above the V-neck of her sweater.

But he was looking directly at Kenya. "Word up!" he hollered. Kenya panicked, wondering how to act, what to say, how to stay cool. Phil did the bump on her, rather violently, she thought.

"That's the word!" she finally thought to say, but by the time she spoke, probably too quietly, he was boogeying away. "Whoo hoo!" he yelled.

"Oh my God!" said Phyllis, elbowing Kenya.

"That was Phil McCartney," hissed Lolly, spit flecking Kenya's ear.

"Say it, don't spray it," said Kenya, trying not to smile. Nearby, Lizzie Canwell and Lindsey Carroll whispered together, looking at her. It had been said that Lindsey Carroll used to go out with Phil McCartney.

There were a couple of good-looking and self-composed black boys, but most were either aggressive nerds, loud good-time types, or some Frankenstein of both, like LeVaughn Smith, who had gotten on the front page of the local paper for a patent he took out on a science project but who also tried to grab the DJ's microphone at dances. Unlike the white boys, who ignored her, these boys seemed specifically to hide from Kenya, occasionally venturing forth to ask Lolly, with her bulging hazel eyes and knobby knees, to dance. She went with them grudgingly, always returning to complain that "no cute boys" ever asked.

Kenya didn't blame any of the boys for disregarding her. She had eyes just like anyone else, and her house was full of mirrors that Lars claimed "enlarged a space." She was not tall or cutely miniature, and she had a completely average B-cup chest. Her skin was not light, her brown eyes unremarkable, her hair standard-issue nappy; at dances she wore it in a ponytail with bangs that kinked up fiercely if she began to sweat while dancing. Despite her mother's new look, Kenya was not allowed to perm her hair until high school. But she didn't think it would matter anyway. For her, "boys" was Tyrell Smith walking away while Phyllis was introducing her. And the only time the idea of a "boyfriend" really came up for her was when Teddy asked about it, which he started to do repeatedly. "Don't make me have to use my bat to break some boy's kneecaps," he'd say.

"What's the worst thing about him?" Zaineb asked Kenya about Teddy Jaffrey one day at lunch while Kenya was complaining about her mother's boyfriend. In the summer before and into eighth grade, Kenya had begun talking to Zaineb more than the other girls. Zaineb had never believed in Santa Claus and was reasonable about everything except New York City, about which she harbored outrageous fantasies of Bohemian life.

"He does seem really irritating," Zaineb continued, "but, like, what's the number one worst thing?"

"I mean, if your mom is happy, does any of this really matter?" asked Phyllis, reminding Kenya why she preferred conversations with Zaineb alone.

"Well, maybe it's weird to have to hang out with a guy that's not your dad," said Lolly. "My dad is, like, *so great*. I can't imagine."

"It's not that," said Kenya, looking at Zaineb. "He's just— it's just . . ."

"I just wonder if you're trying to, you know, be difficult?" asked Zaineb. "I mean, I can't stand my dad, but I'd be so pissed if they broke up and my mom brought someone else home."

Kenya wondered. Was there no way to like Teddy Jaffrey? She tried to imagine how it might be to appreciate having him around. She would enjoy it when he came into the house and got her involved in some confusing handshake. She would find it charming when he asked her if she'd ever been to Kenya and then laughed at his own cleverness. She would understand why her mother looked at him, pulling at her flattened hair, her eyes glazed over with—what? Love?

"I don't know," Kenya told them. The conversation turned to a new boy, Whitby Bradford, who knew all of the Beastie Boys' songs by heart. Later that night, while Teddy Jaffrey and her mother were upstairs, Kenya called Zaineb.

"He's not himself," she told her, without saying hello. "That's what I don't like. You can tell that he never says what he's thinking. He says something else."

"Maybe you don't want to know what he's thinking," said Zaineb.

Once upon a time, back when they lived in the city, Kenya had breathlessly watched a cartoon miniseries of *The Lion, the Witch and the Wardrobe* and become convinced that the White Witch lurked in the upstairs hallway. Kenya didn't remember the day she forgot her fear of the witch, who made it always winter and never Christmas (which it also never was in Kenya's real life). But she recalled the taste of terror in her mouth she used to get as she climbed the lonely stairs in the old house, when she woke one night in her new house to find someone in her room.

It was a Saturday night, after Katherine Stein's birthday party at Radnor Rolls. Kenya had skated almost nonstop, pleased to discover something she could do that made her feel like she was flying. And, unlike at school dances, there was no question of being chosen or spurned. She didn't mind that Katherine's mother kept giving her that smile, the one that convinced Kenya that she'd been invited out of a sense of racial charity; she didn't even care that Phyllis Fagin was trying to create a drama between herself and a scarily blond guy in a letter jacket who looked like the villain in *The Karate Kid*. "It's like he doesn't even know I'm alive," Phyllis whined, a well-founded complaint. Kenya ignored her, whirling around, yelling "Nineteen-ninety-nine, don't you wanna go?" She skated faster and faster, flying into the barricade. She fell, laughing.

After the party, Kenya found herself pleasurably exhausted but also cranky that life offered opportunities to do things like roller-skate only in the briefest of intervals. Instead one's time on earth was taken up with sitting at the dinner table with one's mother and her boyfriend, eating boiled hot dogs and listening to him complain that all of the guys he knew who'd failed the real estate licensing exam (like him) were black and that the guys who passed it were white—and Chinese. Of course the whites might let a few Chinese pass, he complained. It was black men they were afraid of.

"May I be excused?" asked Kenya.

"I'm sorry, Kenya," said Teddy Jaffrey, putting back the laughing mask. "This talk might be a little strong for you."

"Kenya knows how things are," said her mother. "We—I— never hid anything from her."

"I'm just tired," said Kenya. But then maybe she was the one—not Teddy Jaffrey—who never said what she thought. Because she was thinking that he was a petty, stupid man. Was being black and not passing the real estate licensing exam his idea of a racial conspiracy? She remembered the majestic narratives her father had spun, aligning presidents, the pope, and the local court system—actual conspiracies. It made Kenya miss him suddenly, so sharply that it was a pain in her side. The shame of being alive was listening to Teddy Jaffrey's woes and watching her mother ooze sympathy.

But she had skated and felt good, so Kenya looked at her mother's boyfriend and said something she did not mean. "I'm sorry about the exam. I'm sure you'll pass next time."

Then Kenya went upstairs and collapsed in bed, where she slept so heavily that it felt like minutes later when she woke to find a man standing over her in the dark. She tried to wake herself up from this bad dream, but the figure was still there.

"Baba?" she whispered.

"You fell asleep with your clothes on," said Teddy Jaffrey. "I came to turn off the light."

"Thanks," said Kenya. Fully awake now, she felt ashamed that she had called her father's name.

"You're welcome." He sat down on the foot of her bed. "You went to bed early. Must have been tired. Pretty fun party, huh?"

"Yes."

"Let me help you into your PJs," he said, reaching for the covers, but Kenya held them tightly.

"Teddy, where's my mom?" she asked.

"Asleep," he muttered.

"Teddy."

"So, folks, even though she never says it, she knows my name," Teddy said to an imaginary audience, whispering in his jocular voice. He managed to laugh in the same whisper.

"Teddy, I'm going to go to the bathroom," Kenya said slowly, quietly, and clearly. "I guess you should go to bed."

The figure disappeared.

The next day at breakfast, Teddy Jaffrey was exactly the same person he'd been before he came into her room. He was not especially fawning over Kenya; nor was he indifferent. He sang along with the Luther Vandross record her mother played, always coming in a little too early. It was, Kenya thought, as if he wanted to be sure everyone knew that he knew the words.

"Since I lost my baby," he sang.

(*Since I lost my baby*, repeated Luther Vandross.)

"You are *no* Luther," said Sheila, stacking pancakes on a plate next to the stove. Aunt Jemima on Sunday morning, same as back in the city. Kenya knew now that she should be grateful for the things that had stayed the same—especially now that her mother also cooked a pile of bacon for Teddy. Sometimes Sheila even ate a piece of it, sitting at the table with her permed hair in a scarf and rollers, a woman Kenya had never known.

Kenya sat at the kitchen table nearest the stove where her mother stood, and though she didn't have anything in mind to say, she was suddenly gripped with the fear that if she were to speak, her mother would not be able to hear her.

Devi Warren was an extreme rarity at Barrett: a midyear transfer. Her family had moved from New York City and the rumor, an unusual one, was that they were very rich. No matter how echoey and marble-floored the mansions she'd been to, no Barrett girl yet had admitted to being rich. If it came up, which it rarely did, they said, with the same inflection, "I'm not *rich*," as if the word *rich* were like the word *dumb* or *dirty*. Kenya had done the math on her own situation; she knew that her mother's salary was $37,000 and that they were not paying for the house or their old Subaru, or for much of the tuition at Barrett. If these girls who hired cotton candy machines for their parties and had Porsche convertibles in their rounded driveways weren't rich, what did that make her and Sheila?

Of course no one would ask Devi Warren to confirm or deny, but she did look the part in a way that Kenya would not have recognized back before Barrett. "The more money these kids have," her mother had declared once, on their way home from a school picnic, "the worse they look. The ones who look like orphans in Dickens—there's your Rockefellers." Devi Warren wore a gray kilt like everyone else, but her Tretorn sneakers had been battered almost beyond brand recognizability. It looked as if someone had eaten part of the collar of her dingy white polo shirt, and her short brown hair was streaked with a dirty blonde that *actually* looked dirty.

For about a month, leading into winter break, Devi Warren ate lunch at one of the two center tables in the dining room. Her air of glamour and mystery had earned her a probationary period among the popular girls. Meanwhile, at Kenya's table, Phyllis whispered, "I heard she's, like, the biggest lesbo." The class had recently learned that word—distinct from the all-purpose insult *gay*—and the accusations had immediately begun. In retrospect, Kenya found it remarkable, in the way of ant colonies and elephant funerals, that the girls never accused Tuff Wieder and Sharon McCall of being lesbos, even though they'd been holding hands on the swings and sharing a sleeping bag at slumber parties since anyone could recall. (Of course, that might have been because no one wanted to anger Tuff, who cursed casually, played rough at lacrosse, and had a mysterious scar over her right eyebrow.) When Devi materialized, with her David Cassidy haircut and brusque manner, it was as if the use of the word had called her into existence.

"I heard she has a boyfriend in New York," said Zaineb, her eyes going soft at the prospect. "That's pretty much the opposite of being a lesbian."

"But she totally looks like a guy," said Lolly.

"Maybe that doesn't mean anything," Kenya said. "People are not how they seem." Kenya had recently begun making several versions of this statement. It was all she could bring herself to say about Teddy Jaffrey. She had not told anyone about what had possibly not happened the Saturday night after the roller-skating party. The only person she could imagine telling was Zaineb, but Zaineb was not a vault. She was just an eighth-grade girl who sometimes ran out of things to talk about just like anyone else. Kenya could easily hear her saying, "You know Kenya's mom's boyfriend?"

She had not told her mother. She had not put into words why, not even in her journal, where she had written only "Teddy Jaffrey." Kenya loved her mother and her mother alone. It was a variety of images, scenes from possible outcomes, that kept Kenya silent. She imagined her mother saying an enraged and tearful goodbye to the dazzlingly handsome Teddy, throwing an accusing glance back at Kenya, who'd sent him away. She imagined her mother living out her days as a single woman, enjoying an occasional can of beer, wearing the same clothes year after year, like some of the unmarried teachers at Barrett.

Yes, it would be Teddy's fault. But really it would be Kenya's.

Then there was the image of her mother, face contorted in pain, clutching her bleeding shoulder, the one in which she'd been shot. Kenya's fault, too.

All of this was bad. And there was another scene that sometimes intruded upon her, one where Sheila asked "But did he *do* anything to you?" and kept asking until Kenya had to say "Wasn't that enough?" Where would they be then?

Nor did Kenya mention to her mother that she had been having trouble sleeping. That would mean explaining that she was trying to stay awake just in case Teddy Jaffrey came into her room again. She negotiated a later bedtime, which some-times meant that she stayed downstairs after Teddy Jaffrey and her mother had retired. She went up dutifully at 10:30, but instead of sleeping she lay in bed imagining a conversation where she asked Sheila for a lock on her door. In the imagined conversation, her mother would frown slightly and ask, *Why?* To which Kenya would say, *You know I'm getting older, just for privacy,* and her mother would ask, *Why? Why do you need a lock on your door?* Then, instead of telling her why, Kenya would start the reel in her head from the beginning. *Mom, can I please have a lock on my door?*

It was not clear whether the popular girls tired of Devi Warren or she tired of them. In any case, after winter break, Kenya encountered Devi in what was traditionally her seat with the other girls at lunch. Kenya usually sat next to Zaineb and across from Lolly and Phyllis at one of the long tables at the edge of the room. Now she had to sit on the fringes of the group, the last in an ungainly row of three. Across from her was Dorrie Futter. Kenya thought that Devi would quickly move on to another, more interesting group of girls so she could reclaim her seat. But she came and plopped herself down day after day for a week. The other girls listened to her talk about her life back in New York with rapt attention. Kenya thought she was, as they used to say when she was growing up, "on herself."

Zaineb had an unusually alert expression on her face as she listened to Devi complain about the Upper East Side, which she'd hated, as it was full of snobby old ladies and little dogs. Her best friend in the neighborhood was a bum named Artie, to whom she used to give part of her lunch money. She had gone to a school called Dalton, which was, she said, a "rich skank pit."

"We moved just in time. They were about to kick me out—just because I didn't fit in with those moronic rich sluts."

Kenya tried to catch someone's eye—Zaineb's—because, again, wasn't this someone rich pretending otherwise? But of course she had never discussed this issue frankly with Zaineb, whose family was rumored to own several luxury hotels in Europe, though she always said her father sold rugs. Besides, she knew the look on Zaineb's face as she listened to Devi. It was hunger.

"Did you ever go to, like, Greenwich Village?" said Zaineb, trying to put a shrug in her voice. Kenya thought that if

Zaineb ever succeeded in getting Devi into her house, she'd first have to take down all of her New York posters, including the map of Greenwich Village.

"It's Gre-nich, silly," Devi said. "Yeah, I was actually born in the Village. We lived there until I was five. It's cool. That's where all the gay boys are."

"Don't a lot of them have AIDS?" asked Phyllis.

Lolly hit Phyllis. "*God*, Phyllis! Shut up!"

Phyllis's eyes glistened briefly as she caressed her injured shoulder. "God, Lolly!"

Devi pushed her hair back. "I guess a few of them do. It's actually really sad."

"Not all gay people have AIDS, Phyllis," said Zaineb.

Kenya thought of Teddy Jaffrey and her mother watching a news special about the disease. Teddy Jaffrey had declared that it wasn't just prejudice anymore; he could now decline to shake a faggot's hand for health reasons. "Don't say *faggot* in front of my daughter, Teddy," Sheila snapped, standing abruptly from the couch and walking into the kitchen. "I was just kidding," Teddy muttered to no one. Finally he, too, went into the kitchen and Kenya held her breath, waiting with excitement for her mother to deliver him a tongue-lashing. Instead there was a long silence followed by giggling.

Looking at Devi, Kenya asked, "Why didn't you fit in at your school?"

"A lot of reasons," Devi said.

"Like what?" Kenya said.

"I don't know, Kenya," the girl said in a nasty voice, "why don't you fit in at yours?"

Later Kenya would think that what happened next was

very weird. She had never in her life so much as hit anyone, and of all of the cheek-burning, stomach-sinking things people had said to her at Barrett, this was hardly the worst. Yet, barely missing a beat, Kenya got up, went around the end of the long table, and tried to pull Devi out of her chair by her raggedy collar.

"What the fuck?" Devi screamed. The startled expression on her face gave Kenya a lightning thrill. Then the girls were hitting each other amid squeals of "Oh my God" and "They are totally fighting." It drifted through Kenya's mind that there had never been a fight at Barrett in the whole time she'd been there. Then Mademoiselle Lambert (*Lom-behr*, Kenya knew to pronounce it, after nearly four years at Barrett), the tiny but powerful French teacher, who also taught dance, had each of them by the ear.

"Are you the crazy?" she asked. "We go to Matron Wells's office. Now!"

In the waiting room outside of the office, Kenya heard loud breathing that she eventually realized was her own. *Am I here?* she wondered.

"What did you mean by that?" she said to Devi. "How do you know whether I fit in here or not? You just got here."

Devi sighed for a long time. "Duh, Kenya. Hello? I'm part black."

"No you're not," Kenya said.

Devi laughed. "Are you 'the crazy'? Why would I lie about that?"

"I've seen your parents. Are they somehow black, too?"

"Ever heard of adoption?"

Kenya twisted her mouth to the side in a way she'd seen her mother do when in doubt.

Devi folded her arms. "Fine, don't believe me. I don't give a fuck," she said, hitting *fuck* just as the matron's door was opening. She regarded Devi and Kenya and cleared her throat. "Mrs. Appleton," she said to her smirking secretary, who sat in the outer room, "can you get Mrs. Warren's and Mrs. Price's telephone numbers?"

"So tell me what this is about," the matron said when the girls were seated in the two hard chairs in front of her desk.

Kenya's bottom lip trembled at her proximity to the displeased matron, a tall woman who might have been a stern female John F. Kennedy. There was no point in trying to defend herself. She had tried to dump the new rich transfer student out of a chair and beat her up.

"I started it," said Devi before Kenya could speak.

"Yes?" asked the matron.

"Kenya said something kind of mean about my old school. But it wasn't her fault—she just said—well, implied that maybe it wasn't as good as Barrett."

"Kenya, why would you speak that way?"

Devi spoke again hurriedly. "Well, it isn't, Matron. It isn't as good."

"But Dalton is a fine school. Excellent, in fact. Kenya, I have not heard you speak yet."

Kenya had been stunned into silence. The new girl was lying for her. She looked over at Devi again. Her nose definitely looked broader and her blonde-streaked hair curlier. Kenya wondered if everyone else at Barrett knew that she was black.

White people were extremely bad about this sort of thing. That slut Cindalou had told a story about working in a meat plant where the white women she sat near had felt free to say all kinds of nigger-this and nigger-that because she was, as she put it, "a little yellow."

"I'm sorry," Kenya said. "I shouldn't have said . . . what I said."

"You'll find," the matron said, "that you build nothing up by tearing others down."

Kenya felt Devi trying not to laugh.

For a few weeks after that, Devi and Kenya circled each other. Devi continued to sit at their table, but she now recognized Kenya's seat and moved down one, taking Dorrie Futter's seat, displacing her to an empty table by the window. Kenya continued to study the new girl for signs of blackness. Some days she thought she saw them. She realized she finally believed her when she found herself wondering at the fact that she, Lolly, and Devi all belonged to the same anything at all. *Race*, she thought, *race race race*, until the word became strange.

"Sometimes I just wonder, would it be so bad to be dead?" asked Devi.

It was a chilly spring morning and girls were running the perimeter of the middle school athletic field in their gray gym kilts, their knees goose bumped.

Kenya was intrigued. "So instead of waking up and getting on the school bus, just waking up, like, dead?"

"But you'll go to hell if you kill yourself," said Lolly.

Devi clarified. "I didn't say anything about killing myself. I just wonder what it would be like to be dead."

"It wouldn't be like anything. You'd be dead," said Zaineb.

"It would probably be better than gym," said Kenya.

"You guys are so maccabee," said Phyllis.

"I don't think that's how you say that," said Zaineb. "In fact I'm sure it's not."

Kenya remembered the failed suicide with the mangled face and his motivational speeches. She told Devi, who thought it was terrifically funny. "Don't miss," she repeated gleefully. Zaineb tried to laugh. Lolly and Phyllis ran ahead, giving each other a look.

"How would you do it?" Kenya asked Devi at lunch.

"I said I wouldn't."

"I know, but if you did."

"Well, I saw a movie once where a guy ran a really hot bath and then slit his wrists. I could totally take a hot bath even while my parents were home and no one would notice until—*oops!*"

Kenya found herself laughing. "But you'd have to cut your own arm a bunch of times. What about poison? That seems much easier to me."

"That shit—I mean crap," Devi said, scanning the room for Mademoiselle Lambert or some other enforcer, "totally burns up your insides. And who knows how long it would take you to die? It could be hours."

"You guys are talking about this *again*?" said Zaineb, who had stopped genuflecting before Devi and her life in New York. ("I just think," she had said to Kenya in Algebra, when Devi was not around, "that she's, like, disturbed."

("Like Damien in *The Omen*?" Kenya asked. Zaineb had once confided in her that *The Omen* had given her nightmares for weeks.

("Yes, Kenya, just like Damien in *The Omen*. Don't be an A-hole, okay?")

Kenya knew Zaineb was jealous. She and Devi were getting closer every day. They had even talked about the fight—Devi had admitted to being bitchy because of missing her boyfriend, who was friends with the guy who managed Run-DMC.

Devi had also confided in Kenya that while she could stand Zaineb better than Lolly and Phyllis, she was a little "tightly wound." Kenya found Zaineb, despite her jealousy, calm and reasonable. But she told Devi that she *totally* agreed.

"Am I going to what?" Kenya asked. It was August; light streamed in through the glass walls of the sun porch at Devi's house, illuminating Devi's mother from all angles. Sun dripped off her oddly stiff, long, dark hair; it seemed to shine out of the sharp bones of her neck. She wore a black wrap dress that appeared coated in light. The sun even seemed to stream out her eyes, a bruised purple color that looked like Devi's. She had asked a question in her strangely high voice, a voice that might be described as sunny.

Kenya and Devi sat at a glass table nibbling at brownies that tasted strange to Kenya until Devi clarified that they were sugar-free. A black dachshund called Sally paced hopefully underneath the table. Kenya was vaguely worried, having heard somewhere that chocolate was poisonous to dogs.

"Get married before the rapture?" the woman repeated. Devi sighed. She picked up another brownie but put it down when her mother looked pointedly at it.

"What is the rapture?" asked Kenya.

"My goodness," said Mrs. Warren, in a laughing voice. "I'm sure glad you came here today, Kenya."

"Mom," Devi pleaded.

"Mom, what? Devi, will you tell this smart, beautiful young lady about the rapture already—you know, before it happens?"

"Can we talk about this later?" Devi asked. "I think we're going to go get ready for swimming."

Though she didn't make a sound, Mrs. Warren's face changed. In Kenya's memory of this moment later, clouds briefly eclipsed the sun, the porch went dim, and Sally barked. Though the serene, sparkling pool was only on the other side of the glass, it suddenly looked very far away.

Devi sighed. "The rapture is when Jesus comes back to earth to claim his true followers and take them to Paradise."

"And the rest will perish," Mrs. Warren continued, smiling again. "So you see why it might be important to get married before that."

"Oh" was all Kenya could muster.

Kenya had been all over the Main Line. In her first couple of years she had visited many of the girls' houses. She had not specifically been invited back to a lot of those homes once everyone's curiosity was satisfied, but there were always parties. All told, she had done a thorough tour, and she had gradually gotten used to the many things that seemed wrong. At Trinity Howell's house, she had eaten something that she seriously suspected was a pork chop and pretended to herself that it was chicken. Cynthia Malder's older brother and sister called each other *cunt* and *dickface*. In several of the girls' basements, where parents never seemed to go, she had watched R-rated movies involving naked teenage girls and once, at Tuff Wieder's house, part of a porno, which Tuff helped narrate while her cut-buddy, Sharon McCall, giggled. Kenya had helped make prank calls to local boys and, to Sheila's horror, eaten doughnuts for breakfast. She was often the only one who took a shower the morning after a sleepover. None of that made the floor tilt as much as this.

Though Johnbrown sneered at Christianity, Sheila had made Kenya understand that being fanatically religious was a reasonable choice for black people who didn't know any better. ("I don't buy it," Sheila had once said about the six churches in a three-block radius back in their old neighborhood, "but I get it.") Less seemly, but no less predictable, was the rabid Christianity of tacky white people, mostly in the South, generally fat and flushed, who gave money to Tammy Faye Bakker with her mascara-scarred cheeks. But Mrs. Warren was a thin, stylish, and exceptionally rich white woman in the suburbs of Philadelphia who lived in a house with six bathrooms (and counting). Kenya found the incongruence terrifying.

"So just consider it," the woman said. "You know, getting married before all of *that* goes down. And in the meantime, I may join you both for a dip if that's okay."

"Sure, Mom," Devi said in a flat voice.

But up in her room she said, "Maybe we should just climb out of the window and never come back."

Kenya glanced at her first actual best friend. By the time that school year had ended, they were speaking on the phone every night and trading Led Zeppelin cassettes back and forth. They sat together whenever they could; during one assembly they gripped each other's hand, using their nails to keep from collapsing in ugly laughter at the kids from the special school down the road performing a concert. Kenya imagined herself and Devi in an edgier version of the "best friends" McDonald's commercial.

Kenya had told Devi things about her life that she hadn't told anyone else at Barrett. She had broadly sketched out the Seven Days and mentioned during one late-night summer phone call that her parents had never married. But Kenya hadn't told her *everything*, which now seemed fortuitous, because, frankly, Devi had left out a lot of important details when it came to her own situation. Here is what Kenya knew: Devi hated her parents—but didn't everyone at Barrett? She hated her mom more than her dad (but again, didn't everyone at Barrett?) but was stuck with her a lot while her dad traveled for his job. Her mom used to model in Paris, which was the only cool thing about her. She didn't even know why her parents had adopted her. Devi had never mentioned that her mother was what Johnbrown had called an Atonist, let alone to such an intense degree. Kenya had been to Devi's house before, but Mrs. Warren had never been there. This time she was.

Kenya was too freaked out to be polite. "Maybe we could just stay up here and play cards?"

"My mother would come looking for us. She doesn't like me up here alone with other people."

"Girls!" called Mrs. Warren right on cue.

As Devi and Kenya passed through the sun porch, they

could see Mrs. Warren on the other side of the sliding doors. She wore a black bikini, large sunglasses, and a floppy hat.

In clothes, she had been a slightly stooped stick figure. Now the word *cadaverous* suggested itself.

"Mom, you look skinny," Devi said grudgingly. It took Kenya a moment to realize that this was a compliment.

"Oh, I look old," Mrs. Warren said, waving with a grin toward Kenya. "And it took thirteen years, but I think I *finally* lost the baby weight," she said, pinching Devi's thigh as she walked by.

"Ouch, Mom!" Devi yelled.

Kenya held herself underwater for as long as she could manage, as many times as she could. She came up and Mrs. Warren was challenging them to a race, which she won. Kenya came up again and Mrs. Warren was swimming with the dog. Afterward, Kenya lingered in the shower until Devi banged on the door and asked if she was okay.

At dinner, Kenya ate her first shepherd's pie (a food she resolved never to eat again) as quickly as she could without seeming impolite. She studied Mr. Warren, a thin man with large, sad eyes who said little, even at times when Kenya might have liked to hear his views. Like, for example, when the conversation veered toward yet another thing Devi hadn't mentioned—the fact that the Warrens had left New York to get away from the atmosphere of "usury," a word the class had learned during the *Merchant of Venice* unit in English. Dinner had concluded with fruit, which Mrs. Warren insisted on calling dessert, and now the girls were up in Devi's room, where they had to leave the door open until they went to sleep.

"I can't believe school starts in a week," Kenya said, because what else was there to say?

"You can call your mom to come get you if you want," Devi said in a low voice. "She's going to try to make us go to church tomorrow."

"On Saturday?"

Devi snorted. "You're lucky she didn't make us go tonight."

The dog appeared in Devi's doorway. Sally was beginning to strike Kenya as a tragic figure, aligned as she was with the maniacal Mrs. Warren. Devi threw a Docksider at her and Sally made an injured semihuman sound.

For the first time in years Kenya thought about Charlena. There were so many things she had forgotten to think about. She wondered if the girl was now just as devoted to her parents' religion as they were. To Devi she said, "It's okay. Everybody's parents are crazy."

Devi jumped up off of her bed. "I'm closing this. I don't care." Despite the spirit of her declaration, she shut the door with a soft click. "Devi." Her mother's voice floated up. Devi snatched the door open. "Sally is bothering us!" she whined, sounding somewhat like the dog just had.

Kenya heard laughter from downstairs. Devi shut the door again, this time more loudly, and then sat down on the bed so hard that she bounced.

"I fucking hate it here!" she said.

"You mean in Paoli?"

"In this house. I hate them and I hate *her.* Did you get what she was saying down there? We left the city because there were too many Jews for her. And the Jews there were too many of? My father's family!" Kenya had never seen Devi so upset; the bottom of her face stretched longer and longer. Then she flopped down on her bed and turned her face away from Kenya toward the wall.

Kenya felt desperate and loose, the way she had felt when she attacked Devi. "My mother's boyfriend tried to molest me," she said.

Hours seemed to pass before Devi Warren sat up slowly, wiping at her face. "Oh my God, what happened?"

As best she could, Kenya told the story, which, as she listened, didn't quite sound like a story. What was the plot? Climax? Resolution? But Devi's eyes and mouth were perfectly round. "Didn't you say he was really cute?" she asked.

"So?"

"That seems weird. I mean, you'd think he'd be, like, a loser. Didn't you watch that movie *Amanda's Secret*? The dad had just lost his job and he was getting fat so his wife wasn't—"

"He's not like that."

"Is he, like, an urban type?"

"What the hell do you mean by that?"

"Don't get all weird, Kenya."

"I'm not, but maybe we shouldn't talk about this anymore."

"Why not? I mean, now you know how messed up my family is," Devi said. "I shouldn't have even . . ." she started to say.

"It's okay," said Kenya, though she didn't know if it was. Then they talked as they usually did: Barrett gossip, celebrity talk, New York memories, until Kenya could tell that Devi was drifting off to sleep. If she didn't ask now about Devi's being adopted, she never could. But if she asked, what could the girl say? What on earth could she say?

"Devi?" she said quietly.

The only answers were Devi's deep, even breaths.

"I shouldn't have said what I said," Kenya said, her heart pounding in her throat, "but I didn't tell any lies."

"What was it exactly that you said, Kenya?" the matron asked in a voice as cold and calm as a glacier.

"I t-told Zaineb that . . ."

"Yes?"

"She was telling people that my mother was an anti-Semitic religious freak! And it wasn't just Zaineb!"

The road from that summer night at Devi's led back to where Kenya and Devi's friendship had essentially started—the matron's office. They again sat side by side across from her desk, a week after the start of ninth grade.

"Is that what you said, Kenya?"

"I said she was a little religious and that she talked bad about Jewish people. I shouldn't have said those things. I—"

"I should say not. Now, Devi, what did you say?"

"She shouldn't have been calling my mother a religious freak and an anti-Semite!"

"I hear you, Devi. But now I'm asking you a question. What did *you* say?"

Kenya tried her best. "Look, can we just forget about this? I mean, can we forget what she said to me? It's nothing. I don't care." Before she knew it, she was crying.

The matron slid a tissue box toward her with the slightest motion. "I know this must be difficult for you, Kenya, but it's important that I find out what has happened."

Kenya wasn't sure how she'd phrased it or how she got it out of her mouth, but she made the matron understand the rumor Devi had been trying to spread about Kenya and her stepfather.

"Devi, did you say that?" the matron asked in a particular voice, a combination of concern and shock that made the hairs on the back of Kenya's neck rise, even though she wasn't being addressed.

Devi jumped up abruptly in a motion so violent it overturned her chair. "Fuck this!" she screamed. "Fuck you, Kenya! You were supposed to be my friend!"

"How could we be friends? You said you were adopted and that you were black! Why would you lie about that?"

"Do I look black to you, you dumb bitch?"

Then Mrs. Appleton, the daintiest fat woman Kenya had ever seen, was in the room with a French-manicured hand on Devi Warren, all of a sudden seeming more bodyguard than secretary. Devi's eyes had gone black and she was screaming as if to tear her own throat.

Kenya watched Devi Warren overturn a chair, slap away both the matron and her bodyguard, and knock everything off of the matron's desk. It was like ballet, which Grandmama had sometimes made Kenya watch on Channel 12. It was beautiful. It was also the last time Devi Warren was seen at Barrett.

As terrified as she was of her mother's fury, Kenya was still aware of feeling relieved that no one saw Sheila pull up to the school in a sputtering brown Dodge. They had traded in their old-but-decent car to help Teddy Jaffrey lease a navy-blue Mercedes. He needed to present "a certain image" to sell real estate, though Kenya had not heard about his passing the license exam yet. This car was cheap because it was a stick shift, which her mother was still learning how to drive. Kenya was grateful for the start-stop of the conversation, but the ride was perilous.

"Last thing I heard, that girl was your ace boon coon. Now you all are acting so crazy that I have to leave work early? Goddammit," Sheila said as the car jerked dead. "God fucking dammit!"

It was too late to start from the beginning. Her mother was now Mrs. Jaffrey. At the very end of August, around the time of the nightmarish visit to Devi, there had been a depressing little ceremony at the town hall; Alma Lewis was the matron of honor and Teddy's childhood friend Bert, a short white man with a mustache, had been best man. Kenya's mother had bought her a dress that cost nearly one hundred dollars. They had all gone to lunch at the Cedar Grill, where Teddy had repeatedly used the waiter's name, which he always did when the waiter was white.

"I'm sorry," Kenya said.

"Yeah, you are sorry! You need to tell me what the hell is going on."

"Mom, I swear, there's nothing to tell. I was friends with a girl and now I'm not. Just like you said."

"What did she do to you?"

Kenya supposed she could have been grateful for this. The matron could have had a separate conversation with her mother and pressed on the issue of her stepfather. But she'd summoned everything inside of her to convince the woman that her stepfather had not touched her, which he had not. It was just, she claimed, that Devi really hated her own parents and was strangely obsessed with Teddy.

"But you're not overly fond of him?" the matron had asked.

"He's corny," Kenya had said, and then she began telling stories that presented Teddy Jaffrey as the kind of non-lecherous stepfather that a cranky girl would surely come around to loving eventually. Ones that made it sound as if he tried too hard—popping popcorn on the stove instead of the microwave (which he did, with great ceremony), worrying about her when she came home a little late from school (which he didn't). Kenya kept waiting for the matron to show signs of softening toward Teddy. She did not. Nor did she tell Kenya's mother what Devi said. Kenya suspected that she would one day remember the matron as one of the good ones.

Sheila said, "Kenya, this really isn't like you, so I know you must be going through a lot. There have been a lot of changes. And I know Teddy is very different from your father. But this is our life now and you have to give it a chance."

"I haven't said anything."

"Is there something you wanted to say?"

Kenya snapped her mouth shut and observed the glory of suburban fall foliage. When winter came, it would be two years since the birthday when her mother dragged Teddy in from the snow. Kenya couldn't imagine her mother driving this car in the snow. At long last the car jerked into the garage. Sheila cut it off with a final curse.

"I want to talk to Baba," Kenya said.

"What?"

"That's what I want."

"You know that's not possible," Sheila said.

"We could find him. I know we could. They do this kind of thing all the time on TV. We would just go out to where he last was, or find Cindalou's family, or—"

"Kenya, your father is in prison."

"What?"

"He's in prison."

"What are you talking about? You said you didn't think anything would happen to him. Is he there for what I—"

"No. I told you, he and his—Cindalou tagged up a bunch of police stations. Also, even though they couldn't get me to testify against him for the—the shooting, the police don't like it when you skip bail, which he did. I'm sorry."

Maybe she was and maybe she wasn't, Kenya thought, her eyes drifting over the tools neatly hung on a pegboard in the garage. They'd been there since before they'd moved in: different types of saws, pliers and wrenches, a sledgehammer. She wondered what her grandfather the pharmacist had ever done with a sledgehammer.

She got out of the ratty car, slamming the door, which Sheila hated. Her mother looked at her but said nothing. *Just because your father is in prison doesn't mean you can slam the car door*, Kenya thought, feeling the hysterical urge to laugh.

After minutes that passed like years, they sat at the dining room table while Sheila explained to Kenya that her father had been in prison for a year and would be there for at least two more.

"I just don't understand why you didn't tell me what was going on."

Sheila sighed and clawed at her curls. "Like I said, there have been a lot of changes, Kenya. We didn't want you to feel too . . . lost."

"We who?"

"What do you mean?"

"You said 'we.' So Teddy Jaffrey knows about this? You told Teddy Jaffrey something about my father that you didn't tell me?" The heat that rose in Kenya's body pushed her up out of her seat.

"Sit down, Kenya," her mother warned. "I know this is tough. Yes, I told Teddy. He's my husband." *Which my father was not*, thought Kenya. She slammed herself back down in her chair.

"So where's Cindalou?" she asked.

A curtain fell over her mother's face. Kenya was amazed, and in this moment pleased, to find that simply saying the woman's name could still do that.

"She lives in Mount Airy with her—with the child."

Sometimes Kenya forgot about that part of it. Of course there had never been any mention of a child in the cryptic postcards, which, she realized, had stopped coming some time ago. Now she realized she knew nothing about it—not even the sex. She also realized that going further with the subject might hurt her mother even more—so she did. "Is it a boy or a girl? Or should I say, do I have a brother or a sister?"

"A sister. I mean, if you consider her your sister."

"You considered Melvina your sister and you didn't have either of the same parents."

"I think I'm done talking about this for now," said Sheila.

"Oh is that right? Suit your fucking self," said Kenya, knowing she was insane to speak like that. From her ex-friend Devi, she had learned the word *nihilism*.

Sheila froze.

They faced each other. It was all her mother could do, Kenya knew, not to knock her on the floor. Instead she savagely ripped open a drawer on the breakfront and threw a stack of thick envelopes in the general direction of Kenya's face and stormed up the stairs.

The envelopes landed on the table. They were stamped STATE CORRECTIONAL INSTITUTION, GRATERFORD and addressed to Kenya.

From The Key: A Prose Libation for Black Martyrs
Draft #1, "The Martyr's Tale"

I meant to die. When I had dispatched each one of them, I tried to follow. But I was too weak to walk into the fire and too strong to succumb to the poison. Now it is true that searing pain shoots through my stomach and I'm lying in my own filth, but regretfully, I am alive.

I can see through the small barred window that the sun is a crimson ball in the August sky, dropping lower. Earlier there was a crowd of white men cursing themselves hoarse, calling me out of my name. Then the mood turned suddenly celebratory, as if these farmhands and laborers took joy in a rare daytime moment to relax. Despite the early hour, they passed a bottle and made jokes. Then they remembered themselves and dispersed. I know that they will come back. After dark they will fill this cell and tear me apart like animals.

What I have done is worse than anyone I know has done.

I have gone beyond disgrace into horror. And yet I know that white men, even "innocent" ones, are worse. They who have labeled the rest of us savages, they who are always accusing others of eating human flesh, are the true cannibals. They devour the human soul.

Their mouths were bloody on the island where I came from, where my grandparents had worked in the sugar fields in the time of slavery and returned to the same sugar fields after. This was back home, where my father died of a heart attack, so hard did he work polishing a white woman's silver, so eager to prove himself good as any white man. But of course white men did not polish silver where I came from. Where my sallow-skinned mother was so consumed with the life she would never have that she either ignored or beat me cruelly. The mouths of white men were bloody in New York, the filthy, freezing city where my wife, Elizabeth, and I first landed, in search of the something golden promised us in America. And now we are here.

"These will be *good* white people," my wife had said before we arrived. But Elizabeth, no matter how many times I have explained it, does not understand the hollow echoes of the term *good white people*. Like so many foolish and desperate Negroes, she acts as if there were a difference between a foot resting slightly on one's neck versus one resting heavily. "Neither will allow you to stand," I have told her. "Oh, but you are dramatic," she says. Or used to say.

There will not be a trial, so no one will ask why I did what I did, but I wonder what Elizabeth would say if they asked her. I wonder if she would tell them that I was never satisfied. Or defend the Architect's mistress and her ugly, menacing children? I try not to, it makes me clutch my burning stomach, but I can see my wife sitting before a jury of white men, eyes cast down, telling them that I was insane.

But truly it is not me who is insane. In the internationally famous home where we arrived to serve the Architect, where though some rooms blaze with sunlight and sky, we occupied a damp, stifling, and pitch-dark room in the basement (damp, freezing, and pitch-dark in the winter). In the widely photographed and much bragged-about home that the Architect continues to refine, we spent our days going in and out of a kitchen the size of the corner of the shack where my mother cooked our miserable meals. The light and air in that room came from a stingy ribbon of window. Was it insane to complain about dancing around each other (and the large Irish housemaid) in that tiny furnace on a floor slick with steam and sweat? Or about the squat entryway, some kind of perverse joke, that even my wife, in no way tall for a woman, must duck to enter? If I am insane, perhaps it is from the repeated blows to my skull I've borne forgetting to bend down as I go in and out of that dungeon.

I heard the Architect giving a tour to guests who laughed at the size of the kitchen, to which he simply replied, "I don't cook." It was a line he would go on to repeat to visitors several times, to much laughter.

Oh yes, that employment agent, the one who furnished "a clean couple of Caribbean Negroes" to these "good white people." He was a soul devourer, too.

I have a confession. I don't want to tell it but I must. Once, I, too, allowed myself to be led on by the *good white people* here. Not the mistress or her children, who manage to appear both sickly and fat; I knew what they were about when I first laid eyes on them. No: I began to have a kind of faith in the Architect. He was white, yes, but also a man of vision by definition. I let myself imagine that the Architect might see something improbable behind my dark eyes, that he might apprentice me in the design of his buildings. It had been a mistake to mention this to my wife, who warned me that I expected too much even from good white people, and that we should be glad that we weren't diving for pennies in the sea at home. I never did tell her how I sometimes went about my tasks as a servant while dreaming of learning to build mansions and concert halls. The memory of this washes over me in an acid wave of shame at least once a day.

I never did tell her about the conversation with the Architect, when he called me into his study. My heart started to beat rapidly, as if I were a silly little girl, because I thought, *Now is the time; he will talk to me about his craft.* Instead, he showed me a stained, malodorous blanket draped over the chaise longue where he liked to nap, and demonstrated how to fold it just so. He told me conspiratorially that the Irish housemaid had been banned from straightening the room because she could never get the folding right. "I'm counting on you," he said with a wink.

It was after that when I began to see my future as the kitchen with that low entryway and the walls squeezing in to push the breath out of me. Sometimes down in the cell of our room, I would suddenly gasp for air. Elizabeth would ask me what was wrong, but I knew she would not understand. I tried to tell her, Look, just because the Architect is white does not make him more than a man, and just because I am colored does not mean I am less.

And yet . . . I cannot stop the faces from swimming into my mind as they emerge from the smoke I can still smell on my clothes. I cannot help but watch their bleeding faces melt like white-and-red candles. I cannot stop tasting what I did not want to eat: the bit of bloody flesh that landed on my lip as I drew my ax back from cleaving the skull of the little boy.

When I was a little barefoot boy, my mother laughed at me when I said I would become important and make it so that the white people on the island would cut sugarcane and the black people would sit on verandahs, sipping tea. She would not laugh now. I have moved beyond disgrace and into horror and I am ready for the night and the men. Let them come.

Kenya read what her father wrote, each envelope containing a few pages, in stutters. She kept putting the pages down on an impulse to yell down to her mother. But then she remembered she was angry with her mother for keeping this from her. So she did not call out but simply kept reading. It was laughable. But she was not laughing.

She'd never really thought about her father's obsession with the butler. It had been one of those childhood things she had not really questioned, like the rugless hardwood floors in her bedroom that regularly gave her splinters, or the fact that Johnbrown didn't drive. Why had he sent her this and not a single actual letter? Perhaps her mother had been kind to hold this back. It was dated a year ago. But then again, her mother had not known that they were not letters. So no matter what she said, it had been spiteful to keep them from Kenya. And then there was Teddy Jaffrey.

That Kenya was stuck between and among these people made her angry. Her thoughts whirled about in fury, finally resting in the garage, on the sledgehammer. She imagined herself using the sledgehammer to destroy both of the cars. A Mercedes with busted glass and sledgehammer-size dents would at least project the correct image of her mother's husband. But the battered cars, surrounded by their own glass—the bewildered expressions of her mother and her mother's husband—those were secondary. What sent Kenya into a trance was the thought of making contact, the metallic sound of slamming a car with the hammer, the music of breaking glass. That night, just before she finally drifted off to sleep, she saw a flashing image of her father dressed as the TV character Benson, brandishing an ax.

The fantasy of using the sledgehammer was so vivid that Kenya woke up the next morning with a gasp, wondering if she had not destroyed the cars in her sleep. Then she briefly wondered if she'd dreamt up her father being in prison. She had not. Her mother was contrite and, when Teddy was out of earshot, said that maybe one day they could go to the prison.

"When?" asked Kenya, and she knew from the look on Sheila's face that her mother's offer had been only partly sincere. But then one cold Saturday in November, they were driving there.

"So what does he say in his letters?" Sheila asked after getting on the expressway.

"Nothing much," Kenya lied, keeping her eyes straight ahead. "Prison food is bad. He's reading a lot, you know, Malcolm X–style."

"Sounds right up his alley," her mother muttered. "A life of study."

Kenya had not expected prison to be so bright, or their visit to take place in a room so crowded. It reminded her of the lunchroom at Lea School. It had the same ammonia smell, and people were eating things that made their fingers greasy, just as the cafeteria food had. But unlike cafeteria food, these things were homemade. Kenya watched as a withered but sparkling-eyed old woman unwrapped fried chicken and slices of chocolate cake for her grinning son. Kenya hadn't known you could bring care packages to prison as if it were camp. She suspected that her mother had known and still had packed nothing. Her mouth watered as the old woman poured what looked like lemonade from a thermos.

Though there were some extremely hard-bitten white people, the visitors were mostly black women, some with small children. One tiny girl in a lacy yellow dress and a blizzard of white barrettes chanted, "Ma-ma, ma-ma, ma-ma, ma-ma," impervious to a harried woman desperate to show her prisoner that the girl could say "Dad-dy."

Johnbrown appeared in his blue jumpsuit. His eyes, which were bright and sad, triggered something behind Kenya's own rapidly filling eyes. She saw her mother blinking hard. They had been a family. After pausing in the doorway, he moved slowly toward Kenya and folded her into him. "Monkey," he said, his hug engulfing her in a smell of cigarettes and sour milk. He hugged her mother. They sat down at one of the small tables, she and her mother crowding one side, he on the other.

"I can't believe it," he said, wiping away tears. Kenya remembered the one previous occasion she'd seen him cry, just before fleeing her mother's hospital room. How disgusted she'd been and how hurt.

"It's been a long time," said Sheila.

"You look beautiful, both of you," Johnbrown said. Kenya now thought it was absurd that she'd expected him to comment on her mother's hair. Her own she wore in at least one hundred tiny braids with extensions, done by a woman in her house on City Line Avenue, despite her mother's offer to "take her to the hairdresser." It was Kenya's business to say no as much as she could.

"Say thank you, Kenya."

"Thank you, Kenya," she blurted.

Her mother scowled, but Johnbrown laughed. "How is your new school?" he asked.

Kenya was in her fifth year at Barrett. "My new—?" she said. "Oh, it's fine."

"Getting good grades?"

"Kenya is number three in her class," said Sheila.

"I wouldn't expect any less," he said.

"How's prison?" asked Kenya.

Her father laughed his high-pitched laugh. It was so familiar and yet so ancient that it made Kenya laugh, too.

"It is not great," he said. "Not great. And you see who's here."

"Sure do," said Sheila, shaking her head.

"I mean, you know," he said, and Kenya did know exactly

what he would say, but he said it anyway, "that the majority of prisoners in the U.S. are white."

"But it sure doesn't look like it here," said her mother.

There was a pause.

"We don't have a lot of time," he said. "So I want to say—"

Sheila raised her hand. "Let me give you two a minute."

"But what I have to say includes you, too, baby."

" 'Baby'? Oh no, no."

"But I didn't mean—"

"I'm going to be right over there, Kenya. Good seeing you, Johnbrown. You take care of yourself, okay?"

Johnbrown sighed. He and Kenya watched her mother go sit in one of the chairs bolted to the walls. Then her father reached out for her hand and held it. As far as she could recall, it was an unprecedented gesture for him. His hand was moist; she tried not to pull back.

"First, what I wanted to say to you—both of you, really, so please relay this to your mother—is that I'm sorry. I made mistakes that I've had a long time to think about, starting the day I ran away. I hope you never have occasion to feel as sorry as I do. Okay?"

"Okay," said Kenya.

"Second, I'm not going to be in here that long, just a few more months. And when I come out, I want to be your father again. I know your mother's got her own thing, and that's great, but you're my daughter and I love you more than anything."

"I guess," Kenya said without thinking.

"You guess?" Johnbrown laughed.

"Thanks?" It was no one's fault but Johnbrown's that they

were here. Did they really need to make declarations of love? Instead, Kenya screwed up her courage to ask a question. "What about Cindalou and the baby?" she asked.

"Tell you the truth, I don't know what's going on with me and Cindalou. Yes, you do have a sister, and she's not a baby anymore. But none of that changes us."

"What's her name? My, um, sister."

"Amandla. It means—"

"I know what it means," Kenya said, annoyed. Didn't he remember their trip to the Free South Africa Rally in Washington, D.C., by chartered bus?

"Want to know what I love best about Amandla?" said Johnbrown, grinning.

Kenya felt her eyes narrow.

"How much she reminds me of you."

"I'm sure," Kenya muttered, trying to decide on a feeling that wouldn't make her cry. It was hard, though. No more Cindalou. What did it mean? She thought of telling him about Teddy Jaffrey. She kept her mouth shut.

". . . So promise me," he was saying, "that when I get out, we can be family again. It's the only thing I've been thinking about since I've been in here. That and, you know, staying alive."

The mother of the girl in barrettes gripped her daughter's arm, stressing that it was her last chance. The girl began crying. ("*Mama*," she wailed.)

"Baba," she said. "Those letters you sent?"

Kenya's father's expression was a curious mix of cornered and eager. "The drafts? I was wondering when you might ask about that."

"I thought The Key was philosophy and history."

"Well, philosophy and history—those are just ways of telling stories. This is a story, too. You know I met this really cool white dude in here, Garrett Hadnitch. Kind of weird, but mostly in a good way, I think."

Garrett Hadnitch. The name rang a bell, but it was too faint.

Johnbrown continued. "Anyway, he's a writer. He's even written two novels in here, really good stuff. We talk about books. I was telling him about Julian Carlton—and he already knew the story. He's an architecture fanatic, really into Frank Lloyd Wright. Anyway, the story is part of The Key."

"But why are you sending them to me?" Kenya asked before she could stop herself. She tried not to sound how she'd felt reading them at first. It was like when she was little and helped with the laundry, finding frayed edges and holes as she folded her father's boxer shorts. When she was eight, the sight of that ragged underwear had made her sad. It looked like the shame of being alive.

Her father leaned back, looking a little sad. "I'm not sure," he said. "I think I wanted you to keep them safe. I've been working on more. Do you want me to stop sending them?"

"No," Kenya said quickly, unsure if she was telling the truth or not.

The guard announced that the visiting hour was ending.

Johnbrown looked at Kenya, and she watched him pick up his shoulders and force a smile that would have earned Sheila's disdain years ago.

"Don't kill any white people, okay, Baba?" she said, giving him her own brave smile.

"Just in the mind," he said. "Maybe on paper."

As they hugged goodbye, Kenya's father spoke in a stage whisper. "Say, Monkey. What the hell did your mom go and do to her hair?"

Though eleventh grade was the most important for getting into college and her SAT scores had only been okay, Kenya often found it impossible to concentrate on school. Her rank had slipped to near the middle of the class, which stung, but not quite enough to move her to action. Just as at Lea School, where she would have rather felt separate from her classmates because she was a prodigy, she knew she should have been the "brilliant black girl" in her class at Barrett, the heir to those brave children in the South who'd shined their shoes each morning only to get kicked and spat on in their fight for a good education, the descendant of all of those remarkable Negro Firsts. She should have been proving herself more worthy of a mother who had used education to catapult herself from a housing project to a large house in the suburbs.

Alas.

That year, Kenya got a mind-numbing part-time job filing and organizing the supply closets at the office of her grandmother's old friend Dr. Walton. Social life mainly meant getting into a car with Lolly, Zaineb, and Phyllis and going to Bennigan's, TGI Friday's, or the movies. On the nights she stayed in, she read desultorily in her bedroom with Sheila's tiny old black-and-white TV on in the background, keeping her company.

Teddy Jaffrey, who had finally passed the real estate exam and quickly become successful, had offered to buy Kenya a big new color set, but she said she didn't need it. "Kenya doesn't go in for that kind of thing," her mother had said, sounding both nasty and admiring. Sheila herself had initially seemed apprehensive about Teddy's lavish new ways. But she finally warmed to his gifts of jewelry and her first fur coat. As for the kind of thing Sheila herself went in for now, one evening in November she came home to a (leased) black Mercedes-Benz to match Teddy's blue one. He'd actually had a bow tied on it, like in the commercials.

"I couldn't wait for Christmas," he said, because now they celebrated Christmas, as well as a rather cursory version of Kwanzaa.

Teddy convinced Sheila to get rid of the couch that had been one of her signature purchases with Lars after they moved into Grandmama's and replace it with beige sectionals that took up twice as much space. He also offered to pay to put a sun porch on the back of the house. Sheila bubbled about it for months, looking at magazines and drawing up plans. Finally, in the spring, construction workers showed up, filling the backyard with stacks of wood and bags of cement, carelessly squashing Grandmama's rosebushes.

Since Teddy seemed wholly preoccupied with being the Man, Kenya felt sure that he would not come into her room again. Still, what she most enjoyed about going out was the chance to escape him and her mother on weekend nights. Sometimes they entertained Teddy's friend Bert, who sounded like a black person, and his latest black girlfriend, usually a thin, whispering type. Sometimes Alma Lewis and her husband came over to play pinochle. But even if it was just Sheila and Teddy, they always drank wine and got loud. Louder still were the four-foot speakers that Teddy had bought for a spare room upstairs that he now called the Surround Room. Unfortunately, the Surround Room, which had been so designated because it had a particular electrical hookup, was next to Kenya's room. She could hear her mother and Teddy's friends laughing into the nights. She also had to listen to their music, as well as Sheila and Teddy's playful arguments over music. Incredibly, Teddy's favorite song was "Ain't No Stoppin' Us Now," which always made Kenya remember the humiliating May Day performance at Lea School. Back then, while doing the imbecilic steps, she had noticed just how slow and depressing the song actually was. As the fifth grade had shuffled to the right and the left, she had thought of how easily they could be stopped.

Meanwhile, Teddy made a show of "banning" Sheila's music from the stereo, especially her beloved Donny Hathaway.

"That nigger," he said, "can turn anything into a funeral song. I mean, correct me if I'm wrong, but isn't a song called 'To Be Young, Gifted and Black' supposed to sound *inspirational*? Shit makes me feel like eating a gun."

"Or getting really high and falling out of a window," said Bert, and Kenya remembered that this was the story of how Donny Hathaway had died.

"Y'all leave Donny alone," said Sheila. "He was a tortured genius."

"You can play them sad songs downstairs on your sad little stereo," Teddy said.

• • •

Kenya spent the occasional Friday or Saturday at a party that would have appalled Sheila as much as Sheila's carrying on irritated Kenya. Kenya thought about this with some satisfaction one night as she sipped a beer in some girl's crowded kitchen somewhere in Devon. She wanted to go sit down in another room but didn't feel like fighting the crowd that was clumped up in the kitchen, avoiding the music until they got drunk enough to dance. Across the room, she saw Tuff Wieder. She nodded coolly, then went up the back stairs, Sharon McCall hot on her trail.

"Those crazy kids," she said to Phyllis, though she wished Zaineb had been there instead.

"What?" Phyllis yelled. "Oh my God, Zach Vito is here. Oh my God. Did he see me? Is this zit terrible? Where are you going?"

Kenya began pushing her way into the living room. These parties were all the same. They took place at sprawling but not overly interesting suburban houses crammed with extras from John Hughes movies. Tonight, as on many of those nights, she and Lolly seemed to be the only black people in some stranger's house, and Kenya worked to stifle her instinctual fear of too-many-drunk-unknown-white-people—especially boys. As she made it into the living room, where people were beginning to fling themselves around, she could not help but be afraid, for example, that if she spilled her drink on some wild dancer, he might call her something nasty. Maybe it was crazy, but these parties recalled nothing so much as scenes of rabid segregation enthusiasts in *Eyes on the Prize*. It was not comforting that the soundtrack to these nights always included a lot of rap music, especially Public Enemy and N.W.A. Kenya wondered what kind of music the young racists of the fifties got pumped up to before going out to spit on children trying to integrate the schools. Black folks made all the music with a good beat back then, too.

Still, though Kenya sometimes blew off invitations to eat mozzarella sticks or watch horror film sequels, she always rallied to go to parties, telling herself that anything could happen. And yet no matter how frantically she danced, how long her braids, or how tight her pants, nothing ever did.

It was a serious improvement when Barrett social life suddenly brought Kenya back to the city, via Zaineb's cousin Reggie, who lived in an actual house in downtown Philadelphia. Kenya had seen near-mansions on the Main Line, but had never been in anything as chic as a town house in Society Hill. Reggie threw spontaneous get-togethers at his parents' glistening home on nights when his mother was away for work and his father had to report to the hospital. Reggie didn't care much for people, but he loved drugs. He threw parties like nets, to draw in as many as possible.

Partying in the city brightened up Kenya's friends. Lolly would pretend to get drunker than she was and start grinding on the nearest girl, something she never did at parties on the Main Line. Phyllis, who shared Reggie's passion for drugs, had a talent for figuring out who was holding the hardest thing and getting some for free; traditionally, she then made out with whoever had gotten her high. So it was that she became the only Barrett girl known to have tried crack. At the opposite end of the spectrum, Zaineb, the designated driver, was haunted by a TV special she'd seen about drunk driving, which featured a shot of bloody prom dress bits on a lonely highway. She wouldn't touch alcohol, not even the one drink Kenya usually allowed herself, but in the city, she talked more animatedly than usual, preening about her connection to Reggie.

There was always a smattering of black kids at these parties, but, as on the Main Line, the boys seemed not to notice Kenya. Besides the white girls with their obvious allure, there was Cary Benin, a creamy brown Jessica Rabbit type who went to the Catholic school across from Barrett, with her long, shiny, naturally straight hair. Cary dressed in February as if it were August (and don't even ask about August).

Even if no one seemed to see her, Kenya watched everything, and she always noticed the boy, white or black, whom everybody else noticed. There might be a group of contenders, but she always tried to narrow it down to the Man, the one who moved around with the most ease and commanded the most feverish greetings. Sometimes he was cute, sometimes less so. Sometimes he was white, other times black, or even racially ambiguous, as in the era of dashing Vincent Tran-Garcia, with his sumptuous swirl of hair. When Kenya came home, she shunned the bed that Teddy Jaffrey had threatened to climb into, secreting herself in her bedroom closet to entertain herself with deliberate fantasies of how the Man would approach her in the crowd. She didn't even need to get to the part in the sequence when they touched. Just the image of her, the boy, a café table, two hot chocolates with whipped cream, and done.

Of course she had preferences. She was not at all interested in Ned Samuels, for example, who was evidently the most popular boy at a party she ventured out to on a chilly April night. He went to the arts magnet high school in the city and there was a lot of murmuring about his talent as a painter. But with shockingly bright red hair and freckles so numerous they looked painful in the harsh light of the kitchen—where everyone milled near the liquor—Ned Samuels was a stretch for Kenya's masturbatory fantasies. Then she noticed the black boy at his side.

"Commodore!" she screamed.

"What?" he yelled back.

"Commodore!" she called again.

"OOGABOOGAAAAAAAAAAAA!" he screamed, jumping up and down. He was tall, and the jumping made him almost freakishly so. "Oh my Gaaaaaaaaaaawd!" he yelled. They hugged each other, and since Ned Samuels was looking, everyone else in the kitchen looked, too. Kenya felt triumphant as Commodore introduced her to Ned, who nodded and pronounced her name to be sure he had gotten it right.

"Whew, what's it been, a hundred years? You look *great*," Commodore said.

"You look tall," said Kenya, her face growing warm as she exaggerated an effort to look up at him.

"I think you might be the same height you were in, what, third grade? Who knew you'd turn out to be such a squirt?" Commodore said. "Hey, want something to drink?"

Kenya allowed him to make her a second drink for the night, something tasting of Hawaiian Punch. She felt both at home and in outer space as their conversation took them from the kitchen to a quiet corner of the living room.

He went to the arts high school with Ned and had never heard of Barrett. He remembered Yaya saying that Kenya went to "some private school." He lived in the same house Kenya remembered, in the area of West Philly called the Bottom. He told her that the neighborhood had gotten a lot worse.

"It's really fucking scary," he said. "I mean, I don't know who's worse: the basehead zombies or the dealers. Our next-door neighbor got shot standing in her kitchen window. Guess you don't know nothin' about all that out in the burbs."

"We hear about it on the news. You know. We send money," said Kenya. The punch thickened her tongue, but she congratulated herself that her mind still worked.

"So what's it like out there?" Commodore asked.

"Everything is perfect. My mother married this great guy, and we live in a big house and I go to private school and . . ." Commodore's eyes widened.

"I mean it sucks dick like everything else," she said, suddenly feeling as if she might actually blush, having raised such a specter, even in slang.

"Your mother got remarried?"

"Unfortunately," Kenya said. Then she paused. "But actually 'remarried' is not the way to put that. It turns out my parents were never actually married."

"Say what?"

"Yup." It was delicious telling Commodore things that she usually couldn't talk about in the world where she lived.

"Why not?"

"You know, Movement bullshit."

"That's *deep*," said Commodore. It was something the Seven

Days used to say. They laughed. He said, "So not a fan of the new husband, huh?"

"No," she said simply.

Commodore said, "I almost ran into one of those situations myself. A stepdaddy. Well, maybe more of a brother in this case." He giggled.

"Yeah?"

Commodore told a riveting story about how his parents had briefly separated. Yaya had left to live with a local conga drumming legend barely out of his teens, who deserted her after a few weeks. Alfred had let her come back, but he was so angry that he hardly ever spoke. Three years later, they still spent much of their time together in silence. Commodore suspected that Yaya might have another boyfriend.

"I mean, they managed to slap it together again for my sake. But I don't like being in that house, and I don't think they like it either."

"That's sad, Commodore."

"Is what it is. So have you heard from your"—and here he gave a small smile—"Baba?"

"He's in prison."

"*What?*" Commodore stood up and then fell back down. "All I heard is that he ran off with Cindalou. Where does prison come into it? Stop dropping these bombs! Prison for what?"

He didn't know, Kenya realized. Maybe none of the Seven Days knew about the night with the sleepwalking, the gun, and the hospital. Kenya left it in the little sealed box. "Well, there was some madness with tagging a bunch of police stations, and then he jumped bail. I saw him there, in prison. I guess he's probably out by now."

Commodore said, "Maybe he'll try to start it again. You know."

"The Seven Days?"

"Yeah, 'cause obviously these niggers need something in their lives."

Kenya still had not trained herself to not wince at the word *nigger*, though it was a regular feature of Teddy Jaffrey's speech.

"I don't know," she said. "Seems to me that's where everything started."

"I guess you could see it that way," said Commodore. Suddenly he made as if to pour his cup of red juice on the rug. "From the Creator, for the martyrs," he said.

"For the martyrs," she repeated.

They didn't laugh.

"Commie!" screamed a chunky white girl in combat boots and with thin pigtails. "You better fucking dance with me!"

"Excuse me," he said, rolling his eyes but not really. "I'll be back. Or—you should come over in a minute." He leaned close to her. "Save me."

Kenya wanted to go find one of the people she came with and tell them the miracle of what had just happened, but when she tried to stand, the floor seemed to fall away. Across the room, she watched Commodore moving to "Bonita Applebum," a song that made her dizzy with happiness but also made her heart ache. It had a melancholy blackness that sounded like the music her father used to listen to. Kenya found herself wondering what had happened to her father's old records: Doug and Jean Carn, Ornette Coleman, pre-disco Earth, Wind & Fire. Commodore moved languidly with the girl, but quickly enough to thwart her attempts to drape herself around him. Kenya imagined herself dancing with him.

Commodore walked up to say he'd be back. Then he disappeared. She didn't know how much time passed before Zaineb was standing over her saying that it was time to go and asking if she'd seen Lolly or Phyllis. After struggling to get off of the slippery leather couch, and a tenuous walk up the stairs, Kenya and Zaineb found them in the enormous master bathroom. Phyllis lay on the floor laughing and writhing while Lolly groped around under her short denim skirt.

"Oh my God, you guys! Phyllis lost her tampon!" Lolly yelled.

"What?"

"It's true," Phyllis said merrily. "I totally forgot about it and I'm too blasted to get my hand up there! It's been in there, like, nine hours or something."

"It's not funny, Phyllis," Lolly hissed. "You could get toxic shock syndrome."

Suddenly Reggie burst into the bathroom. "Phyllis, did you take those fucking 'shrooms out of my freezer?" he yelled. His eyes were bleary and his bare feet were filthy.

"Get the fuck out of here, you pervert!" hissed Zaineb.

"Phyllis, did you do mushrooms?" yelled Lolly.

"Phyllis, where are my 'shrooms?" he yelled. "Hold on, what are you guys doing to Phyllis?"

"Oh my God, who has 'shrooms?" Phyllis said, pushing Lolly aside and shooting up from the floor.

Kenya closed her eyes and tried to wash it away. Even if they never spoke again, she was glad Commodore was in the world.

She resisted briefly, tried to push it down, but it was still there later when she thought of him, rising in her chest, flooding outward in her body. He wasn't the Man by anyone else's standards. When Kenya tried to mention him to Zaineb and the others, they didn't remember who he was. But to Kenya he was cute. She concentrated on seeing him as he was at the party, tall and slender, maybe with muscular arms, cigar-brown, with a high, neat fade. And he was like her. He knew her in a way that no one else did these days. Or at least the way no one else—namely Sheila—admitted to knowing her.

Commodore had been in the rooms filled with eccentric black people from Kenya's childhood, and now inhabited the ones filled with drunken white people. She thought again and again of their conversation on the leather couch, her head swimming pleasantly with punch, surrounded by dancers who seemed to push her and Commodore closer together. She had gotten so absorbed in touching and retouching the fantasy version of the scene that she experienced something like fear one Sunday afternoon two weeks later when he called her. Kenya, who had her own phone, but not, like every other Barrett girl, her own line, didn't even hear the phone ring. She was, at that very moment, dreaming of Commodore over her American history textbook. Her mother's voice floated up to her through the door.

"Who is it?" Kenya asked, though it was always Zaineb.

"It's Commodore," Sheila said, her voice full of wonder, moving closer.

By the time Kenya picked up the phone, Sheila was knocking on her door. She came in before Kenya could answer.

"Ooga Booga!" Commodore said.

"Oh hey," said Kenya, feeling crazy. "Hang on." Sheila was looking at her with wide eyes. "Mom," Kenya said, "can you go hang up the phone?"

"Tell him I said hello," Sheila said, backing out. She shook her head as if she, too, had been interrupted in a reverie.

Kenya felt as if she were the main character in one of the novels she hated but still read, the ones where the plain girl dreamed and her dream came true. He was calling to invite her to hang out downtown. She nearly tripped on the carpet going down the stairs, though she had tried very hard not to rush at all.

"Mom," she said, catching her breath, "can I have a ride to the train station?"

"You didn't tell me you saw Commodore," Sheila accused. She looked up from where she liked to sit on her new furniture with the Sunday paper while Teddy watched basketball for what seemed like the entire day. During commercials he paced to the back of the house and glared at the lack of progress contractors were making on the "sun porch."

"Who's Commodore?" Teddy said. "I thought you were too hip for Lionel Richie."

Kenya addressed Sheila. "I saw him at a party."

"Well, how did he seem?"

"Fine. He goes to Creative and Performing Arts."

"Do they still live in the same place?" Sheila asked. She did not speak the name Yaya or Alfred.

"Yeah. Commodore says it's pretty bad over there."

"I should say so. This crack business," said Sheila.

"Uhm!" affirmed Teddy.

"So," said Kenya, "can I get a ride?"

"Well, you know I don't like to go out on Sundays," her mother said, as she had perhaps ten thousand times, just before taking Kenya somewhere on a Sunday. Sheila never said anything about it and never asked questions, but it was clear that she would sacrifice even her at-home Sundays so Kenya could have some kind of social life.

"Please?"

Sheila raised her eyebrow.

"I mean, it doesn't really matter," said Kenya, too late. Her mother was already smiling.

They met in Rittenhouse Square Park, where Commodore waited with Ned, an overweight black kid named Peter, and a whispering white girl named Dawn, who mostly looked out at Ned from under her bangs. When Kenya walked up, she heard Commodore saying, "I *hate* him."

"Who?" said Kenya.

"Oog—I mean Kenya!" said Commodore. "What it *do*?"

Ned said hello and extended his hand with cute formality, as if they'd never met. Kenya shook his hand and didn't remind him.

"So who is this that you hate?" she asked Commodore.

"Ugh! This kid Oliver, at school. He is *the worst*!"

"He's not that bad," said Peter, who had a rumbling bass voice.

"He really *is* that bad," Commodore said.

The girl Dawn whispered something.

"Of course he's nice to you, Dawn," said Commodore. "He wants to poke you with his long weird curvy penis!"

Ned threw back his head and laughed. "Come on, Commie, what do you know about his dick? That's a little gay."

"I don't need to be gay. I can just tell that it probably looks like one of his gross dreadlocks. That guy is so wannabe, but wannabe what? Punk? Rasta? Pasta? A tragic mulatto indeed."

"Bro, you are *wrong*," said Peter. "Ain't he wrong?" he asked Kenya.

They were sitting in a circle on a patch of grass. An older white man stood nearby looking at them pointedly while his large dog sniffed the ground in a preparatory fashion.

"We need to get in out of the elements," said Commodore.

"Agreed," said Ned.

Kenya followed them to Ned's parents' condominium high above the park, with its exposed brick walls and gleaming honey-colored floors. The windows, which were taller than Kenya, looked down on the park. Kenya stood in the huge open space that seemed to be the main room, trying to look nonchalant. Commodore went to the kitchen and asked if anyone else wanted a Screwdriver. Dawn took off her sneakers. Peter flopped onto the suede couch and used several remote controls to turn on the television.

"I'm going to bake cookies," said Dawn, who was easier to hear indoors.

"My dad rented a bunch of movies just before he left," said Ned. "This one's about the Sex Pistols. Might be okay."

"Ugh—you know who loves the Sex Pistols?" said Commodore.

"Dude, you are obsessed with Oliver. Should I be jealous?" Ned said, winking.

"I'm just saying, what black person in their right mind wears a leather jacket with a swastika on it?"

"Isn't that supposed to be a punk thing?" asked Dawn. "Isn't he in a band called Niggerpunk?"

Kenya tried not to flinch.

"Niggerpunk, indeed," said Commodore, who didn't seem bothered by a white girl's voice saying "nigger."

Peter began singing "Thin Line Between Love and Hate," a song whose clunky title made a bad thing much worse.

Except Kenya, none of them sat particularly still while watching *Sid and Nancy*. Ned fiddled with a joint; Dawn baked cookies from premade dough; Peter complained about punk music; Commodore worked on his terrible British accent. At first, Kenya, who sat next to him, was distracted by his nearness. But he didn't appear to notice, and soon she found herself absorbed in the movie, which was very gross and poignant. Though her family had taken three trips to New York, she'd never felt strongly about it, had never caught Zaineb's zeal. But she was struck by the bombed-out scenes at the end of the film, the purgatory where Sid Vicious danced with chummy black kids, then took a taxi to punk heaven with his dead girlfriend, whom he'd stabbed in a drug-fueled haze. She teared up briefly as the credits rolled. No one seemed to notice.

"What kind of shit was that?" Peter asked. "That's the kind of movie your dad watches? What if I made my Jamaican grandma watch that? I can just hear her now. 'But why de boy don't take 'im shower?' " he said in a rich, feminine voice.

"That heroin must be something else," said Commodore.

"I'm going to try, like, every drug just before I die," said Ned. He stared off dreamily into the middle distance.

"But it wasn't just the drugs," said Dawn. "They were addicted to, like, their love. That was what killed them." She sat on the floor and gazed up at Ned on the couch.

"Heroin," said Ned. "I'm trying that first."

"What'd you think, Kenya?" asked Commodore.

"Worst couple in history," she said, hoping that Dawn wouldn't feel insulted.

Commodore laughed.

Kenya hung out with Commodore and his friends at Ned's house several times that spring, happiest when it conflicted with some invitation from the girls. She loved to say no to them in order to hang out with high school seniors who went to school in Philly. She was no longer socially desperate.

When she was with Commodore and his friends, they talked endlessly of the other people at their school. While a lot of it was dull, she listened carefully for hints that he had a girlfriend or anything like it. They smoked pot (except Kenya) and baked cookies, played cards, and after the *Sid and Nancy* incident and, even more disturbingly, the *Blue Velvet* incident, only watched movies they'd already seen: *Monty Python and the Holy Grail*, *This Is Spinal Tap*, *Gremlins*, and *Nightmare on Elm Street*. During comedies, everyone worked hard at laughing, flopping around and gasping for air. They narrated the horror movies using funny voices, calling the characters "douchebag" and "dipshit."

It was almost always the five of them, give or take Peter, a tuba player who sometimes had weekend band practice, or Dawn, who was intermittently angry with Ned.

"She wants a relationship, but it's just not the time for us," he once told the others in her absence; this reminded Kenya of speeches she'd heard on *The Young and the Restless*.

Kenya waited to hear how Commodore would respond to that, but all he said was "Uh-huh." He never seemed terribly interested in Ned's relationship with Dawn.

When her mother asked if she and Commodore were "an item," Kenya tried to act nonchalant. While it was true that they were alone only when they spoke on the phone, they had begun talking nearly every night. At first they reminisced a lot about the Days and the way it had been with their parents.

Then they talked about other things, arguing about whether rap music would outlive soul, or making lists of their favorite movies. Commodore had snuck into *Angel Heart* and would never forget Lisa Bonet naked or bloody. Kenya thought *The Lost Boys* was high art. Sometimes Commodore complained bitterly about Oliver with what Kenya felt was an unhealthy intensity. Kenya spent more time than she wanted to trying to picture this boy. (Based on Commodore's description, she could picture only a photo she'd once seen of Jean-Michel Basquiat.) Though the bulk of Commodore's complaints involved Oliver's terribly named band and his affected British accent, it became clear that Commodore's rage was a competitive one. Oliver was always garnering a teacher's compliment for his work or an art prize that Commodore felt he deserved, and then there were confusing stories about Oliver "trying to flirt." A girl named Pippa figured heavily in these anticlimactic tales.

"What does Oliver's flirting have to do with you?" Kenya asked.

"I just hate seeing that big dork make such a fool of himself. It offends my sensibilities," Commodore said.

After getting off the phone Kenya sometimes stayed up late dozing over her homework. The morning after one of these marathons, Kenya slept through her alarm and woke up to Zaineb, who usually drove her to school, outside honking her horn and Teddy knocking on her bedroom door.

Though Kenya had vowed never to cause Teddy to come near her room, this particular conversation had been worth it.

"How do you meet guys?" Commodore had asked suddenly. "You know, going to that school?"

"I don't meet too many," said Kenya. Up until that moment, she hadn't known how she would handle this question. Should she demur and make herself seem normal? Or should she tell the truth, which was that nothing—not a kiss, not a date, and certainly not sex—had ever happened to her.

Commodore had two ways of talking, even on the phone. Sometimes he was clearly distracted. Now his focus sucked the air out of the space between them. "Do you, ah, date outside the race?" he asked, and Kenya could feel him waiting for her answer.

"Not really," she said.

"Hmph. So you don't approve of that sort of thing?"

"Do you?" asked Kenya.

"Well, you know I love black women," said Commodore.

"I *love* my black women. But I keep my options open, you know?"

"Is that how you put it?" said Kenya.

Commodore gasped in a dramatic fashion. "You would judge me? After I opened up to you? I can't believe this."

"Settle down, Miss Scarlett. So you date white girls?"

"I didn't say that!"

But during the next conversation, she learned about Hannah (two dates), Scout (sophomore dance), and Tessa (they just kicked it sometimes). They'd all been special in their own way, and all white, apparently. But none of them mattered, he said, because thoughts of other girls had gone away when he met Pippa.

"That jawn almost broke my heart. Bruised it, at least. At least!"

"You really want to call a white girl a *jawn*? Just doesn't seem right," Kenya said, trying to smooth the edge out of her voice.

"So mean! I almost lost my mojo over that one. I'm over it now, though."

It was hard for Kenya to put together either a picture or a personality for Pippa through Commodore's description. Mostly "there was just something about her." Listening to Commodore, she pictured a faceless white female presence. Several months later, when she finally saw Pippa at one of Reggie's parties, Kenya noted her long, thick blond hair and her large, globe-like breasts.

"I mean, it seemed like we were getting close for a while, you know. I would walk her to her classes and put these sweet notes in her locker. I know it sounds corny. But then she just, like, started dodging me. She switched lockers without saying anything. I can't believe I'm telling you this stuff. I must really feel comfortable with you . . ." Commodore said, trailing off. Kenya made listening noises, not knowing how else to respond. Later, she kept thinking about it, how she should have acted. Because after that conversation, Commodore didn't call for several days.

"Where's your boyfriend?" asked Teddy Jaffrey.

Where's yours? thought Kenya.

"Don't tease her," said Sheila.

Barrett had let out for the summer and Kenya had a week off before going full-time at Dr. Walton's office. Commodore would still be in school several more weeks. It had been five days since she'd spoken to him. She told herself that after a conversation like the one they'd had about his love for every other girl in America, she should wait for him to call.

But she didn't.

An angry male voice answered the phone: Alfred. Though he hadn't talked much in the old days, a wave of nostalgia nearly knocked the phone from Kenya's hand. Then Commodore was on the phone, sounding as if he had a cold.

"I have to call you back," he said. As he hung up Kenya heard angry voices in the background.

Kenya wanted desperately to know what was going on. She had scribbled Ned's number down somewhere once. She thought of calling him to get the story. But soon enough the phone rang.

"Wait till you hear this bullshit," Commodore said. "I have to be quick. I'm not even supposed to be on the phone, but they went out to get something to eat and left me here."

"What happened?" exhaled Kenya.

"What happened is that you can't trust *white* bitches."

That afternoon Commodore had been called into the principal's office—incidentally, another white bitch. Pippa had been there, "looking like someone had strangled her dog." Her tight-lipped mother and Alfred were there also. Also there: a large folder of the notes Commodore had slipped into Pippa's locker. Words like *harassment* were used by the principal, particularly in reference to the notes, which quoted both Henry Miller and Amiri Baraka extensively, and which had been found by Pippa's mother, who kept lamenting that something had to be done, since she couldn't *afford* to transfer Pippa to private school.

"Oh my God," said Kenya, who felt the shame of being alive on Commodore's behalf. "Did you know any of this was going to happen?"

Commodore laughed bitterly. "What kind of question is that? I guess I should have known when she started acting funny. But, I mean, if she didn't want me, fine. I don't know why she had to get school administration involved. That's the white girl part of it."

"I thought you were over her. That's what you said last time."

"Well, if I wasn't then, I sure as fuck am now! So I'm grounded, but when I get off punishment, can I see you? Like, just us? I haven't really felt like hanging out with Ned and them since this went down. Those cats are cool, but they don't *really* know what's up."

"What about Peter?"

"Peter is black and everything, but he grew up in the

Northeast and he basically discovered he was black in sophomore year. He's not like us," he said.

"Not like us," Kenya repeated.

"He's new to this," said Commodore. "We're true to this."

After his two-week punishment ended, Commodore suggested they meet at the art museum, where Kenya had not
been in years. It was an unnaturally warm Sunday, the day
before Memorial Day. She tried to dress alluringly without re-
vealing that she'd tried. She wore old jean shorts with a new
silky peach-colored blouse about which Sheila had been especially enthusiastic. Walking from the train station that afternoon, she realized it was a poor choice for a hot day. She beat
Commodore to the museum, so she ran to the bathroom and
did her best to towel away the visible wet spots under her arms.
When she emerged into the grand entrance hall, she saw him
and smiled, her arms locked tight to her sides.

"Hey, you look good," he said. "Stop trying to make me
look like poor relations."

"What's wrong with what you're wearing? It's Bohemian."
His red polo shirt and loose jeans were both perfectly nice, if
paint stained, and he smelled good. Kenya wondered if he was
wearing some kind of man perfume, but the smell was gone
almost as soon as she detected it. She thought maybe it was
just her fevered imagination.

"Correct me if I'm wrong," he said, "but that's a blouse you're
wearing. You're wearing a blouse."

"Please stop saying *blouse*. It sounds like *slacks*." Kenya
shuddered.

The museum was cool and empty. They made it through a couple of floors, pausing to look at paintings that especially interested Commodore. He particularly liked ones with a hint of a horror story. He and Kenya stood forever in front of a huge canvas on which a bunch of white men in dark clothes, whose old-time look registered as "slaveowner" to Kenya, performed a bloody operation. It did not look as if they were helping the patient. The painting was aptly titled, Kenya thought: *The Gross Clinic*.

"I don't think she's going to make it," said Kenya.

"I think that's a dude they're operating on," said Commodore.

Kenya wasn't so sure. "What am I supposed to think is good about this?"

"It's like there's so much going on. Look at the mother there, and that guy in the back. And it's just so fucking *real*."

Nearby, an older white couple with unkempt curling gray hair and matching sandals stood smiling at them.

"Let's get out of here before they try to adopt us," Commodore murmured.

"Or sponsor us," Kenya said.

"I could use a sponsor," said Commodore. "A patron."

For lunch they bought hot dogs off of the cart out front, agreeing that even though these were beef—not pork—meat from a cart violated an unofficial Seven Days–type dietary restriction. They sat eating at the top of the steps, where people took snapshots of each other posing like Rocky.

"Maybe your art will be in there one day," said Kenya.

"What are you, my grandmother?"

"Okay, maybe you'll die broke and unknown. How's that?"

"What are you, my parents?"

"Is that really the kind of stuff they say to you?"

"Not in those words, but they're pretty pissed about next year."

"But you have a full ride to a good school!" protested Kenya. Commodore, who had not gone to private school, and consequently had not been held back a year like Kenya, had gotten a scholarship to Tyler, Temple University's art school. "And it's not far away, so they can't complain about that."

"Well, I don't think they would have minded me moving to Jupiter, actually. And they wanted me to go to a black college. They're not big fans of the company I keep, especially these days, with the shit happening at school. But mainly, they're just scared. It's like they made up this whole way to be, them and their crew. And they raised us with it, but since they made it up, they don't really know where it goes next. Like, they don't want me to be some kind of blue-collar grunt, or city bureaucrat like them. But they know I'm never going to study law, and since I barely passed ninth-grade science, med school is out. Of course they would never fix their lips to say 'Corporate America.' It's too late for that."

"My mom would fix her lips to say that."

"Yeah, your mom went another way," Commodore said, smiling. "I think mine is a little jealous, tell you the truth."

"Yeah, well, my baba went another way, too. Is she jealous of that?"

"Well, see, that's another reason they're scared. He was their Fearless Leader."

"And he was a nut."

Commodore looked thoughtful in the pause.

"I think about him sometimes," he said.

"My father?" Kenya squeaked.

"Yeah, he was kind of like an artist. I mean, he was an activist, or whatever they all thought they were, but he had a kind of thing to him like an artist."

Kenya thought about The Key and rolled her eyes. "He didn't make any art."

"No, but he was trying to do more than just make things better for black people."

"Wait, is it a bad thing to 'just make things better'?"

"No, not at all." Commodore laughed. "That's not what I meant. Making things better for black people is the only reason a chickenshit like me can even, like, exist. If it was the fifties, I would have just opened my eyes and died right there after being born."

Kenya laughed. "I think I would have made it home from the hospital maybe . . ."

"But your dad—excuse me, your baba—he had what they call a vision. He had a vision of another world. That's why he was always fighting with them."

"How do you know that? I don't remember you being there when they got into fights."

"I would hear about it later, though, mainly from my dad. He was not the biggest Johnbrown Curtis fan."

"Alfred talks?"

Commodore laughed again. Then he looked at her as if they'd just met.

"You feel like hanging out some more?" he asked.

Despite what Commodore had said about not wanting to see his school friends, they wound up at Ned's in the late afternoon. Ned answered the door in what looked like pajamas.

"Ned?" Kenya asked. "Do you actually have parents?"

"Unfortunately," he said. "Make yourselves at home. I think Dawn might be over later. Or not. I'll go shower," he said, yawning.

"And brush your teeth," said Commodore. "Please!"

"Please," Ned mimicked in a high voice. Then he said, "Commie, why don't you make yourself useful and roll us up something? Shit is in that drawer," he said, pointing to a heavy wooden chest. "And don't be makin' it all baggy like you usually do. Respect the herb like *you* paid for it." With that, he peeled off his shirt and padded into the bathroom. Kenya observed that his chest and back were muscular.

"What are you looking at?" asked Commodore with exaggerated petulance after the bathroom door had closed.

"A *lot* of freckles." Kenya imagined saying something to make him jealous, but it would have been absurd. Ned had nothing on Commodore, who, she'd decided, was beautiful in his lanky way, and also probably her soul mate.

When Ned emerged from the shower, he made grilled cheese sandwiches, and then they half watched *Xena: Warrior Princess* while Commodore and Ned smoked a joint. Kenya wanted to smoke with them, but she was terrified that she would find herself drooling all over Commodore. She was also terrified that maybe he would not even notice. In fact, he became quite absorbed in a monologue about how he had to "get back to my art. Like, really start taking it seriously again."

"When did you not take it seriously?" Ned asked. "It's embarrassing how much Mr. Yoder falls all over your shit in class. And you got a scholarship to Tyler; probably fucking affirmative action, but still."

Commodore ignored the dig. He said, "I mean I think I just let this Pippa shit distract me. But me and Kenya went to the museum today, and I was looking at some of that shit and thinking about, like, twenty years from now . . ."

"Dude, if anybody could do it, you could," said Ned before Commodore could finish the thought. It struck Kenya that Commodore had never said anything about Ned's art. Though she'd heard people at parties talking about his great paintings, he hadn't gotten into Tyler or any art school, and he was going to a school called Reed all the way in Oregon. Ned's face darkened as Commodore talked on and on, blithely vowing "to work till my fingers bleed" at school next year.

Ned cut him off. "So what are you guys up to the rest of the evening? Gonna go get started on Michelangelo's *Ghetto David*?" He didn't *quite* sound nasty, thought Kenya.

"Naw. Working on my nude studies. Your mom said she'd pose for me." Commodore mimed a woman's curvy figure with his hands.

Ned laughed. "Oh yeah? I'm pretty sure you'd pay her to put her clothes back on."

As if trying to move past the prickly moment that had just passed, the boys fell into each other laughing. When Commodore asked to borrow his bicycle, Ned seemed to make a point of loaning him the newer, fancier one.

"That was getting a little fucked-up," Kenya said when they were safely on the elevator.

Commodore shrugged. "Yeah, Ned's jealous. But that kid is crazy talented in his own right."

Kenya gave him a side eye. "That's not what I meant."

Then Commodore spoke matter-of-factly. "Oh, Ned's a little racist. They all are. Well, some are more than a little. But what I found out is that racist white people—I mean the ones without guns—are not as scary as our parents made them out to be. And let's be real—not all black people are that cool."

"I guess," said Kenya.

"Sometimes I don't really like Ned's vibe," Commodore said. "But his house is a dope place to hang out. And he always has the dope." He laughed at his own joke as they emerged onto the warm, dark street. "Do you have to go home now?"

"Not really," Kenya said, though it was getting close to dinnertime, which was when she told her mother she'd be back.

Commodore pointed to the bike. "So get up here. In front."

"Couldn't we get a ticket or something? And aren't you high?"

"Up!" barked Commodore, rolling his eyes.

"Where are we going?"

"My cousin's barbecue. And I'd like to get there before it ends, already."

By the time they got to Overbrook, all that remained of the barbecue were a few dried-up burger patties and the dregs of some mayonnaise-heavy salads. But the party, in Cousin Jamal's blue-lit basement, was just beginning. Girls in brightly colored short sets with Tilt-A-Whirl permed hairstyles clumped together; guys in sunglasses and exaggeratedly preppie summer outfits—one wore an ascot with a short-sleeved rugby shirt—clumped nearby. Commodore's cousin, whose fade was higher

even than Commodore's and who wore a leather Africa me-
dallion, greeted them with "Peace, God, peace, Earth." He
complimented Kenya's name.

People danced erratically without commitment, some in
couples and some solo. Then the opening guitar sample of "My
Part of Town" slashed the air, and the DJ got into a frantic
groove. Commodore, who had toured the room, distributing
pounds to some of the boys and hugging a couple of loud girls,
pulled Kenya into the crowd and they danced together, not
quite touching, to music that throbbed and shrieked. The crowd,
some doing a lazy two-step, some jumping in the air, kept cheering as if Big Daddy Kane, KRS-One, Queen Latifah, and EPMD
were actually there and not just vibrations trapped in vinyl.
Kenya remembered how exhilarated she'd felt skating that night
before Teddy Jaffrey came into her room. But this was better.
There were the parties she was used to, and then there was this
blue planet, where she was neither a black hole nor a curiosity.
She might not be beautiful, but she was a girl, dancing.

The spell ended when the basement flooded with red light
and then Kenya heard the murky opening strains of "Piece of
My Love," where it sounded as if Aaron Hall was saying *dumb
bitch*. Couples clutched each other and started grinding hard.

"Phew," Commodore said, deftly maneuvering them off
the floor. "I still gotta bike you to the train."

"Yeah, I *really* have to go now," Kenya said. But then she
proposed a stop on the way.

A couple of weeks later, when nothing had happened, and
Commodore called with ecstatic talk of Pippa and then not

again for weeks, Kenya couldn't believe it, and also couldn't believe that she couldn't believe it. What was she tripping on anyway? All it had been was an afternoon at the museum, which had free admission on Sundays. And Cousin Jamal's had been, for Commodore, just another party.

Besides, what had it meant to him that he'd stood beside her on Irving Street, in front of the house where she had grown up? The short, narrow block looked shockingly shabby, especially since Kenya had learned that aluminum siding was for people with limited tastes, poor black people, ethnic whites. Standing in front of her old house, which looked tiny and generic with its white paint and dark green trim, Kenya realized she had never really looked at it. Then she noticed that heavy-looking drapes had replaced the boards on the windows. There was no hint of who had once lived there or what had happened to them. Now it looked like the home of normal black people: Christians, patriots, eaters of pork.

"That's that," Commodore had said with a shrug, so she couldn't exactly be shocked now that he seemed to have vanished. But his arm had grazed hers.

And the bike ride to the train was just a way of avoiding the unpleasant fluorescence of a city bus. So what if their bodies had been touching, and the city had suddenly seemed both mysterious and like home? So what if the smell of his cologne and his sweat made her dizzy? So what if at the time she had thought, *I know he feels this, too.*

During a long, air-conditioned summer spent sorting out the dentist's files while the receptionist listened to the excruciating oldies station, Kenya made a daily mental tally of what she had lost. She had not given anything up to Commodore that really mattered. She had never actually told him she was a virgin or that she felt they were made for each other and that fate had united them again. She had never told him about Teddy Jaffrey or about the gun and her mother. She'd never gotten drunk or high or sloppy in front of him. She tried not to imagine how she fared in conversations he had with Pippa, but she couldn't help it. He probably said she was "crazy cool" or something equally patronizing. Then it struck her with almost physical force that he'd probably never mentioned her to Pippa at all.

Since she'd all but completely abandoned Zaineb and the others, her own conversations about him were usually with herself, and sometimes they made her dig her nails into her palm or speak aloud. They had only just begun to let up in August, when he resurfaced, announcing that he was now really done with Pippa, who'd gone to California for college and was never there when he called. And that he wanted to hang out with Kenya and "catch up."

Walking by his side down South Street, Kenya concentrated on not hoping for anything until she spotted something that made her breathless.

There were three boys walking in front of her and Commodore. "Uh-oh!" one of them yelled, elbowing his friend. "It's Public Enema!" Kenya's eyes followed the taunt.

Two young hippie types sat in front of the beading shop with a strangely sleek and well-fed-looking black dog slumped between them. The boy alternated between two chords on the guitar, over and over, singing some melancholy thing without a chorus. Verse spilled into verse, linked by the words *and the.*

And the frog will dance with the fly, and the earth will spin a web, and . . .

Kenya stopped short and grabbed Commodore's arm to steady her suddenly wobbly stance. "I know that girl," she said.

It was Devi Warren on the tambourine, singing "Oooooooooooh." Her hair was long and matted, bedecked with a single daisy. She was very brown with sun, reminding Kenya of her bizarre lie. Her purple eyes were both calm and empty. She sat cross-legged in a long cotton skirt, from which her grimy bare feet peeked out.

They sounded terrible. Kenya's legs wobbled and she took a deep breath, and she finally understood that the lie was how Devi had felt. And now, brown, broke, and abandoned, she was on the outside what she'd felt on the inside. *That could happen to you,* Kenya thought as she and Commodore hustled past. She let his arm go.

"Man," he said, "you know the singer from Public Enema? Ooga Booga, you never tell me about your connections!"

"She went to Barrett. I can't deal."

"And she can't sing," Commodore observed. "But she's kinda cute. You know, in a scruffy way."

"Com, you are so fucked," said Kenya.

"What about *you*, Dad?" he said, a joke from *The Breakfast Club* they sometimes lobbed at each other. "What about you?"

"No, I mean it," Kenya said, her voice growing surprisingly icy. "There is something really wrong with you."

"Wait a minute," Commodore said, "what just happened? Who is that girl?"

"It doesn't matter," Kenya said. "None of it matters."

"None of what?" he asked.

A thought struck Kenya as she sat eating deliciously salty fries at midnight in a café on Wesleyan's campus during her visit in the fall of senior year. She was with two pretty dark-skinned girls, one black and one Indian, who were complaining about a male English professor and his constant attempt to find the lesbian subtext in everything they read.

"He tried to find the lesbian subtext in *Lolita*," the black girl, Candace, said.

"He could find the lesbian subtext in those fries!" exclaimed the Indian girl, Karen. Kenya threw her head back and laughed, and she could tell that this made them happy. As she laughed, she had the (unhappy) thought that it had been a long time since she had truly looked forward to something.

There had been a few weeks with Commodore, which later started to seem like some kind of sickness, but before that, what? Lame parties? Dinners with her mother and Teddy Jaffrey? She had sent her father a letter after hearing he was out of prison and in a halfway house in Yeadon, but she had heard nothing back. Since that was going on two years ago, she'd long since stopped looking forward to hearing from him. But as of this moment she was looking forward to coming to this school.

Back home from her visit, at dinner, she announced that she would apply to Wesleyan Early Decision.

"But you've only visited two places, and one was Penn. So it barely counts as a visit."

"Yeah, but I want to go to Wesleyan."

"Well," Sheila said, looking sad and dreamy, "I guess that's a pretty good school."

"Isn't that all girls?" asked Teddy Jaffrey.

"But?" Kenya asked her mother, ignoring him. "'I guess that's a pretty good school' but?"

"It's just—well, Alma says that Grace is only applying to Ivies."

"Well, maybe if I don't get into Wesleyan, I can use Harvard as a safety," said Kenya.

"Watch it, Kenya."

"I'm sorry, Mom. But, um, have you seen my grades?"

"Your grades are fine. And it's not just about grades. I just want you to keep your options open."

"By applying to Ivy League schools?"

"You know what I mean."

Teddy Jaffrey, who had not finished college, gave a speech about how "people make different choices." This kind of pointless utterance was his specialty. Kenya often wondered if the nature of her mother's feelings toward him had changed. She had seen a movie on TV where a man had proclaimed his love for a woman, explaining that he found something new to love about her every day. She found it hard to imagine her mother saying this about Teddy. In fact, Kenya was fairly sure she sometimes saw Sheila's eyes cloud over when he spoke.

Kenya got into Wesleyan. Despite the matching Mercedes in the driveway and the money Grandmama had left, it seemed that both she and Sheila would have to take out loans. The college provided just enough aid for them to scrape by.

After a brief spell of self-righteous anger over the fact that Wesleyan hadn't recognized Kenya's genius with a more generous financial aid package, Sheila became sentimental.

"The little girl is going off," she said once, brushing a braid from Kenya's face. "Going off and leaving me."

"No, I'm not," protested Kenya, but she was leaving, and she was not sad about it. She imagined that being several hours away would bring her and her mother closer than they'd been for years. She hoped Sheila would come to visit without Teddy.

The year dragged on toward its inevitable conclusion: prom and graduation. Kenya was equally disinterested in both and went to prom with Zaineb, who was not allowed to date. Phyllis Fagin brought a balding man she kept insisting was younger than he looked, though she did not deny the rumor that he dealt cocaine to the best schools on the Main Line. Lolly's parents had handpicked her date, a beige-skinned nerd who was distantly related to Thomas Jefferson.

For Kenya, whose college plans were set, watching the keyed-up anguish and hope of Barrett girls whose futures lay in the balance was more entertaining than prom. Lolly was wait-listed at Penn. Zaineb was off to Northwestern. Dorrie Futter had gotten into Yale, where China (who had finally gotten over Prince and now had a serious boyfriend) had gone. Generally, though, Kenya was surprised at how extremely unprestigious things had become for many of the girls. Boston University? Um, *okay*. Bryn Mawr was a good enough school— but it was literally across the street from Barrett. Then there was some talk of something called a gap year. Phyllis Fagin was taking one of those. She hadn't gotten into any of the fifteen schools to which she'd applied.

"Guess you can't buy everything," Sheila said.

In the midst of all this, two things materialized. The first was a letter addressed to Kenya from Johnbrown.

The letter was long and detailed, but also elliptical. He hadn't contacted her, he said, because he was trying to get his life settled, but he wanted her to come for a visit as soon as she could.

"Mom," she asked one night as the two of them sat half watching a TV movie, "where is Freedom, Pennsylvania?"

She grimaced. "Beats me. Why?"

"That's where Baba lives, on a farm. He says he wants me to come out there for the summer."

"A farm?" Sheila said with a little laugh.

"That's what it says here."

"So when are you going?" Sheila asked. Kenya could tell that her mother had committed herself to a supportive pose. Her eyes were painfully wide in an "excited" way, and she kept blinking.

"I'm not sure if I want to go. I mean, why did it take him so long to get in touch with me?"

"I don't know," Sheila said. "But you could ask him yourself if you went up there."

Kenya knew that he wasn't alone on the farm, as the letter employed the word *we* in descriptions of pruning peach trees and caring for chickens and a cow, but he didn't say who else was there. He told her to call him collect so they could schedule her visit. Kenya sat in silence with her mother and told herself that she was deciding whether to go, but she knew that she was allowing herself to get used to the idea of it, and preparing herself for what she might find there.

"Will you be okay if I go?" asked Kenya.

Sheila laughed. "I mean, it's your last summer here. Yes, I'll be lonely, of course, but I can spare you for a few . . . weeks."

"You'll have Teddy," Kenya said, trying to sound as if she meant it.

"He's not my only daughter."

More frequently it seemed that only Sheila *or* Teddy was home. Kenya and her mother often dined alone together at night while Teddy and Bert, now his business partner, entertained clients. This was odd, because Teddy seemed to be working less during the day. Other times, her mother, who seemed to be taking on more at the library, didn't make it home for dinner. Left on their own, Teddy and Kenya ate takeout while watching TV. Kenya usually scarfed down her food and went up to her room.

These dinners coincided with the second thing that arrived that spring: a foul change in Teddy Jaffrey's overall mood. Kenya had always scorned his mask of joking cheer; she was convinced that he'd be easier to live with if he wasn't always trying so hard. But this proved not to be the case. If "charming" Teddy Jaffrey was annoying, then the Teddy who slammed doors and drawers, snapped at Sheila, and complained daily that the contractors who had long ago left the pile of crap in the backyard that was now supposed to be a sun porch had stolen his money was just this side of menacing. Though she didn't try to cross his path, Kenya didn't quite stay out of his way either. She was curious to see if he'd direct his ire toward her.

One night Kenya's mother stayed late at work doing inventory. When Teddy called upstairs that dinner was ready, Kenya headed down to the kitchen for her TV tray. She stopped short when she saw that Teddy had set the dining room table with a neat array of Chinese-food cartons. He sat unshaven at the table in his pajamas: a football jersey from his brief college career, and boxer shorts.

"Why don't we sit at the table like civilized people?" he proposed.

"What about watching TV?" Kenya suggested, though there was just *Entertainment Tonight* and game shows.

"Ain't nothin' on but game shows and *Entertainment Tonight*."

Kenya pulled out a chair and sat down.

"How is everything?" Teddy said.

"Fine. Is there lo mein?"

He rolled his eyes playfully. "Isn't that your favorite?"

For a few moments, the only sound was forks hitting plates. Then Teddy asked, "So are you looking forward to going away to school?"

"Yesh," said Kenya, her mouth full of noodles.

Teddy's laugh was hollow. "Getting away from your evil stepfather, huh?"

Kenya looked at him.

"No answer, huh?"

Kenya shrugged.

"I know what you think of me, *Kenya*. But I've always treated your mother right. And I've tried with you, I've really tried."

Kenya forged into new territory. "Tried what?" she asked.

"Oh, you're funny now. You being funny?" Suddenly he was standing and yelling. "Look, I'm not some genius like your father, I know that. But I work hard. And I'm tired of being disrespected in my own home!"

Kenya yelled back. "If you don't stop screaming at me, I'm going to call my mother."

"Oh yeah, what are you going to tell her? She already knows you're a little sulky brat!"

"Teddy, if you don't stop, I'm going to—"

"You're going to what? Get a gun and pretend to shoot me in your sleep?" Now he faked a high-pitched laugh.

It made sense, she knew, that Sheila would have told Teddy about all of that. After all, strictly speaking, it was what got them here. But still, she'd clung to the idea that Teddy didn't know. What Kenya did next was directed at the both of them: Sheila for telling one of her worst secrets, Teddy for being the other.

She stood from the table slowly and her hands began pushing things off it: containers of noodles, rice, and the gravy-soaked (and ever-disgusting) egg foo young, an open bottle of soy sauce, plates, an open bottle of cranberry juice all poured onto the dining room rug. Teddy was frozen. It was as if they were in a shared trance; she could not stop doing it and he could not stop watching. Just before she knocked the glasses to the floor, hoping they would splinter into hundreds of pieces, her stepfather jumped up and grabbed her to him. Her throat filled with terror as she struggled in his arms. He pulled her tighter into his sour all-day-pajamas smell. Then he made an angry noise and pushed her away.

As soon as he let her go, she ran upstairs, shut the door, and put a chair against it. Lying on the floor, she sobbed with rage. For what seemed like hours, she listened to the sound of Teddy cursing as he cleaned up, and then finally she heard her mother come home. Teddy told Sheila nothing of the fight, and that made Kenya sure of something she'd suspected. When Teddy had pulled her to him, he'd had an erection.

The next morning during the rush out the door, Kenya told her mother that she'd decided to spend the whole summer at her father's.

"But what about your job at Dr. Walton's?"

"They'll find someone else."

"You're going to need spending money at school, you know."

"I have some savings. Other than that, I'll just skip the fall wardrobe or whatever."

"Well, you know I'm not going to let you do that. But I mean, Kenya, this is your last—"

"Mom, I'm sorry, but I can't live in this house with *your husband* anymore," said Kenya.

"What are you talking about?"

"Why don't you ask him?"

As was typical these days, Teddy was not there to ask; he slept during the hours when other people got ready for work. He could be roused only to take calls from Bert. But that wasn't the point, Kenya knew. Sheila donned her steely glare. "I'm asking *you*," she said, her voice rising. "I'm asking you to tell me what you're talking about."

The air was dry and the house seemed very bright. Kenya pictured herself across from her mother, a deep crevasse between them. If she spoke, who would fall? How would they get out? She had already shot her mother. Again she felt as if she was sleepwalking.

Would her mother kick Teddy Jaffrey out so that it would be just her and Kenya again? The way it had been in the Ardmore Arms?

What if she didn't and he just stayed and nothing happened?

Remembering the ragged crying she'd heard only once, Kenya choked back her own tears and babbled something she'd seen on a blended-family sitcom once, about her stepfather taking her mother away. Her mother held her. Two days after graduation, she was on a Greyhound bound for western Pennsylvania. Her mother and Teddy waved grimly as she pulled away.

Freedom

The town that greeted Kenya when the bus turned off the highway was dismal. Every other store on the main street was shuttered, and the handful of slow-moving shoppers had a grayish tinge to their skin. The families in the bus terminal sported heavy metal T-shirts and jagged, fried hair. Both of Kenya's parents, but especially her father, had taught Kenya to fear the Philadelphia kin to these people and the neighborhoods where they dwelled: Roxborough, Fishtown, Kensington. But there in the center of this bus terminal, which reminded Kenya of the prison visiting area, was her father, a paperback under his arm, his hands in his pockets, as if he belonged there. He managed to look relaxed, though he stood straighter and taller than Kenya remembered.

"Look at you," he said, pulling her into a rough hug. "Look at you."

"Hey," said Kenya, not wanting to call him Baba in the bus terminal. His hair was a little too long—an inch or two shy of Frederick Douglass–style—and full of gray. When he smiled wide, which he did repeatedly, he showed a missing tooth. But as shabby as he should have looked, there was something expensive and gracious-looking about his old, soft T-shirt and jeans, about his sweet, woodsy smell.

This is my father, Kenya thought as they climbed into a red pickup truck. *I'm here with my father.* Johnbrown asked her about the bus ride, about Sheila, graduation. She answered, listening to the sound of her own voice.

The house had Johnbrown's same wood smell and a rustic glamour, with high, exposed ceiling beams and rough-hewn floors. Despite its old homey look, it also seemed to have a powerful and quiet air-conditioning system. It reminded Kenya of the Urban Outfitters store in University City. Kenya's parents had told her that Urban Outfitters used to be a tiny hippie shop featuring a barrel from which you could take old clothes. Now it was impossibly chic in a way that seemed to go with its grand barn look. There was even a new downtown outpost of the store, where cute white salesgirls followed you around if you were black.

"We're home!" Johnbrown called as he and Kenya passed through a room full of muddy boots and jackets into the kitchen. They were all there around a table covered with what looked like a large meal in the making. Cindalou, who'd gotten heftier, clasped Kenya tightly, while Amandla, a chubby dark brown girl in glasses, gave a more mannered hug.

There were three other people, too: a wiry white woman with a cloud of blond-going-gray hair floating around her shoulders, and two small sand-colored children. Kenya tried not to flinch as her father, who had not warned her of this at any point, told her their names. She wasn't sure if the boy was Nannie or the girl was Dennie, but she knew the white woman's name was Sharon and these were her children. Johnbrown's children. Sharon took Kenya's hands into her own. "So wonderful to meet you," she said.

Though Sheila had often said that *black men loved themselves some white women*, Kenya's only previous point of reference for this, besides mixed celebrity couples, was a specter from child-hood. Back in West Philadelphia, she and her mother had sometimes seen a sunburned-looking woman with a thin pony-tail and missing teeth on Fifty-Second Street, begging near the McDonald's with her three ragamuffin reddish-brown sons. "What happened to her?" Kenya asked once when she was little. "Some Negro," Sheila had answered.

"It's good to meet you, too," Kenya told Sharon. Then there was a pause where everyone waited for something.

"Can I show Kenya the Zen room?" said Amandla finally, still studying her sister.

"Why don't you let her settle in?" said Sharon.

"Isn't that where she's settling in?"

"Don't you have some beans to snap, Amandla?" said Cindalou.

"We can all have a good visit at dinner, Monkey," John-brown said to Amandla. "I'll take her back there."

"Okay," the girl said, pushing up her glasses and staring intently. It was a different stare from those of the two younger children. Kenya wondered if Amandla was looking at her hair, or rather her head, which she'd had shaved almost bald the day after she graduated from Barrett. She had imagined her-self emerging from the barber chair looking like one of the first black supermodels in the 1970s, but sadly, no matter what pose she struck, she knew she only looked like a boy.

The small room was at the back of the skylit second floor. It was sparsely furnished, with a few covered baskets and a large, low wooden chest topped by a large red-stone Buddha figurine, some candles, and framed photos. A deep purple rug sat in front of the Buddha. The biggest thing in the room was a kind of bunk bed with no bottom bunk, suspended from the ceiling by thick chains.

"I built this myself," Johnbrown said, gesturing toward it. "You use this to get up there," he said, pointing to the metal ladder resting against it.

For a few years, Kenya had assumed that she was no longer sleepwalking. But given what had happened in their family, it hit her with a force that her father must have completely forgotten. Or perhaps he was daring her to bring it up—the fact that she could, in her sleep, try to climb out of bed and go crashing to the floor, the same way she had apparently taken a gun and shot her mother in the shoulder.

Kenya would not be the one to mention it. Instead she heard herself ask what the Zen room was usually for.

"Amandla was the one who named it. I meditate in here, but everybody uses it. Sharon does yoga in here. Sometimes we send the kids in when they need to calm the hell down. It's also for guests."

Kenya looked down from the floor to the height of the bed. "I guess you have pretty adventurous guests."

"Actually we have about zero guests. Well, that's not true. Sharon's parents came once but they were really too rickety to climb up there. But you'll love it," he said. "I would sleep there myself, but it's only built for one person."

"Are you married to both of them?" Kenya blurted. She slapped her hand over her mouth but it was too late. The tension at home with Sheila had left her in knots. When she'd decided to come here, she'd promised herself that she would ask no serious questions of Johnbrown—or of any of these people, for that matter. But this one had overcome her like a belch.

"It's okay." Johnbrown shrugged. "What I can say is that we're a family," he said. "Amandla, Nneka, and Denmark are all my children." He looked at her.

She nodded.

"Monkey," said Johnbrown, "you can't know how happy it makes me that you came."

"Baba, maybe you shouldn't call me that anymore, okay?"

"Can I ask why not?"

"Well, not to be petty, but a special nickname doesn't seem as special if you're sharing it with other people."

"Oh," he said. They both heard a small throat-clearing sound from the hallway. Naturally it was the other monkey.

"Oh hey," said Kenya, feeling bad. She liked the girl, and not only because she found her instantly preferable to the sandy-haired imps.

"Hey, Amandla," Johnbrown said. "Since you butted your nose in, why don't you show Kenya how to get up there?"

"I'm sure she knows how to use a ladder, Baba," Amandla said, wrinkling her brow. "Kenya, they said don't worry about dinner if you're tired. We can warm up a plate for you whenever you feel like eating."

"Well, are you going to have dinner with everybody else, Amandla?" Kenya asked.

"Of course," the girl said, pushing her glasses up on her small round nose. "I always have dinner with everybody else."

"Well, then so will I."

Amandla cracked a smile.

"What's so funny?" asked Johnbrown.

At dinner, Kenya noted that the kitchen was clearly the heart of the place. She compared it with her mother's house, where she felt most comfortable napping in front of the television on the pantyhose-colored sectionals when no one else was home. That was no heart compared with the spacious and bright room where she now sat in a very upright chair. Filled to bursting as it was with stuff and people, it was harmonious, or at least controlled. They sat at a thick table, set with matching plates and glasses and an array of colorful cloth napkins, each slightly different.

"Mama made this," said the imp girl, holding hers up for Kenya to admire.

"That's very nice," Kenya said, taking the chance to study the twins, with their hooded gray eyes that made them look older than four. They both had wild hair, the girl's in a messy ponytail, the boy's in a shape that evoked Prince with bedhead or a post-concert Little Richard. Sharon had her children's eyes, thin lips, and strangely small teeth. The three of them looked like frolicsome woodland creatures, though given their golden coloring, Nannie and Dennie could have easily been Cindalou's children. The person they did not resemble was Johnbrown.

"Mama made all of the napkins," said the boy.

"They're very pretty," said Kenya.

"Dennie and Nannie," said Sharon. Her tone was corrective, but she grinned. "When you meet someone for the first time, you're supposed to ask them questions about themselves, not just talk their ears off." To Kenya she said, "The problem with homeschooling, you see. This one," she said, indicating Johnbrown, "took the time to teach them about the ancient civilization of Khmet, but he forgot basic manners."

Johnbrown rolled his eyes with a smile.

"Uh-huh," said Kenya.

"Kenya?" said Nannie.

"Yes?"

"How old are you?"

"One hundred," she said. No one laughed. She coughed. "How old do you think I am?" Kenya asked.

Nannie made deliberating noises and played with her counting fingers. She looked at the different people at the table as if that would help. "Mama, how old are you?"

"Well, I'll give you a hint," said Sharon with a wink. "I've told you about thirty-six times."

"*Mama!* How old are you, Mama Cindalou?"

"Thirty-two. But *I've* told you about thirty-two times that a woman who tells her age will tell anything."

"You're thirty!" Dennie yelled at Kenya.

"Now, Dennie," said Sharon, who had turned a blotchy red.

"She's nineteen, Dennie," said Johnbrown. "Much older than you, so be sure to listen when she tells you to do something. You, too, Nannie and Amandla."

Cindalou said, "Kenya, can I get you some more of the green bean and tomato?"

"Actually, yeah," Kenya said. "Everything tastes really good."

"Girl, you say that like you surprised," said Cindalou. "You forgot my cooking?"

"Cindalou puts her foot in it nightly," said Johnbrown.

"You put your feet in the food?" said Dennie, looking frightened.

Nannie spit masticated chicken onto her plate. "Ewww!"

Amandla sighed. "It's an expression, you dummies."

"Enough, Amandla," said Johnbrown. "*Put her foot in it*, it just means she's a good cook."

Kenya was relieved by this scuffle. It meant she didn't have to remind Cindalou that she'd never tasted her cooking. How would she have, back then? Maybe Johnbrown could have brought home a plate from their clandestine meetings?

"Are you a cook, Kenya?" asked Sharon.

"No, not really."

"Well, this is a good place to learn if you're interested," said Johnbrown.

"Baba, you don't know how to cook," said Amandla.

"You sure are sassy tonight, 'Mandla," murmured Cindalou.

"This is true," said Johnbrown. "I don't cook. But *you* don't know how to wring a chicken's neck. Each according to need and ability," he said, pointing a drumstick at her.

"You can wring a chicken's neck?" asked Kenya.

"I taught him that," said Cindalou. "This African right here was scared of chickens."

"I still am! Those mammers act irrationally and they have beaks and claws."

"Truly, I don't see how you all do it. I don't see how you kill them, don't see how you eat them," Sharon said, shaking her head. She was eating only corn bread and vegetables.

"You see it nearly every day," said Johnbrown. "We are

some chicken-eating people right here. But for Sharon's sake," he said to Kenya, "we did experiment with vegetarianism some years ago."

"The fried tofu was pretty good," said Amandla. "I liked that."

"And the pounds just melted off," said Cindalou sadly.

"Why'd you start eating meat again?" asked Kenya.

"Oh God," Sharon said. "Here we go. I was breast-feeding twins!"

"Turns out this one had been sneaking off to eat ribs," Johnbrown said with a smirk, now pointing the bone at Sharon.

"And bacon!" Cindalou laughed.

Johnbrown laughed, too. "I mean it was a whole swine *binge*. If I hadn't smelled it that time, she would have got down to chitlins."

"Enough, enough. We don't need to talk about chitlins at the table," said Sharon. "Now I don't know about the rest of you, but I think it's wine time. Any objections?"

"None over here. Objections, I mean," said Cindalou.

"Kenya, do you—" Sharon started.

"Um, I think not," said Johnbrown, a shadow crossing his face. A similar shadow crossed Sharon's and she held her tongue.

"What's for dessert?" asked Nannie. "Are we having birthday cake?"

"Nannie," Amandla despaired. "Your birthday was"—she counted quickly on her fingers—"seven months ago."

"It's okay, my love," said Sharon to Amandla. "Nannie has a small person's sense of time. Like you used to. Remember last year you sent away for those stickers and asked me about them every day?"

"They never came," Amandla muttered darkly.

"Nannie, would you like some peach cobbler?" asked Cindalou. "I made it special for Kenya, but I think it might be almost as good as birthday cake."

"I want birthday cake," said Nannie.

"That's fine, because nobody is getting any peach cobbler unless their name is Johnbrown Curtis," said Johnbrown.

"No, Baba," cried Dennie. "Peach coddler is my favorite."

"Dennie, you've never even eaten peach coddler," Johnbrown said. "You kids are insane."

"They come by it honestly," said Cindalou, winking at Kenya.

After the cobbler with ice cream (homemade, of course), and after she'd sat at the table until she could sit no more, Kenya begged off to the Zen room. As she attempted to scale the bed, she wondered if there actually was some trick Amandla could have shown her about getting up into the loft. Gripping the metal ladder immediately hurt her hands, and one rung shy of the top, she was sure she would fall. But when she finally got up there and felt her bones melting into the mattress, she forgot all of that.

She could hear the noises coming from different parts of the house: a toilet flushing, a sink turned on and off. From the kitchen she heard the clatter of plates, then voices of her father and the women (his women?), the low hum of jazz. She thought she recognized a song Johnbrown used to play.

Space is the place
Space is the place!

She was wondering how he had kept his records all of these years—in jails, prison, and halfway houses—when her name jumped all the way from the kitchen up the stairs and into the loft.

". . . *just like you*," said Sharon's voice. "I mean a spitting image!"

". . . can see Sheila," said Cindalou. Then she said something about Kenya's hair. Kenya could not tell if it was a compliment or not.

Kenya's body tensed with listening, but now they all seemed to get quieter. She heard her father's voice, and then only the plucking of bass strings in a long pause. When they began to talk again, it was clearly of other things.

She imagined herself making fun of them for someone, a new, imaginary person—not Zaineb, Commodore, or Sheila, but someone else who could understand just how absurd her father was, from failed revolutionary to imprisoned novelist and finally contented interracial polygamous family man. She imagined mocking Sharon and her strange children with their sharp little teeth and Cindalou, the now-obsolete home-wrecker who was still hanging on.

Even before she got to the farm, Kenya had been waking up confused about where she was. In the moments before opening her eyes, she didn't know if she was a small girl in her tiny bedroom in West Philadelphia, if she'd slept over at Zaineb's, if she would wake up to the yellow walls of her room back at the Ardmore Arms. Now she was alarmed when she opened her eyes and found that she was way above the floor—and that someone was standing in the doorway.

"Good morning," said Amandla. She pushed her glasses up on her nose. "I didn't mean to scare you."

"It's okay," said Kenya.

Amandla looked down, studying her sneaker.

Kenya said, "You can come in."

"Amandla!" called Cindalou. "Let that girl sleep!"

"She's already up," Amandla called back.

"I'm glad you woke me," said Kenya. "If I sleep too long, I start to have bad dreams."

"Me too!" said Amandla.

"Amandla!"

"Shouldn't you go see what she wants?" said Kenya.

"I'll go in a minute."

The night before, when she'd studied her at dinner, Kenya had seen Amandla as a browner Cindalou. But now, looking at the girl's jaw, she saw Johnbrown as a preteen girl. She had his slanted eyes behind her glasses, and shared his faint air of disdain. She looked somber for someone wearing a T-shirt bearing a large pink flower at the center.

"Did you sleep well?" Amandla asked.

"Very well, thank you. What about you?"

Amandla made an *okay, not great* motion with her hand. Because of Barrett, Kenya thought *comme ci, comme ça.*

"Do you ever sleep up here?" Kenya asked.

"Once when I was sick I got to sleep up there with my mom."

"Well, maybe we can have a slumber party sometime. I mean, not if you're sick."

"Really?" said Amandla.

"Why not?"

"Well," Amandla said, with a frown, "Nannie and Dennie might want to come, too, and we can't all fit up there."

"Why can't they just sleep in the woods with the other fawns and foxes?" she asked.

"What?" Amandla said, but she giggled anyway.

It occurred to Kenya that she was being reckless with the little girl. But perhaps not as reckless as some had been with her.

For a week, Kenya ate, slept, and observed her father's new life at what they jokingly called Curtiswood. She noted the changes in Johnbrown, who was now the type of man who could build a loft bed. His outdoor work here had tanned him more deeply brown than she remembered, and his arms looked powerful. He also had gray hair at his temples and a paunch packed with Cindalou's food.

Kenya thought of her father's old daily schedule when she saw the large, complicated chart that hung in the TV-less den, where the family often gathered after meals. According to the chart, everyone except Dennie and Nannie took turns waking up early to milk the lone cow and tend to the chickens. Cindalou cooked and did the shopping, and she was also in charge of household finances. During the fall and winter, Johnbrown homeschooled the children, but in the summer he took care of the crops alongside local and migrant workers hired during planting and harvesting seasons. Sharon was a working artist. Otherwise, she yelled at the kids to make their beds and pick up their toys, and she made the house presentable for the woman who cleaned every week.

The kids had chores, and even though it was summer, Johnbrown had loaded them down with reading and math exercises. They also had to take cooking lessons with Cindalou and do art with Sharon. Everyone had time in the day, at least forty minutes, when they were permitted to do whatever they liked. Nannie and Dennie played little games in the woods; Kenya imagined them reverting to a wild state, snarling and howling. Amandla, whom Kenya wrongly assumed to be an avid reader as she had been, wandered about the house, appearing to play hide-and-seek with herself and singing endless made-up songs in her flat but appealing voice. Sharon used Kenya's room if she wasn't in it to stretch or meditate. Johnbrown was still working on The Key. She wondered if he was still making up stories about the butler but felt shy asking. Their meeting in the prison visiting room seemed so long ago, as if they had been children who had since become orphans.

Each afternoon during her siesta, Cindalou fell asleep on the couch in the den with a book. One late afternoon, Kenya noticed that it was *Remembrance of Things Past*.

"Ugh," Kenya said when she saw it. "We were supposed to read part of that in French class this year. But our teacher, Mademoiselle Lambert, said we were trampling it up like ignorant elephants and we wound up reading a children's book."

"That must be some school you went to. I've been reading

this on and off for about—is that right?—five years. One of your father's recommendations. I could tell he thought I wouldn't finish it." She rolled her eyes.

"We were just reading part of it."

"Yeah, but you know how to say *trampling all over it like ignorant elephants* in French."

Kenya laughed a little, and then felt awkward in the silence that followed. She stood abruptly from the big chair she'd been sitting in, the one that the kids had argued over the night before, cramming in and jostling each other. "I don't want to disturb your quiet time," she said.

"I think the quiet is something you can share," said Cindalou.

Kenya lowered herself back into the chair and opened up an early Alice Walker novel she'd plucked off a shelf in a room the kids called the Free Library. That was as opposed to Johnbrown's library, where borrowing a book involved actual paperwork and solemn vows about returning the book in such-and-such condition.

Cindalou glanced over. "Whew. That one makes *The Color Purple* look like that French children's book you were reading." Kenya didn't tell Cindalou that when the title character, a little boy, died at the end of the children's book, Mademoiselle had wept about it. Cindalou went on. "I'm tellin' you, early Alice is *rough*. I mean, if you think about the ending, *Color Purple* was obviously her idea of a fairy tale."

Cindalou and Kenya turned pages, drifting in and out of conversation about *The Third Life of Grange Copeland*. ("Let Hollywood try to turn *that* into a movie," Cindalou muttered.) But just when Kenya relaxed, feeling that silence between them was okay, she heard Cindalou say, "Your mother turned me on to Alice."

Kenya was trapped.

"I'm pretty sure you don't want to hear this," Cindalou continued. "But I miss her. I been missing her this whole time."

"Uh-huh," said Kenya. And then, to her horror, Cindalou was wiping away tears. "You know, not in a sexual way of course, but I think I was just as much in love with her as I was with him. But everything got so . . ."

They heard footfalls on the stair and then the shuffle of the Chinese slippers Sharon wore around the house.

"My goodness, what's wrong?" she asked.

"We're just catching up," Cindalou sniffed.

Sharon placed a hand on her chest and looked sympathetic. "You all must have *so much* to talk about. Don't let me, you know, stanch your flow." Then she fidgeted in the doorway to the kitchen, looking uncomfortable. "So," she said, "would you like me to start dinner?"

"Yeah, Sharon. I want you to start dinner," Cindalou said in a hard voice.

"It's just 'cause the kids—"

"You think I don't know what time the kids eat?"

"Come on, Cinda, don't be angry. I didn't *mean* anything."

"You never do, Sharon." Cindalou got up and stormed past Sharon into the kitchen. She slammed cabinet doors and pots, muttering loud enough to hear: *no-cookin' ass if I want her to start dinner can't nobody eat that mess . . .*

Sharon smiled at Kenya and rolled her eyes. Then she poked her head into the kitchen. "Rarf!" she said. "Rarf! Rarf!" She whimpered, holding limp paws in front of herself. She glanced back out at Kenya, who remained pinned to the chair, smiling weakly.

The back door to the kitchen opened and the sounds of the children and their father filled the downstairs.

"In the doghouse again, huh?" he said. Nannie, delighted with her mother, commanded her to sit.

"I have a suggestion," Johnbrown announced on a Sunday at the beginning of Kenya's second week at the farm. He had decided that Kenya would shadow each member of the household for a week (even Nannie and Dennie, so they wouldn't feel left out) to see what they did all day and how she might fit in that summer.

"Me first!" said Cindalou. "It *would* be nice not to have to hire that smelly German lady to help with the canning."

"I thought maybe we'd let Kenya choose first."

"Okay," said Cindalou. "But last year 'Mandla said she saw that woman pick her nose."

"Mama, *you* saw that."

"Well, somebody saw it."

Kenya imagined being a captive audience for Cindalou, Sharon, or her father. "Well, I don't want, um, nose picking in the jam," she said. "But I thought I'd spend some time with the kids."

"Yay!" yelled Dennie. "Ken-ya! Ken-ya! Ken-ya!"

She had meant Amandla, but it was too late now.

By Monday night, Kenya was exhausted. Despite the elaborate chart in the den, it wasn't clear to Kenya what Nannie and Dennie usually did all day, because their time with her seemed to revolve around getting her to do things with them that the other adults either wouldn't do or wouldn't do for long. Instead of doing the exercises they'd been assigned, they demanded that she read them every storybook in the house and then tell stories of her invention. They wanted to play dress-up in the attic clothes, dry-rotting castoffs that would probably never make it to the nearest Salvation Army—180 miles away—and they wanted her to dress up, too. Dennie demanded that she play an idiosyncratic version of backgammon for kindergartners that "my baba" had taught him. Chess was Nannie's game; "my baba" had taught her that, too. Both of the twins were intolerable, weeping losers and horrible winners, and they were never more distraught than when they suspected that Kenya was letting them beat her.

On Tuesday afternoon, which was blistering, they wanted Kenya to walk them a sweaty fifteen minutes down to the creek, where they were allowed to play only with adult supervision. Kenya, whose main experience in the wilderness had been on a Barrett trip to the Pocono Mountains where the cabins had microwaves, immediately despised the creek's muddy water, which was lush with thick, slimy weeds.

"Do you all think the creek is, um, sanitary for the kids?" she asked the adults that night after the kids had gone to bed. She had showered hours ago but still felt itchy.

Johnbrown laughed. He said, "We can cut their 'week' short, you know. I'm not sure they'll know the difference."

"Please, Baba, you're their teacher. Nannie definitely knows how many days are in a week," Kenya said. "And it's only Tuesday. I'll survive."

At the beginning of the week, they listened to her. In addition to the matter of obeying Sharon, Cindalou, and John-brown, who reminded them every day to respect their big sister, they had made pleasing Kenya a competition. But as the week progressed they began to challenge her. By Thursday, Kenya was beginning to feel hysterical; they were back at the creek, where the kids demanded to go every afternoon. The weeds caressed her legs, and the same horsefly kept landing on her arm. About a foot away, Nannie listlessly whipped her body back and forth, making herself a human sprinkler.

"That's it, guys," Kenya said. "It's time to go back and get washed up for dinner."

"Can we stay a little longer?" said Nannie.

No matter when Kenya announced that it was time to stop one thing and move on to the next, Nannie always tried to bargain for more time. Kenya had learned to start preparing the kids to stop what they were doing before it was necessary, in order to accommodate Nannie. But now she thought she would scream if one more insect buzzed in her ear.

"I think now, Nannie."

"But I'm not *ready*."

Dennie didn't care much for the creek. One of his earliest memories was of his mother holding him in a pool in New Jersey, and it was evidently the country of his soul. He usually raced Nannie into the water, splashed around, and then exited quickly. He would dry off carefully, clean the mud from be-tween his toes, and sit down to imitate birdcalls.

"Maybe we should go," he said.

Kenya said, "I really appreciate that, Dennie. We have to wash up for dinner. You know Cindalou doesn't like us sitting down to eat with creek water on us."

Nannie looked up at the sun, as Johnbrown had no doubt taught her. "It's nowhere near dinnertime. And it's *Mama* Cindalou." She kept moving back and forth, whipping up water. "Why don't you call her *Mama* Cindalou?"

"Because she's not my mother," Kenya said. Heat rose in her chest and throat and she folded her arms to tamp it down. Nannie folded her arms in imitation and crossed her eyes. Then she cackled.

"Let's go, Dennie," Kenya snapped, reaching for the boy's hand. Then she turned away from Nannie and began walking toward the house.

"Nannie," Dennie cried, twisting back toward his sister. "Come on!"

"Bye, y'all," yelled Nannie. "I'm swimming to the other side!"

Kenya stopped short and weighed her options. The shallow creek floor dropped in the middle and Nannie couldn't swim—not really. Dennie made a whimpering noise and she realized she was crushing his small hand. She dropped it when she heard loud splashing and turned to find Johnbrown striding into the water. He had appeared out of nowhere just in time to see Kenya abandon Nannie.

"Baba!" the girl cried happily.

He didn't say anything. She kept saying his name and he kept ignoring her until she turned it into a sob, *Baba, Baba, Baba,* but Johnbrown remained silent, his face a bland mask. At dinner, he was in his usual calm and expansive mood. He did not reprimand Kenya or even address the incident. She never found out what he told Sharon or Cindalou. But he must have told somebody something, because the next morning she found herself being ushered out to the Paul Bunyan super-market in town with Cindalou.

"We were thinking you must be tired of them wild beast kids," Cindalou said with a laugh as they walked out to a maroon station wagon, one of three cars in the gravel lot. "Wear' you down to the gristle, don't they?" she said.

"It wasn't that bad," Kenya lied.

The car door closed and before Kenya could stop it, Cindalou started talking.

"I didn't know nothin' about nothin' when I came up to Philly," Cindalou began, as if she and Kenya were in the middle of an interview. The narrative continued for the rest of what was meant to have been the twins' week, as they ran errands in Freedom's semiabandoned shopping district, with its dilapidated bars, junk stores, ancient post office, and sour-looking white people in yesteryear's fashions. It continued organically into a week of shadowing Cindalou as they sorted enormous piles of laundry, made chicken stock, and drove around in the car. Cindalou would pull on a thread of her narrative, drop it to pay a vaguely hostile cashier or issue a cooking directive, complain about the multitude of country stations on the car radio, and then pick it right back up.

In the drugstore, she said: "Your father was the smartest person I'd ever met, white or black. He wasn't slick. I knew a lot who were slick, but he was smart. That really impressed me then."

As they hulled the strawberries without the aid of the German woman, who had gone off to open a restaurant, she explained: "But I'm not trying to say that he tricked me into anything. I was a grown woman.

"I felt so bad, though," she said as they walked back from the chicken coop. "Your mother had been so kind to me. I was used to girls hating me. All the girls in Greenwood called me a conceited yellow bitch and thought I was trying to steal their boyfriends. My only friend was this other light-skinned girl who actually *was* conceited and *did* steal this one girl's boyfriend. But them boys wasn't shit anyhow. I was just the closest thing to a white girl they could get their hands on without getting lynched . . .

"Me and your mom had the best talks," she recalled as they sat at the kitchen table. They were supposed to begin preparing a stew for lunch, but all Cindalou had done was take out carrots. "It was like having a sister. Now you know, my real sister was eleven years older than me, but with your mom, it was like we'd grown up together.

"And the thing with your dad—I mean, we cared for each other deeply, but we were out of our minds. It would be funny now if things hadn't gotten so crazy—a grown man spray-painting police stations while I was the lookout? I don't know if you remember that terrible woman Marjorie, but I hooked up with her just to have someone to talk to about all of this. Anyway, when I found out I was pregnant, I thought hard about not having it, but that wouldn't have been my first time doing that. The other time was down South in some dirty woman's house and I nearly bled to death. And I had that stupid Marjorie talking in my ear about murdering babies . . . so I was just going to break it off with him and then move back home to have the baby. I wasn't even going to tell him. But he guessed. And then . . ." Cindalou paused, making some calculation. "Then he told me he and your mom were on the verge of breaking up anyhow and it wasn't because of me."

Oh did he? thought Kenya, wondering if that had been true.

"And then he told me about his idea. Now it seems totally crazy, like did I really think somebody as together as Sheila would go for it? But it was such a beautiful vision. We could all be together. We could raise our children together. They would be my family. *You* could be my family. I mean, I hope you feel like that now."

Cindalou suddenly looked at Kenya, as if just remembering that she had been there all along. "Well, do you?" she said.

"What?" said Kenya, her eyes darting around the kitchen for some help. She saw that it was nearly noon. Everyone congregated at the table at half past twelve. The stew would have to be very quick.

"Feel like I'm your family?"

"Well, I guess Amandla's my sister. I guess you're sort of like my stepmother? Or one of them?"

Cindalou's eyes went flat.

Since that had already happened, Kenya asked, "Where did Sharon come from?"

Cindalou sighed. "The Graterford Prison Visual Arts Initiative."

"But . . . ?"

"She's mostly okay. She means well. Some of them do mean well, you know. That was even true in the South—maybe even more true down South. But it's also true that if you'd have told me ten years ago that I . . ." She trailed off and rubbed at her temple, looking weary and innocent, like a very tired small child.

Kenya remembered the feeling she used to get from being near Cindalou, always wanting to laugh. Back then, she had seemed so excited that it made you excited to be around her. She remembered her attempts at Sheila's hairdos. Now her hair was long and she wore it in a bun, like Charlena's mother used to. But where Charlena's mother's bun had been immaculate, Cindalou's was sloppy, and Kenya could swear that her hairline was receding.

Cindalou sighed again and looked at the kitchen clock. "Guess we'll have sandwiches," she muttered. Then she picked up the carrots and walked to the refrigerator, which she opened forcefully. When she spoke she seemed to address the food inside of it.

"You know I do love Sharon. And I think of Nannie and Dennie as my own."

But? thought Kenya.

Cindalou slammed the refrigerator shut.

Kenya steeled herself to shadow Sharon.

"Amandla will be very relieved," Sharon said. "She usually gets stuck helping me with this."

Sharon was weaving a wool tapestry based on some Incan method she'd learned traveling across Latin America in her twenties. According to Cindalou, she sold the tapestries for outrageous amounts. "Don't get me wrong," she said, "they are pretty, but we're talking, like, ten thousand dollars for a rug." Kenya had seen some of the ones Sharon had not sold hanging around the house and had to agree: they appeared to be regular old rugs.

Sharon looked like a different person in her studio, wearing large black glasses, her wispy hair atop her head. Since, according to Cindalou, she shunned deodorant and used a soap that was as close to no soap as possible, the warm room was redolent with a ripening white girl smell so familiar from her Barrett life that it made Kenya feel surprisingly wistful. It also smelled like wine.

There was a desk in the office and two chairs, but Sharon sat on the floor against a kind of pillow apparently called a husband. The loom sat on her legs. There didn't seem to be much for Kenya to do, but Sharon gave her the job of helping keep the wool threads in their place with a tiny wooden stick and using flat larger sticks to keep stretching the fabric.

"You got it," she kept saying.

"But I'm barely doing anything," said Kenya.

"You're doing plenty. And I hope this is a nice break from all that studying you did at Barrett. I heard that is *some* school."

"Yeah," Kenya said.

"I went to a school like that in New York," she said. Then she sighed. "Bad old Dalton."

"Did you say Dalton?" Kenya said, feeling a ghost move through her.

"You heard of it? It nearly killed me," she said lightly. "You're doing a lot better than I was after graduation. They had to scrape me up off the floor to pack me off to college. And that wasn't much better."

"Where did you go?"

"My parents wanted to send me to Dartmouth, because my dad went there and it was far away, but I told them if they made me apply to a school in freaking New Hampshire I would make the application a suicide note. So I went to Penn, which was the only other Ivy that would take me."

Kenya sucked in a breath. Sharon looked concerned.

"Oh, I know what you're thinking," she sang. "No, I did not know your father back then."

"I wasn't thinking that," Kenya lied.

Sharon shrugged. "It's fine if you were," she said, smiling. "Anyway, I thought Philly was a backwater, but it saved my life. I would probably be shooting up in some basement on the Lower East Side if I hadn't gone down there.

"Tell you the truth," said Sharon. "It was a backwater. Still is; no offense. But it was exactly what I needed. I took a lot of art classes at school and I loved that, but I didn't hang out there. Outside of class, I used to run around with these crazy hippies wandering around barefoot, giving out flowers. That's where I got into yoga and gave up meat. I was even a raw fooder for a while. I was like a walking garlic clove." She laughed. "I stunk to high heaven. My roommate moved out."

"Luuuuuuuuuuuuunch!" called Cindalou.

"But, Kenya, hold on a minute." Sharon spoke with theatrical singsong inflections most of the time. But like other people Kenya had known—even some black ones—Sharon sounded whiter when she wanted to get serious. The only time Kenya had heard her call her children "Nneka" and "Denmark" had been in these clipped tones.

"I don't want to waste this time we have together. I want you to know that I will answer any question you have, okay?"

The idea, Kenya supposed, was intimacy. But she felt like Sharon was preparing to give a deposition.

And of course Kenya didn't have to ask any questions. The next day in the studio, Sharon resumed the story of how Philadelphia had saved her life.

His name was Forest. He was the janitor at the elementary school where Sharon volunteered at an after-school art program. Sharon hadn't known that a janitor could be so young. The ones in the Upper East Side building where she'd grown up and at her school had been older than her father—though of course they called him "Mr." and her mother "Mrs." ("Always hated that, even when I was a little girl," she said.)

Also, she hadn't known that a janitor could be so good-looking, but there he was. And there was Sharon, hanging around every day, lingering and hoping to get a chance to talk to him. She had felt so worldly before, coming to Philadelphia from "big, bad New York," but he made her feel like a clumsy little girl—especially when she compared him with the boyfriends she'd had. The most interesting ones had fancied themselves rebels of one sort or another, but they were all milk-fed brats. Even the hippies knew they could always go home to their rich parents, and eventually most of them did.

Forest, on the other hand, had just returned from two years in Vietnam. He wanted to go to college, but he had to work two jobs to help support his family. She couldn't believe it when after months of their "little talks," he asked her to go for a walk.

Yes, she'd lived in New York City, but had she ever actually known a black person, besides Beatrice, who cooked her family's meals? There were no black students at Dalton, though there was a diplomat's daughter with the prettiest olive skin. So it seemed incredibly embarrassing now, but Forest was her first black friend. She was terrified that he'd find out she was nothing but a paper doll, but he always treated her with respect and interest. She fell hard, but not just for him. Where he'd really gotten her was when he brought her among his family, when she met his mother.

"I always remember her arms. They were so feminine, but also incredibly muscular. It was like she spent her days carrying the world or something. I could not stop staring at them. And she was so *funny*! She called me That White Girl. No, really, it was hilarious. She'd say, 'Hi, That White Girl.' She didn't mean me any harm. I mean she called Forest and his brothers and sister the Lil' Nigs. She'd say"—and here Sharon put bass in her voice—"'You heard of Diana Ross and the Supremes? Well, this is Forest and the Lil' Nigs.'"

Forest didn't care much for the Baptist church in which he'd been raised, but he made the mistake of taking Sharon once; she loved it and wanted to go all the time. It was wrong, she thought, how movies were always making black religion out to be a freak show. When she went to Forest's church it was solemn, "but joyful, you know." It was the first time she felt God.

"Uh-huh," said Kenya.

"I can't believe I'm telling you all this stuff," Sharon said suddenly, shaking her head. "I haven't talked about this in years! I guess since, well, since I met your father."

Kenya shifted in her seat.

"Hey," Sharon said softly, "I'm not freakin' you out too much, am I?"

"No."

"Is it four yet? Oh, what the hell," she said, taking a gulp of warm white wine that had been sitting on her desk in a jelly jar since the day before.

"Anyway, the pressure of everything going on at that time was too much for the family. Forest's dad went and got himself strung out. And his mom picked that time to start drinking, so they took away two of the children. Forest tried his best to raise them himself but it was really too much. I tried to help. I told my parents I needed extra money for art classes, but I really couldn't support his whole family. So you know, Forest wanted . . . got into . . . some street *shit*. And by the time I was graduating, he was headed up to Graterford and it was just all a big fat sad cliché."

"Oh," said Kenya. And then, "Do you mind if I take a break?" she asked, not knowing what else to say.

"You don't have to ask. This isn't a sweatshop, you know," Sharon said with an edge to her voice. When Kenya stepped into the long hallway, Cindalou was right there, fussing with a framed poster of Denmark Vesey hanging outside of the twins' room. She pulled Kenya into the room and closed the door. Then she held her stomach and shook with quiet laughter.

"What? What is it?" Kenya asked.

"God love white folks," said Cindalou, wiping her eyes. "She in there telling you about that pimp and how much she learned from him?"

"What?"

"That dude was a big-time pimp. I mean major. White girls! He was like *the* connection in the community. That's why he went to jail!"

"Did he pimp Sharon?"

"Well, supposedly he never could get her to do that. But as you can see, he did turn her out."

Cindalou laughed even after it seemed as if she had to force herself to do so. Kenya made her face smile and shook her head. In middle school, she'd gone on a field trip to a nursing home. A woman with wild blue eyes and a stiff helmet of dyed brown hair had seemed desperate to keep her there, repeatedly calling her Louise and reminding her about all the things she needed to do for Harry. She mustn't forget Harry. No one had told her, but Kenya had known that Harry was dead. The feeling she'd had then was the one she had now, in the company of the women in this house.

Besides a couple of quick check-in calls when she'd first arrived, Kenya hadn't spoken to her mother. Slowly it began to dawn on her just how angry she was with Sheila. But after listening to Sharon talk, she imagined laughing with her mother over the folly of Johnbrown's white(!) wife(?). They would probably laugh less over Cindalou's muted desperation.

Kenya never did get the chance to call.

After dinner, on the last night she shadowed Sharon, Johnbrown yelled for Kenya when the phone rang. He said she could take it in his office. Kenya wondered if he'd answered and what on earth her parents had said to each other. She steered around Johnbrown's books and papers and picked up the phone, feeling suddenly excited.

"I was totally just about to call you," Kenya said.

"Baby, it's so good to hear your voice," Sheila chirped.

Things sounded strange on her mother's end. She hadn't even stopped to mock Kenya for saying "totally" in a totally Barrett fashion. Also, the house was quiet even though it was Teddy Jaffrey's traditional TV hour. Or one of them, at least. And it sounded to Kenya like her mother was using one tone of voice to paper over a more hysterical one.

"What's wrong?" asked Kenya.

"Nothing," she said. "Nothing," she repeated. "I want to hear about your summer. What's it like out there on your father's compound?"

"Weird." Kenya had imagined herself doing an imitation of Sharon, but she realized she'd have to work up to it. "Did you know he lives with another woman besides Cindalou?"

"I knew something about that," her mother said blandly.

"Did you know that she was white?"

"He didn't come right out and say it. I'm not surprised. So did Cindalou finally get fat? I always felt she might get a little hippy in her old age. She always tended that way."

"She's kind of the same," Kenya said, feeling strangely protective.

"Uh-huh," said Sheila, but it didn't sound as if she was listening.

"Mom, what's going on? You sound weird."

"Kenya, you have to give me a minute," Sheila said, alarming Kenya.

"What are you talking about?"

"I just need a minute."

No matter how taut the terror, the fall proceeds to its dregs.

Kenya had been reading a book called *Maud Martha*. Nothing much happened in it, but a bunch of the lines stayed with her.

According to Sheila, Teddy knew nothing about the forged title scheme that his partner had been running. Sheila had never liked Bert, for the simple reason that she couldn't imagine an honest white man as rough around the edges as he was going into business with a black man. But Bert had stuck up for Teddy when they were children, he'd said. Because of those long years of trust, all of this had gone on right under Teddy's nose.

"Mom, Teddy tried to molest me when I was thirteen," Kenya blurted.

"What did you say?" asked Sheila. Kenya saw that the sky outside of her father's office had changed from bloody plum to blue. She knew her mother had heard her.

"Well, he . . . came into my room. I had gone to a roller-skating party."

"What are you talking about?"

"Mom," Kenya said, her voice shaking. "Listen. I had gone to a roller-skating party."

"And?"

"I woke up and he was sitting in my room in the dark."

"And then what happened?"

"Well, I didn't let anything happen. I told him to leave."

Kenya could hear her mother breathing. "So nothing happened? He didn't touch you or anything?"

"He offered to help me get into my pajamas."

"But you said you didn't need help?"

"I told him to leave."

"And that was all?"

"Yes."

"You're sure that was all?"

"Did you want more?"

"Did you?"

"What?" gasped Kenya. "What?"

"I mean, you never liked Teddy," said Sheila, sounding out-rageously calm. Kenya thought of her fights with Johnbrown and suddenly felt sympathetic toward him. It was nasty busi-ness being the emotional one. Very nasty.

"Maybe you . . ." her mother began.

"Maybe what? I wanted him to rape me?"

"That's not what I'm saying. I'm saying you never liked Teddy. He's so different from your father. And something like this wouldn't really hurt you, but it would be just enough, you know—"

Then abruptly, Sheila began crying. "What am I doing?" she wailed. "I just don't even know what I'm doing."

"Mom," said Kenya, her throat bubbling with rage. Maybe this was worse than her calmness. "Mom," she said again, sharply.

Sheila's crying quickly dwindled to sniffles. "Kenya, I'm re-ally sorry if something like that almost happened to you all those years ago. But maybe this is something we should talk about when you get home."

"Are you going to tell Teddy? Because he'll just—"

"Kenya—let me deal with Teddy. Will you do that, please? And now you need to listen to me. I called because *I* had to tell you something."

There followed a series of words that Kenya was unable to reassemble later in their proper order: lawyers, Teddy, savings, lawsuits, bankrupt. Then Sheila said, "We're broke."

"Who is *we?*" asked Kenya, now sweating.

"You, me, and Teddy."

"You're still with Teddy?"

Sheila said nothing.

"Okay," said Kenya.

Her mother continued. She had called the college. She'd talked to Financial Aid and they'd done what they could, but it wasn't enough—even if she sold the house, which was all they had left and stood to lose in court.

"Didn't you tell me that there was a little left over from Grandmama for college? Something?"

"We . . ." began Sheila. "I . . ." she said. "It's gone, okay? I'm sorry."

What she had called to tell her was this: that Kenya was welcome to come back home and get a job, but she was on her own for school. She might want to ask Johnbrown about it.

The house was burning!

Without climbing down the ladder Kenya was somehow on the floor and running through thick smoke. The front door was wide-open, but a burning beam fell in her path. They were all outside, but only Amandla was screaming her name. She tried to run back in, but Johnbrown gestured for her calmly to come through. *You won't feel it,* he said.

She started it! Cindalou screamed, pointing at Kenya. *She started it!*

And so she had.

• • •

Kenya fought her way up through layers of sleep at the sound of knocking. Finally she screwed her eyes open to gray light. "Yes?" she said in a crisp voice, as if she'd been awake for hours.

Her father cracked the door and said something about going to milk Rosie. Kenya remembered that it was time to shadow him. Neither Sharon nor Cindalou had woken her for the milking, and of course Kenya had not pressed the issue.

"You could sleep a little more if you want."

"No, I want to do it," Kenya said. "Just let me . . . I need to . . ."

"I'll be back in a few minutes," said Johnbrown.

It was absurd, Kenya knew, the idea that diligent farm-handing might help her father decide to send her to college. She didn't even know if he had the money. Sure, they'd renovated this big house and they owned land. But the children wore JCPenney store brands and the house was in the middle of nowhere. Kenya lowered herself down from the loft and tossed on the holey T-shirt and jeans that had become her work clothes. She usually wore an old pair of Cindalou's boots for going out to the chicken coop or the barn.

Her father sat in the kitchen, reading *The New Yorker* and nursing a mug. "Do you drink coffee?" he asked. "I used to hate the stuff till farm life."

Sheila had always been a coffee drinker. But she'd never let Kenya have any, claiming that caffeine made children's hearts jump out of their chests. When Kenya was in tenth grade, she had countered that some of the Barrett girls had been drinking it since eighth, and Sheila had retorted that they had probably been snorting cocaine since then as well and did Kenya want to do that, too?

"I'll try some," she told Johnbrown.

It was vile and muddy tasting, even with sugar, but she drank it anyway. And some fifteen minutes later, her armpits were soaked, her pulse racing, and she was already thinking hopefully about tomorrow. Would there be another offer of coffee?

Out in the damp, chilly barn, Kenya jiggled her foot on the dirt floor. No, she confessed, feigning shame, neither Cindalou nor Sharon had shown her how to do this. She tried to listen to him explain the protocol for touching a cow. She looked at Rosie's bored eyes. Was she generous, or just too oppressed to care? There were flies everywhere; one balanced on Rosie's eyelash.

Kenya had formed an elaborate plan about the winding conversation she would initiate this morning. It would gradually present the case for why Johnbrown should pay for her to go to college without mentioning that this was the only way she could go. It would be the beginning of a stealth campaign that would continue for several days, the rest of her time shadowing him. Then she'd wait for his offer. If he cared about her at all, which she thought he did, she would never even have to ask.

"I need you to pay for me to go to college," she blurted as soon as Johnbrown had finished his explanation and was gloved and seated at Rosie's full udders, in demonstration mode.

"What?" he said without pausing. Milk splashed in the pail. His new biceps bulged.

"I'm sorry. I didn't mean to just—I guess I need to talk to you," said Kenya.

"Well now, I don't ask anyone to stand on ceremony. But that's quite a request to make before seven a.m."

"I'm so sorry. It's the coffee. It's like that stuff they use in the spy movies—"

"Sodium pentothal?" Johnbrown laughed. "This watery crap I make? I hope you're better with your liquor. Seems like you might be a bit of a lightweight, like your old baba."

He wasn't answering her question about paying for college. "Why don't we get everything squared away with Rosie and then talk about this other thing?" he asked. "Give her a squeeze."

The sun had seemed unimaginable when Kenya and Johnbrown had set out for the barn. A few hours later, it was near full July blaze as they filled baskets with what might have been the last peaches of the season. Every task on the farm took longer than it seemed it was going to, and Kenya was never quite ready either mentally or sartorially for what the day would bring. Earlier she hadn't been wearing enough clothes to venture forth in the semidarkness, but now she could wring the sweat out of her jeans.

"Can you imagine being a slave?" her father said just then. This was something he used to say on hot days back in the city when they had to walk somewhere far or do something else unpleasant.

"No," said Kenya, thinking that a slave was somewhere laughing his head off at what they were doing while other black people in the world were sitting in air-conditioned offices and tapping cash registers in mall stores.

Johnbrown moved along with a ladder while Kenya followed him, picking the low-hanging fruit. Looking down at her through leaves, he asked, "Did you come up here to ask me for money? I mean, it's not a problem if you did."

Kenya took a breath. "I did not."

"No?" asked Johnbrown, seemingly to the tree next to her, instead of looking at her in the eye. Kenya kept picking, through vision that was suddenly watered and blurry.

"Baba, I didn't know we needed money."

"Did something happen?"

As fucked-up as things were with Sheila, Johnbrown was the one who had run off and left them. She did not want to tell him what had become of Sheila. She could not even, to him, say the word *Teddy*. Instead she said, "I thought we had the money and we didn't."

"Weird."

"You don't know the half."

"Monk—Kenya, I'm not trying to be shitty, but we need to be honest. You know a lot about where dishonesty can lead people."

"Why don't *you* be honest with *me*? Why don't you want to help me?"

"I do want to help," he said. "I have to talk to Sharon."

"And Cindalou?"

"And Cindalou, of course. But come on, Kenya. I'm sure you've figured out that it's mostly Sharon's money." His voice was matter-of-fact, with a hint of vinegar. "I know you're curious about that. But it's not a big deal. If I had to live without all of this—any of it—I would." He laughed. "I really would. Anyway, give me a few days."

For the rest of their week together, Johnbrown said nothing about Kenya's request. It took an almost physical strength for her not to press him. Then the shadowing was over and Kenya more or less went back to eating, sleeping, and reading and dared Johnbrown to ask any more of her. She did occasionally help Amandla with the kids and run a couple of errands with Cindalou. Also, after the week with her father, she found it hard to sleep in. So she sometimes wandered out to the barn and did her best to milk Rosie. This was especially helpful to Sharon, who was sometimes too hungover to stir before eight.

Some afternoons when it seemed too warm to move around, Kenya sat on the shaded back porch reading *Silas Marner*. Sometimes she read it aloud to Nannie and Dennie, who fought over her lap and claimed to understand the story.

One late morning, Kenya sat on the porch, looking down the road from which no one ever came, and Johnbrown appeared. He handed her a fishing rod. "Let's go for a walk," he said.

"Are we going fishing?" she asked nonsensically.

They headed for the creek. Kenya's face burned when she thought of the time weeks ago when she'd turned her back on Nannie. She hadn't been down to the creek since.

"Don't people usually start fishing a little earlier in the morning?" she asked, her body prickling with heat as they settled on the mud by the water. Johnbrown had opened his tackle box and was selecting lures.

"I don't know. What time do *you* usually set out?" he asked with a teasing grin.

She had the urge to tell him that she'd ridden horses, tossed about on sailboats, and gone skiing, both downhill and cross-country. But she knew he'd only say she'd never been fishing, so she rolled her eyes. Johnbrown fiddled with flashing objects.

Without looking up he asked, "Kenya, how do you like it here?"

"Down at the creek?"

"Ha, ha. I mean at the house," he said, gesturing vaguely.

Kenya told herself that getting to college did not depend on what she said in this moment. Still she spoke carefully. "I like it."

This was mostly true.

Then she added, "I'm glad to get to know my brother and sisters." This was one-third true.

"And me—how are you feeling about me these days?"

"I'm understanding more about you since being here," she said. But she didn't say that what she'd come to understand is that her father now seemed to be the leader and only full member of his own cult, a man with whom she shared little except for memories from another world and a fondness for Cindalou's cooking.

"I'm glad to hear you say that," he said. "So I know this wasn't the plan, but I'm wondering if you might want to hang out for a while. Maybe take some time, get a little job in town, save some money."

"Sharon said no, huh?"

"Actually, she said yes. You know how Sharon is. Well, maybe you don't. But in any case, she was fine with it."

"So what's the problem?"

Johnbrown finally stopped playing with what looked like

dangerous cat toys, wiped sweat from his brow, and looked her in the eye. "Well, it's not up to her, really. I mean we're well cared for, but your request will mean we have to lean on her parents more than we already do."

"And they said no?"

The wrinkle in Johnbrown's forehead passed so quickly that Kenya wasn't sure it had been there. "Look, we didn't ask. Okay, so maybe Sharon could get money from her millionaire developer daddy to send the daughter from my ex—I meant first—family to college, but I can't accept any more money from those people than I have already. Just can't."

"Will you take their money to send Nannie and Dennie to college?"

"I don't want to. But those are their grandchildren. I can't stop them."

"How about Amandla?"

He was silent.

Back at her mother's house, Kenya had begun aggressively daydreaming about the campus. Sometimes she would sit down and focus all of her energy to think about it. There, at college, she would dress, talk, and act like a completely new person. Of course she'd fantasized about becoming a new person every summer since she had started at Barrett—but this time it would be real. Except for the wonderful Candace and Karen, no one at Wesleyan knew her. And even Candace and Karen knew only some bubbly, anything-goes version of her. No one knew that her absolute party limit was two drinks, or that she listened to classic rock and old Stevie Wonder records and thought LL Cool J was boring. They wouldn't know about the bullshit she'd gone through with Johnbrown and Sheila or

Teddy Jaffrey. They wouldn't know the old her at all. Now they would never get to know the *new* her either.

Kenya tried to snap the rod, which took more strength than she'd imagined. Frustrated, she hurled it toward the water.

Johnbrown looked pained. "There are going to be some very sad children when news gets out about that fishing rod. That was Amandla's favorite. She named it Rodney." He laughed.

Kenya scrambled to her feet and began walking away from the house, toward the woods.

"Kenya," said her father as he fell behind her swift steps. He said her name again, but not louder. He had not raised his voice since Kenya had been on the farm. It had taken her weeks to notice that he never yelled, not when Dennie and Nannie got the notion to "decorate" their playroom with toilet paper, not when Amandla slept through Rosie's morning milking twice in a row. She could hear sometimes a female voice rising somewhere in the house, battered back by the measured current of his words. She remembered how back when he was her father, his arguing voice had been high and shrill. She thought it would be interesting to see her parents argue now.

She broke into a run but fell almost instantly, tripping over her feet. Her father was over her, extending a hand. She brushed it aside and struggled to her feet.

"Why don't you ever say you're sorry?" she yelled in his face. She noticed, for the first time, that she was now nearly as tall as he was. "You haven't said that to me *once* since I've been here!"

"Because I'm not sorry."

"What?"

"I haven't said I'm sorry because I'm not sorry."

"But what about what you said? When you were hiding out from everything in fucking prison?"

"What did I say?"

"That you'd made mistakes."

"I *did* make mistakes. And actually, you're saying I never said I was sorry, but if memory serves, I did apologize then. But I didn't mean to. I hadn't figured things out yet."

"Now you're saying you didn't mean to apologize?"

"Look, Kenya, I am sorry about the things that you had to go through because of me. But everything that happened got us here. I mean, look around. Don't I seem like a more stable person to you? All of this might not be your thing, but don't I seem like I have more to offer as your father?"

"Except money! Or a simple fucking apology for what you did to my mother!" Kenya shrieked and covered her ears at the same time. Johnbrown gently pulled her hands off of her ears.

"Kenya, your mother and I loved each other. But we were young and times were downright perilous. My brainwashed parents raised me thinking all I had to do was keep my nappy hair cut and wash behind my ears and try to be as white as possible, but there was some fucked-up shit going on in America, in Philadelphia. Brothers were getting their skulls busted by the police for no fucking reason. *I* nearly got my skull busted a couple of times, just for walking around my—"

"You mean the time you gave the police that card and got to go home?"

"Your mother told you that one, huh? Did she tell you about the time I found myself in a police station right near where she lives right now, getting my ass cheeks spread?" His voice cracked.

Kenya stared at him as if unimpressed.

Then he was calm again. "Look, you don't need to hear my war stories. All you need to know is that I was really scared of white people and I was really angry with black folks for not doing more."

"Seems like you made your peace with those white people after you left us," she said, with less acid than she had hoped.

"I loved your mother," Johnbrown repeated. "And I mean whatever happened with us was my fault, too. I don't know what I was doing that drove her to stay in touch with my mother behind my back, for example, but it must have been bad. And as much as I loved her, Sheila could bring out the absolute worst in me. She made me feel like the things I *had* to do, things I never minded doing before her, were things that I was doing only to please her. Other things that I needed, well, she made me feel criminal for wanting them."

"Like other women?"

"Like being a real activist, or like my *work*, which was the main thing keeping me together. Every time I suggested new directions for the Seven Days, she shot me down, humiliated me, in front of the others. And then she tried to be supportive of The Key, but it was obvious she didn't really believe in it."

The fucking Key!

"Maybe you don't believe either," he said. But Kenya barely

heard him. All of this time, she had imagined that the answer for Johnbrown's defection lay somewhere on the person of Cindalou—her soft hair and freckles, her easy ways, which had hardened with time. But The Key?

She said, "I don't even know what the fuck The Key is anymore. I mean, I thought it was some kind of philosophy. But now it's just about your butler arsonist?" She could see that Johnbrown's Zen mask was starting to crack, and it made her happy. She laughed.

"Don't do that, Kenya. Please." He looked stricken. "This is important."

"What are you talking about? What are you *ever* talking about?"

"Look, just so you know, all that stuff, the philosophy—I got rid of that when I went to prison. I was too fucked-up back then to be telling people how to live. I didn't know who I was. But the story of the butler: that was real to me then and real to me now. That is The Key, or *a* key. Maybe it's a blueprint, maybe a cautionary tale, maybe it's nothing. I don't know. But what I'm also telling you is that I'm not making it up. It's coming from me, but I'm not making it up."

Kenya remembered when they'd talked back in prison, how he'd been under the tutelage of a man named Garrett Hadnitch. She had learned later why his name was familiar. The newspapers covered his grim circus of an appeal hearing, complete with the parents of the one Puerto Rican and two black women whose partial remains had been found in his freezer. There had been a picture of him, looking like an extremely dirty Jesus, on the front of the *Daily News*.

Kenya made herself laugh. "Baba, you know that guy in prison, your writing guru, he was—"

His face turned grim. "I know. I didn't know, but then I found out. We're getting way off track here. This isn't about him, or even about The Key. I'm trying to tell you about what happened with your mother, with our family. I've wanted to talk to you all summer. I'm sorry it's happening in this way now, but—"

"Please go on," Kenya said drily. "What else have you been dying to tell me?"

"Look, I don't want you to misunderstand me when I say this, but another part of all of it was that I wasn't quite ready to be a father when you were born."

"You didn't want me," she said.

"Of course I wanted you."

"I have to get out of here." Kenya started walking again but changed her course, heading back through the cultivated land to the house. "Somebody needs to give me a ride to the bus. Not you. I'll throw my shit in a bag and you can get a member of your harem to take me."

"Maybe we should finish this particular discussion before we get back. I know you have a lot more to say to me and I'm ready to hear it."

"Actually I think I'm done talking to you. Like, forever."

Now they were at the house. Kenya moved swiftly past the kids, playing jacks on the porch, and Cindalou, who kept saying, "What's wrong what's wrong," and up into the Zen room. She slammed the door and then yanked open the drawers and closet as savagely as she could, throwing dirty and clean clothes in a pile on the floor. As on the first night, she heard murmurs downstairs that concerned her, but she couldn't make them out.

She meant to stay in motion, but she lost her spirit, surrounded by her things in haphazard piles. She was satisfied, however, that the room looked the way she felt; a pair of her underwear dangled on the Buddha, covering one of his eyes. She clambered up into the loft and fell sobbing into a fitful sleep.

Johnbrown must have warned them to stay away, because everyone did. Kenya awoke to find her stomach growling. When she heard what sounded like lunch happening, she slunk down to the kitchen. Just as she walked in, she heard Johnbrown praising Cindalou's bean salad. All eyes turned toward her.

"You need to try some of this," her father said, adjusting his belt.

"How are you feeling?" asked Sharon.

"Fine," Kenya muttered, wondering what her father had told them. It was impossible to know.

"Do you want some tea?" asked Sharon. "I have a chamomile mint blend that's good for anything that ails you."

"I just need to eat," Kenya said. Rage and sadness had made her ravenous. She tried to seem distant while shoveling cold beans that were annoyingly delicious into her mouth.

"What's wrong, Kenya?" said Nannie, oblivious to the fact that the adult women had not asked. Kenya wondered what she must look like that even a four-year-old would inquire after her well-being.

"I'm leaving tomorrow," Kenya said.

"You really don't have to," said Johnbrown.

Kenya had come downstairs so spent that she'd felt almost calm. All she'd wanted to do was eat and go back to sleep. But sitting with these people and their rustic-gracious living on their forty acres of land, watching her father enjoy his lunch after all that he had said to her, turned corn bread to dust in her throat.

"No, I really do have to go."

Johnbrown finally put down his fork. "I want you to think about what you're doing, Kenya."

"What am I doing, *Baba*?"

"You're storming off angry because I can't give you money."

"Do you need money, sweetheart?" asked Sharon.

"Sharon," said Johnbrown.

Kenya fumed.

Everyone stayed where they were. No one ushered Nannie, Dennie, or Amandla out of the room. But as far as Kenya was concerned, just she and her father faced each other.

"So were you ready to have kids when you got Cindalou pregnant?" she said suddenly.

Cindalou made a curious noise.

"Of course not. I was committed to another woman."

"But of course by the time *Sharon* got pregnant!"

"What? That's supposed to mean something about the fact that she's white?"

"I think that's enough," Sharon said. "Johnbrown, Kenya, that's quite enough. If you guys want to continue—"

"I'm saying this in front of all of you," Johnbrown said, his voice rising angrily. "In fact, I was the least prepared when Sharon got pregnant. I had just gotten out of prison, but—"

Kenya stood up from her chair. "So you didn't want any of us," she said. "He didn't want you," she said, pointing at Amandla, who looked interested rather than distraught.

"Kenya," snapped Cindalou.

"Well, it's true and you know it. But why are you even talking to me? Your whole confused Kentucky Fried act! You knew exactly what you wanted when you met my mother. The good man she had at home. Or rather the good man she thought she had at home. Or the man in her home she thought was good!"

"Daddy, did you want me?" asked Nannie. "Did you want us?" Dennie echoed.

"Of course I wanted you," barked Johnbrown, though he clearly hadn't meant to. Dennie started to cry.

"I hate you, Kenya!" yelled Nannie.

"Nannie," Kenya said, listening to herself with equal measures of horror and glee, "you're a fucking brat. And didn't you hear what your baba said? He *just* told me that he wanted you least of all. But you guys are the golden eggs keeping the goose here."

"What the hell is *that* supposed to mean?" snapped Sharon, looking especially feral. She had stood and for some reason was holding a bottle of wine.

"You're the goose," said Kenya.

"Oh *my* God," said Sharon. "Oh my God, why am I sitting here listening to this?" She finally jumped up from the table, sweeping the twins out of the room with her. Cindalou walked out as well, but Amandla didn't budge, even when her mother growled her name. She sat looking at Johnbrown, as if he was an agitated creature in a cage.

"You're not making any sense," said Johnbrown, "but you are causing irreparable damage!" Finally he yelled, "Get out of the kitchen, Amandla!"

She slowly rose from the table and strolled out, and Kenya made as if to follow her.

"Where are you going?" Johnbrown said. "You started this and we're going to finish it!"

Now he was standing in front of her, his jaw thrust forward. She had never seen her father do anyone physical harm, and she knew he wasn't about to touch her now. But she thought about Teddy grabbing her. In a way, that was Johnbrown's fault. All of it was.

She punched him—not as hard as she meant, but low. "That is it! I'm calling the police!" yelled Sharon, who stood in the doorway. Johnbrown doubled over, making a soft, surprised sound, then snapped at Sharon that the cops were rednecks. In that instant, an unfamiliar wave of memory broke and washed over Kenya. She knew then that she'd been aiming the gun at Johnbrown and that Sheila had gotten in the way. Well, she'd finally hit her mark.

No one followed her back into the Zen room, but she could hear their voices raised at one another. Kenya packed her things and fell heavily into sleep. When she opened her eyes, the moon had burst in through the blinds as if it couldn't help itself. Instead of being alarmed, she felt calmer when she woke and saw Amandla sitting below her on the rug, flooded in moonlight.

"There's some water," said the girl. The glass was in the window cubby up in the loft. Kenya marveled that Amandla had gotten the glass up there without waking her. She gulped it down, hurting her throat.

"What time is it?" she asked.

"It's nine o'clock," said Amandla. "I'm supposed to be in bed."

"Jeez. Feels like the middle of the night. What's up?"

"I thought you might be thirsty."

"I'm so sorry," Kenya managed.

"Well, they're really upset," Amandla said. "But I'm not."

You just don't know it yet, Kenya thought. *It might take you years.*

"It was so dumb," Amandla said. "My baba seemed like he wanted to tell Nannie and Dennie the truth. He wouldn't just say that you had lied. Sharon was getting so mad at him. And my mom just kept shaking her head and saying she knew this summer was a bad idea."

That bitch, Kenya thought. "Amandla," she said. "I feel so bad about what I said to you. It isn't true at all."

"Yes it is," she said sadly. "I used to pretend that he wasn't even my real father. When he was in jail, my mother started dating this other guy for a while, Mr. Taylor. He was boring but he was normal. I used to pray that he would be my dad. I mean, I love my baba and I know he loves me. He's supersmart, but he's a spaz. *You* know. And he makes my mom act like a spaz. She's *so* different when he's not around."

Kenya wondered where the girl had learned the word *spaz*,

considering she didn't go to Barrett—or any school at all. And then she remembered a few weeks ago, describing Phyllis Fagin while Amandla laughed, grabbing her stomach.

"Plus everything is so weird," Amandla continued. "We live with Sharon. She's okay, but when I grow up, I'm never doing anything like this. I'm either going to live by myself or there's just going to be one other person. I used to want to go to school in town, but then I was like, what am I going to tell the kids in town about how I live? I mean, it would be bad enough being, like, the only black kid."

"Yeah," said Kenya with a sigh.

"Why'd you get so mad anyway?"

"Baba didn't say?"

"Not really."

"It's a long story," she said. But maybe it wasn't. Maybe it was a short story that was too petty to tell, but it was still breaking her heart. She imagined herself having dinner with her mother and the awful Teddy Jaffrey every night. It made her want to howl with misery. But she couldn't stay here.

"When are you leaving?" Amandla asked.

"Tomorrow," said Kenya. Earlier, she had hatched, and then quickly abandoned, a plan where she left the house in the dark. She liked the idea of scaring her father, who had breezily mentioned a Klan stronghold to the west of the farm. Let them find her, she'd thought then. Let them string her up.

"I wish I could go with you," said Amandla.

"You really don't."

•   •   •

The next day, after a round of hugs ranging from stiff to hostile (except for the embrace of a quietly weeping Amandla), Johnbrown took Kenya to the bus station. They said little. She didn't discover until he was gone that he'd put a manila envelope containing a sheaf of papers in her backpack. By then it was too late to rip them to pieces and let them fly out of the window in his face.

Disgruntled

Perhaps it began when I was born black on that island across the sea. Perhaps it began when my father dropped dead and my grandparents told me that soon I'd have to leave school and join them in the fields. Perhaps the thing was well under way when the mistress told me that my services were no longer needed. This seems like years ago; it was merely this morning.

"We are grateful for the service you have given us," she said. "But we are going to have to let you go."

I knew if I asked why she would only tell a falsehood, and I did not want to say anything that could be mistaken for begging. I wondered idly also if she had talked to the Architect about this decision. He was out of town and I wondered if he would feel differently. Not fully wanting to, I asked, "Is there anything I can do?"

We were in the large, square room where they entertain. She sat on the couch that was her favorite place to sit and I stood in front of her, the sun spilling in on all sides. She was waiting for me to say "ma'am."

We looked at each other.

"No," she said finally. "There's nothing you can do. We will pay your passage back to New York. We are happy to provide letters of reference," she said.

"I will pack my things," I said, thinking that I would not trust those letters. I'd once heard a story about a young, educated Negro searching for a job in New York who was chased around by letters informing people that they should not hire him and that they should not tell him about the content of the letters.

"There's no rush," she said. "The new man doesn't arrive until later in the week. We could use your help for several dinners before then. The furniture needs one more polishing, the rugs one last cleaning. You'll need to train the new man as well. Of course you will receive your final wages and then some."

"Of course," I said, bowing like an idiot. As I was walking away, she called me back.

"Julian," the cow said. "I'd like a word with Elizabeth. I'd like to explain."

"That won't be necessary," I said, taking a tone with her that I now felt free to take.

"I'd prefer to," she said, forcing her thin, pale lips into a hard smile.

I went to the kitchen in search of Elizabeth, feeling violence in my hands. When she was not there, I went downstairs and groped my way to our room. As I entered the room, dark in the daylight, I heard the sound of someone retching. I, too, nearly became sick as I heard liquid hit the pail we used at night.

"Elizabeth?" I said.

"Yes," she said in a small voice.

"I have to tell you something."

"And I you," she said. That was how I found out about you.

• • •

You will not believe this, but in that moment, it was I who was happy. A child! Your mother's voice was sodden with despair. And so I was even more sorry then, to tell what I had to tell her. I did not light a lantern so I would not have to see her face. I could hear the look in her voice.

"Oh, Julian," she said. "What will we do?"

"She says she'll pay our passage back to New York."

"And then what will we do?"

"She says," I began with a smirk no one could see, "that she'll provide letters of reference."

"Does this amuse you?" Elizabeth snapped. "Are you pleased?"

A familiar and unpleasant jolt went through my frame as I wondered if this woman to whom I had sworn myself would ever understand me. "No," I said simply. "I'm not pleased, but . . ."

"But. What?" she said, each word a small harsh sentence.

"But perhaps this is not what I'm meant to do."

"And what are you meant to do? And how are we meant to live?"

"I know we are not meant to live like this. I know that I was not meant to live like this."

I heard her snort in the darkness. Then we heard the sound of a large stick hit the floor above us. This was how they summoned us if we were downstairs.

"She wants a word with you," I said.

My wife took one look at me, gathered her skirts, and walked up the rickety stairs. I paused alone in the dark. Then I went up as well. It was getting on time to prepare for the afternoon meal.

I could tell the Irish housemaid knew, though she said nothing about it. I knew she was hoping now to work with more grimy white people like herself and her bedraggled compatriots, the hired men.

Elizabeth came into the kitchen and set about rinsing vegetables. I looked at her back, which was slightly stooped, and I loved her. I felt comforted that though we might travel the whole earth, we would travel it together.

"Do you know how many are eating?" I asked. I realized I had forgotten to ask the cow if there would be others besides herself and her horrible children. Well, it was not true that both were horrible; the girl was a shy child with a sad expression. But knowing her mother, I felt I knew what she would become. I thought, as I looked at Elizabeth, about parents and children. She had stopped her work to look out of the window. She glanced at me as if still looking through the clouds. "Seven."

"Are you well?"

"I'm fine. And you can set the regular plate. The other guests are just the men."

Sometimes the cow, in the absence of the Architect, dined with the white groundskeepers. She had never extended this wretched courtesy to Elizabeth and myself, the excuse being that we were always required to serve. This was well and good; I never wanted to break bread with any of these people. I have to admit, however, that it galled me to have to gently place plates before men with barely a tooth between them, who had to be reminded by the housemaid to wash the grime from their faces and hands before they sat down to the Architect's table. In these people's eyes, I would never be as good as these men, who were not much more sentient than the horses and cows they watered and fed.

I was not thinking much of them then, this morning when the day began. I was thinking of Elizabeth and our child as the kitchen clouded with Lucifer's sweat. She was making the hot soup that the mistress required, even in August. She had confided in my wife that it was part of a regimen she followed hoping it would help her conceive a child, though she was past natural childbearing years.

I leaned in close to your mother and made a motion as if to wring my handkerchief into the soup. She said my name sternly.

"What can they do?" I asked her. "Dismiss us?"

I sought a smile, but she began to weep!

"I know this is hard," I said. "But you must trust me. If this woman doesn't want us in her—"

"It's you, Julian, she doesn't want in her house. She does not think you fit here," Elizabeth whispered harshly, tears streaming down her face. "She has asked me to stay on and I have said yes."

I am not sure, but I think I staggered back onto my heels. I remembered once when I was quite small and knocked over a bowl of dry beans through which my mother was sorting. She was very angry. As I was on my hands and knees, picking up the beans, she kicked me. Though she had been in a rage when I turned the bowl over, I could tell that the kick was casual, an afterthought.

I loved your mother, but I could see behind her eyes. Though her cheeks were streaked with tears, I could tell that she had said yes quickly. While I was down there groveling among beans, she had kicked me. Or perhaps the groveling among beans was what I was doing with my days and nights in the service of the Architect, and the mistress's firing me was the kick.

"Does she know you are carrying a child?" I asked in a hoarse voice.

"She has offered to help."

"She has offered to help *my* child?"

The housemaid was in the kitchen wiping sweat from her frizzy brow. "Julian Curtis, the table is waiting," she announced. She then looked at Elizabeth with an expression I could not quite read, but it had the feel of a conspiracy.

"Please go," said Elizabeth.

I hit my head on the way out of the kitchen.

A thought occurred to me while I stood in my usual position on hand as the mistress, her children, and the Cro-Magnons scratched their fleas and ate their dinner. I thought that before I left I would burn the Architect's blanket, and instead of waiting until I was meant to leave, I would do it today. I would say it was an accident. It was as if the mistress heard my thought, for she looked at me strangely.

"That will be all for the moment, Julian," she said. "Please come back in a quarter of an hour."

"If you please, ma'am," I said. "I will start on the rugs."

"Very well."

In the shed, I found the gasoline that we used to clean the rugs. Then the ax caught my eye, and I imagined breaking up the Architect's precious chaise longue. The place where a person like him could lie down in the daytime. When I walked back through the kitchen, Elizabeth was there alone, icing the small cakes beloved by the little girl. I watched her lovely profile for a minute. I was speaking before I could catch myself.

"You must not do this," I said, trying to keep my voice low and out of the dining room. "You must not leave me."

"I am carrying a child," she said, her voice even lower. "I cannot leave here right now."

"My child. That is why you must come with me."

"I'm sorry, Julian," she said. She looked around the kitchen, as if she'd find something to say there amid the clutter of cooking. Then her eyes rested on the gas can and the ax. "What are you going to do?"

"Clean the rugs," I said.

"What are you going to do, Julian?" Elizabeth asked again, her eyes getting wide.

I looked at her. And then I saw myself take shape in her eyes as someone terrifying.

"Please," she said.

In a way, then, it was her idea. In a way, it was your mother who pushed me to do it. Because as I looked at and smelled her fear, I suddenly knew that I would not only burn up the blanket but burn this house to the ground. I also knew that because of you, I would spare her.

"I cannot forgive you, Elizabeth. But if you leave this house immediately, you and the child will live."

I clamped a hand on her mouth before she could scream. I hated to touch her like that. The dining room bell rang again, making a tinny, impatient sound. I felt her go slack in my arms. And then I pulled her to me for the last time in this life. Our clothes and skin stuck to us unpleasantly in the steaming kitchen on that August day.

It was the instinct of an ignorant animal that made me go back into the dining room at the sound of the bell. The mistress spoke sharply to her son, for singing at the table. I could see from my position all of the crumbs that the dairyman had dropped at his place and the nails of his nephew, which were ringed black with manure.

"Julian," said the mistress, "it has been nearly an hour. I know Elizabeth made something special for A—. If you would please clear the table and bring it. The men need to get back to work."

I did not trust myself to speak. I picked up an armload of plates and took them into the kitchen. I heard the little girl's voice: "Mama, why is he so mad?"

The kitchen was empty.

Elizabeth.

I stood at the window, straining to see the receding figure. But the waves of grass were still and empty. She had disappeared, leaving behind the tray of iced cakes, which I brought to the dining room.

I pictured it before I did it, pouring a thin trail of the gasoline along the bottom of the study wall, and from there throughout the house. Then it was happening. I threw a match and the flames answered. Through the smoke I made my way back to the door out of which your mother had fled. I posted myself sentry with the ax. Those who made it through the smoke and flames at the front of the house would try to get out of the back. But none would make it past me and the ax.

There was nothing to do now but wait.

. . .

Commodore had been admitted to Tyler for his realistic, colorful paintings of the people in the neighborhood where he grew up. Despite his obsession with the Eakins painting, he made pretty pictures of black folk: churchy grandmothers, empty-eyed men on the corner, drug dealers dripping in gold. All of them had similarly haunted eyes. The one his teacher labeled his "statement piece" was a glum-looking baby who wore a heavy gold chain and an equally heavy-looking diaper. He grasped a gun in his little brown fist.

Once in art school, after he'd seen the ironic pornography his classmates were making, he'd become mortified by his portfolio. ("I wanted to take that gun and shoot the baby.") He dedicated himself to a series of charcoal drawings of stick figures being executed that he called the Hangman Series. This change in direction was underappreciated, as were the harangues against his classmates' work in his obscenity-laced open letter to the faculty at Tyler titled "A Plea for Black Complexity." He lost his scholarship.

According to Commodore, this was the best thing that could have happened to him. Now he could truly be an artist. "Studying and doing are *not* the same thing," he declared. Of course, after a few days of staying with him, it became clear to Kenya that he was doing neither. If he wasn't toiling at the Green Apple: *a healthy cafeteria*, he was either smoking pot or making plans to smoke. Occasionally he thumbed through a book.

It wasn't terribly surprising to Kenya that Commodore had come to this. It seemed to her that there had been something very wide-eyed about his pursuit of art. It reminded her of Lolly Lewis's violent enthusiasms; this was a girl who had believed in Santa Claus until the sixth grade. Sure, Commodore had spoken passionately at the art museum, and he'd once claimed that he would paint with bloody stumps until he achieved artistic greatness. But none of that seemed real now.

What did seem real, what Kenya could remember sharply, was him as a ten-year-old, waiting for her parents to leave the room so he could call her "Ooga Booga," and being so distracted that he couldn't follow the rules of Uno. She remembered his air of irony even in elementary school. She could not imagine him scowling with concentration at a canvas. The image of him sucking a water pipe, reclined on the couch, giggling at reruns of *Inspector Gadget*—which he had loved at the age of ten—well, it was sad. But it was more fitting.

The big surprise, noted nonchalantly by Commodore, was that he was living with Oliver Gold. Though she was relieved that his roommate wasn't a girl, Kenya nearly fell off of the uncomfortable wooden chair in his apartment when he told her.

"That lunatic?" she asked.

"You know Oliver?"

Kenya shook her head in an exaggerated fashion, as if to clear out the cobwebs. "Com, you mean the Oliver you used to talk shit about all the time? The one who called himself a 'niggerpunk' and talks with a British accent?"

"That's my boy," Commodore said, laughing. "Crazy as hell. But one hundred percent original."

"You *hated* him!"

"I never said *hate*. We don't say that," he said, grinning.

That had been a big thing with the Seven Days. Never

hating—except for the absolute worst white people and black traitors.

"Is he still wearing that jacket with the swastika on the back?"

"Naw. He had to give up his Sid Vicious stylings."

"I just can't imagine why."

"Not what you'd think," Commodore explained. Not the disgusted clucking of black people on the street—he could never please black folks anyway, according to Oliver. Not the skinheads who routinely started shit with him when he went to punk clubs—they had always started shit with him anyway. Not even the Jewish hotheads whom he'd numbed into silence with his complicated philosophical defense of his right to wear the jacket—well, that and the fact that Oliver's mother was Jewish. No, finally an old woman in the Gallery mall drew back her coat sleeve to show him the number tattooed on her arm and then tried her best to knock him over a balcony with her cane. On the way to the hospital, where he received five stitches, the jacket had quietly disappeared and that had been that.

"Yeah, I couldn't really roll with him wearing that," said Commodore. "He told me later that he wore it to an interview for a scholarship from the Alphas."

"Didn't *you* get a scholarship from the Alphas?"

"Well, I wore a suit to *my* interview. But forget about all that. He's cool now. In fact, to be really real about it, he's the man."

"Guess I'll have to take your word for it."

Kenya, who'd turned up on Commodore's doorstep in Powelton Village fresh from the farm, was prepared to deal with Oliver if she could crash in the apartment. When she'd found the address, her heart had sunk taking in the splintered stairs and curling paint. But the inside of the place was sunny and cream-colored, with soft wood floors and a skylight in the largest room. She felt, when she walked in and looked around, the way she'd first felt in the loft at her father's house: like she could hide there.

It was after Kenya read her father's manuscript for the third or maybe fourth time that she decided not to go back to her mother's house. Her father was a dramatic idiot, her mother was a fool, and yet she understood both the butler's feeling of being hounded and his wife's decision to get away from the crazy person who supposedly loved her.

Her parents didn't know where she was. She had led her father to assume that she was going back to her mother's house. She hoped that he'd call to make sure she arrived, only to find out that she'd disappeared. But she knew that he wouldn't. Meanwhile, her mother was not expecting her until the end of the summer. She would find out that Kenya had disappeared only if she called Johnbrown's again. But Kenya felt her mother's shame might keep her from calling back.

On the bus she wavered in her decision not to go home, but then she thought about her last conversation with Sheila, and it made her tremble.

Denial. This had been a favorite word among Barrett girls some years back. They had hurled it at one another for months. You're in denial: the Police are never getting back together.

You're in denial: Mademoiselle Lambert will never let us out early. You're in total denial: this *does* make me look fat!

She was considering her mother's denial, and Commodore had popped into her head as the city came into view. It wasn't quite true that he popped into her head. He was often there, lurking in the shadows, and he had sent her a letter at the farm filled with the kinds of declarations he'd made in "A Plea for Black Complexity." She had kept the letter, which was how she had his address. But on the ride back to Philadelphia he strode to the center of her thoughts as more than a romantic fantasy. She had hesitated at first, not wanting him to think she was looking for more than a couch to sleep on. She didn't want him to think *she* was in denial about who she was, or was not, to him. But as the highway exits became more familiar, Kenya practiced first in her mind, and then in a low voice, the businesslike manner she would use with Commodore. "I wondered if I could stay with you for a few days while I figure shit out," Kenya mouthed, her voice going in and out. Her seatmate, who was wearing a Walkman, tossed her a couple of sidelong glares.

Commodore said yes, but then it turned out that Kenya was beholden to Oliver, not Commodore, for a place on the couch. It was his name on the lease, and he paid extra rent to use two of the apartment's three bedrooms. When he came home from classes at Temple the day she arrived and Commodore mentioned she'd be there for a few days, he simply nodded and said, "Cool." Then he disappeared into his room to make grinding noises on an electric guitar. He kept odd hours, so she barely saw him for the first few days while she flipped TV channels, walked around the city, and watched Commodore get high, all the while pondering the great black maw of her future.

For the first couple of days at Commodore's, Kenya planned to call home. But she imagined her mother answering the phone while Teddy sat a few inches away or, even worse, Teddy answering the phone. So instead, she took to wandering the edges of Penn's campus, near the library where her mother used to work before she'd finally gotten a job in one of the township libraries.

One night she came home to Commodore and Oliver sitting in the tiny kitchen. It had been a week and she rarely saw them together. She had started to wonder if they were actually friends.

"Hungry?" asked Oliver, gesturing toward a pizza. His nasal voice went up and down. He did not speak with a British accent, but his inflections were pretentious.

Kenya demurred. She'd been using her savings to eat McDonald's and the lo mein from the Chinese food truck near Penn's campus that always had the longest line. It was certainly a comedown from Cindalou's cooking, and she constantly had the taste of grease in her mouth, but as a guest she was committed to a certain standard of conduct.

"Suit yourself," Com said, helping himself to more. "I am *starving* like *Marving*." He laughed at his own joke.

"Kenya, you should have some," Oliver insisted. "We can't eat this whole thing."

"Oliver's gotta watch his figure," said Commodore. Kenya noted that Oliver's body resembled a twisted-out hanger.

"Okay," said Kenya, picking up the last slice of cheese pizza. The rest was pepperoni.

"Take my seat," said Oliver. "I'm done eating and I have a crapload of work to do."

"I feel so bad breaking up your—" she began.

"Our romantic dinner?" Commodore laughed and turned to Oliver. "Honey, we never talk anymore."

"Honey," Oliver said with fake emotion, "all you want to talk about is that Mary Elizabeth. Do you know how that makes me feel?"

"Who is Mary Elizabeth?" Kenya asked.

"Some dizzy white broad," Commodore said.

"Your favorite flavor," sang Oliver. "Now if you two will excuse me . . ."

After Oliver closed his door, Kenya wanted to ask again about Mary Elizabeth, but she didn't want to embarrass herself. Instead she gestured toward Oliver's room. "He's okay, I guess."

"Not so bad, right?" said Commodore with a grin. "He must like you okay, too. I mean Oliver's not exactly what you would call a *people* person, but he said he'd clear out of his music room if you want it. There's a futon in there you can sleep on. Of course I told him you weren't planning on staying much longer."

Kenya was silent.

"Ooga Booga," said Commodore, laughing, "what is your *plan*?"

Kenya felt sure that some earlier version of her would have started crying right then. Perhaps even the self that had been at the farm. But there had been too much crying and it had gotten her exactly nothing she wanted. She could hear Oliver's guitar scraping in his music room. *The Sad Dry Blues,* she thought.

"I don't know," she said.

"Well, like I said, you can stay here, and you don't have to sleep on the couch anymore. Oliver said he'd clear his junk out of that second room. And you get the privilege of being in the room next to his. But you might want to get earplugs. This scraping right now is bad enough, but there's talk of a Niggerpunk reunion."

"Oh my God. I'm staying with Niggerpunk?"

"Little-known fact: originally they were Fucksauce."

Kenya pushed her plate away. "What's the rent?"

"Talk to Oliver. It seemed like he was planning to let you stay for free."

"How come Oliver makes all of the decisions and you're the one who tells them to me?"

"I told you. He's the Man," Commodore said. Then he was speaking solemnly. "Are you sure you really want to keep hanging around here? I mean, Oliver's sort of in school for music theory or something, but there's really not a lot going on here, you know, in the immediate future department for our merry band of black depressives."

"Well, the two of you aren't exactly a band. You know, not like Niggerpunk. And what about your art?" Kenya asked.

"There is that," said Commodore. "That is there."

Kenya looked down for another slice of pizza. There was only pepperoni, but she reached for it.

"Hold up! You eat pork now?"

"No, but—"

Commodore snatched the box away. "I can't let you get involved with that."

"Why not? You eat it."

"But I don't want to be responsible for Johnbrown's daughter putting pork on her fork. You can have the pizza. But at least pick the meat off. Please?"

Kenya did as she was told, trying to stifle a smile at Commodore's concern. But the urge to smile disappeared easily as she watched him scarf down the pieces of abandoned meat.

"He's a mess," said Oliver with a wry twist of his mouth, indicating Commodore, who was napping on the couch at eleven in the morning. Kenya and Oliver were moving a jungle of electronic equipment out of the room where Kenya would now sleep.

Oliver continued, shaking his head. "It's really time for him to get back to his art. I mean, unlike me, the kid is actually kind of talented."

"Umf," Kenya said, trying to balance an awkwardly shaped amplifier and a stack of Led Zeppelin records. Oliver made her nervous, but she had to do some thinking to figure out why. It was true that he was odd and slightly gross. Besides being unusually tall, he had a tree trunk dreadlock that stuck straight up the middle of his head. He always smelled slightly of mildew. Though he had nice, shapely hands, the color of perfectly browned biscuits, the starkly irregular lengths of his nails ruined their pleasantness. But none of that was what put Kenya ill at ease. It was that though he also acted nervous, he seemed to want to give the impression of speaking casually. It was as if he had once been shy, but had been forced into a new personality. Conversations with him gave her a flash of Tuff Wieder, Barrett's butchy star lacrosse player, stumbling across the dance floor in her heels at prom.

Kenya took a break from hauling and went to the kitchen to pour a glass of orange juice. She drank it and watched Commodore sleep. She couldn't help musing that if she'd created his face, she wouldn't have done it any differently: not his skin, which *actually* looked like milk chocolate, not his discerning pug nose, not the mole at the side of his eyebrow. She remembered her mother remarking when they were little on the thick fringe of eyelash that had been wasted on him. After high school had ended, he had stopped having his hair cut in a high top like everybody else and wore a little round Afro that reminded Kenya of wooden paintings of Ethiopian Jesus she'd seen in the Penn Museum.

"He's just the cutest. Isn't he?"

She didn't know how long Oliver had been standing in the doorway of his bedroom, watching her look at Commodore. A smile played on his lips.

Kenya rolled her eyes. "So how much do you want me to pay in rent?"

"You got any money?"

"A little. I mean—I'm going to get a job."

"Well, I guess you shouldn't worry about it until you start getting paid."

"Thanks, Oliver."

"No big," he said. Though he did not smile or even look at her directly, Kenya could tell he liked saying that.

• • •

"Would I be, like, a really bad son if I told my mom that I was moving to Alaska?" Oliver asked them one evening after he showed his mother out of the apartment. Though they were all technically adults, Kenya felt like she lived in a home for orphans at Commodore and Oliver's. It was jarring, then, that someone's mother had stopped by bearing brownies.

Commodore said, "Trust me that I know about the need to pull away from the folks now and then. I think Kenya does, too."

"Yup," said Kenya.

Oliver turned to her. "So do *you* think I would be a bad son if I told her I was moving to Alaska? I almost did one summer. I saw this thing in the paper about salmon fishing."

Oliver's mother seemed innocent enough to Kenya. She was thick-figured with dishwater-gray hair and a raspy voice. Kenya thought again of the ruddy-faced hag on Fifty-Second Street, then of Sharon drinking in the afternoon. In contrast, this woman had neat short hair and wore an untucked oxford shirt and jeans in the style of the most forgettable of Barrett mothers. Her crow's-feet looked merry.

"Careful with these," she'd said about the brownies, winking in Kenya's direction. Kenya's first thought was that maybe, despite the woman's suburban demeanor, the brownies were laced with pot. But it turned out that the secret ingredient was a pinch of coffee—decaffeinated.

"Okay, *Miriam*. We'll be careful," Oliver had said, blowing air. Like his mother, just then he reminded Kenya of Barrett. She marveled disapprovingly, as she had in her Barrett days, at the patience of white women with their children.

"She'll just send the brownies to Alaska," Commodore was saying now. "Then we won't get any."

"Oh please, dude, she'd love to bake you your own pan. That woman loves herself some Commodore," Oliver said.

"It's not personal," said Commodore. He and Oliver laughed.

Sometimes when she hung out with them, Kenya felt like one of the kids on *The Cosby Show* whose job it was to act like Dr. Huxtable was hilarious.

"No, it's not personal," murmured Oliver.

"What do y'all mean?" asked Kenya.

"I'm like the black son she never had," said Commodore.

"Heh," Kenya said, channeling Lisa Bonet, whom she'd always found the least convincing of the Cosby kids.

"It's true." Oliver shrugged.

Commodore's parents never came by. He spoke to them every couple of weeks and often hung up feeling depressed. Alfred had steadily increased his drinking. Now he had liver disease and, though they still disliked each other, Yaya took care of him. Commodore thought disapproving of him was what united them.

"Seeing as though they're both pissed at me for dropping out, they're more together than they have been for a long time. It's kind of comical. Even when I talk to them separately, they say exactly the same things to me on the phone, like there's a script." These conversations always ended with him saying the word *school* repeatedly and so nastily that it sounded like an expletive. And yet he was always the one who called them.

Sometimes Kenya feared that Yaya would show up at the apartment and that this would tip off Kenya's mother. Sometimes she hoped for it. But as far as she knew, Sheila and Yaya hadn't spoken in years.

• • •

Kenya opted out of the first party—the first of many, it turned out—they had after she moved in, claiming that she felt exhausted. She did. Earlier that day she'd walked to an interview at the Green Apple on Chestnut Street, midway between West Philadelphia and downtown. She figured she'd be working in a few days and might not have as much time and energy to do things like take long walks. She headed down to Center City after her interview, stopping to buy an ice cream cone.

"Can I have a lick?" said a skinny man lurching along Chestnut Street.

The even skinnier man with him cackled as Kenya hurried on. Though her legs grew tired, she walked all the way down to Penn's Landing. She sat on a bench looking over at Camden, grasping for a memory of a boat ride with her parents when she was six. Her father seemed annoyed that day, though she hadn't been sure why. In retrospect she supposed that it was because the boat trip was a tour of "Olde" Philadelphia, complete with talk about American history and how great it was for everybody. Her mother made a show of ignoring Johnbrown's mood. She ordered Kenya to pose for pictures at the side of the boat, and listened brightly to the Ben Franklin lookalike tour guide. Kenya had been briefly amused by the novelty of being on water, but the boat moved so slowly that she lost interest. All that was left to notice was the humid stink of the river and the little boy in front of them who kept twisting around to stare at them with his mouth open. Kenya thought she heard the boy's mother murmur *kellerd*. Thinking of it now, more than ten years later, she glowered darkly until a man in a blue-collar uniform suddenly loomed in her field of vision and ordered her to smile. She gnashed her teeth in reply.

And so that night, despite halfhearted pleas from Commodore to "come out and play," she listened to the party from her room. Near midnight, she snuck out and into the bathroom, where she encountered some womanly indelicacy smearing the side of the toilet bowl. It made her wonder if Mary Elizabeth— whoever she was—was there. Kenya didn't want to care but was feverish to know what she looked like. She walked into the living room and froze. While she'd heard the buzzer sound repeatedly, and the growing murmur of voices, she was still unprepared for the number of people crammed into the space. It must have been near fifty.

Kenya wondered how it was that she and Commodore, children of the Seven Days, had wound up here. Aside from Commodore and Oliver, there was only one other black man throwing himself around to the music, and he looked a little too old for this party. She thought about the blue-lit all-black space of Commodore's cousin's barbecue, which might have been the best time she ever had. The thought dissipated as she saw Commodore play-fighting with a long-haired boy. Behind him, a small girl with sharp features and spiky short hair was trying to jump on his back. He spotted Kenya. "Double team!" he cried. "Kenya, help!"

On her way back to her room, Kenya saw Oliver. He was sitting at the kitchen table alone, in the middle of the crowd, in a Red Sea–parted type of way. He saluted. There seemed to be some other reality pulsing beneath his and Commodore's languid comings and goings, but she wasn't sure she wanted to enter it.

• • •

"Calm down, homegirl," Kenya's manager at the Green Apple was saying as he used his fingers to comb his goatee. "They're more afraid of us than we are of them."

It was Saturday afternoon, and Kenya was standing in the dim, cluttered office, trembling and near hysterical. "I think it tried to jump at me!" she said. "Like the rat in *Native Son*! Didn't you read *Native Son*? Luther, it was a rat!"

"Look, I want you to call me Luth."

After three weeks of working at the Green Apple: *a healthy cafeteria*, Kenya understood why Commodore was throwing a party or getting high whenever he wasn't there. If the job wasn't an outright nightmare until seeing the rat, it had been an unpleasant dream in which Kenya had to unclog the occasional toilet, be called "homegirl" by her stinky young white boss, and encounter suspicious-looking turds on the industrial-size tomato cans in the storeroom (which now appeared to belong to rats).

As Kenya left Luth's smelly office, and his laissez-faire stance toward rodents in storerooms, she miserably reviewed the reasons she could not quit: it paid better than the mall jobs she had briefly explored and nearly as much as the ones she didn't have the typing skills to get, and was one of the few non-fast-food restaurants that would hire someone with no experience. So when she got home that night, there was nothing she wanted to do more than enjoy the loud oblivion of one of Commodore and Oliver's parties.

Aren't you glad you're not a slave? she thought, sipping her one beer, slipping into the couch, trying to forget the day and the shift she had tomorrow. But the next morning came, and when she opened her eyes and thought of the Green Apple, she screamed. Commodore rapped on her door, yelling her name with alarm.

"I just fucking *hate* work," she called. Then she heard a gravelly female voice ask, "Is everything okay?" Mary Elizabeth.

Kenya found them both in the kitchen, where Commodore was cracking eggs, though Kenya had never seen him cook before. Mary Elizabeth wore a long plaid shirt that fell to her thighs. Below, she wore thick, saggy socks. Kenya hoped there were panties under the shirt.

"I told you," Commodore said.

"Told me what?" Told her that a scantily clad Mary Elizabeth would be there?

"That you didn't want to work there," he said. "Hey, Kenya, this is Mary. Mary, Kenya."

"Hello," said Mary Elizabeth.

"It's nice to meet you," said Kenya, wondering if anyone had ever named their child *Mary Kenya*. To Commodore, she said, "But you didn't tell me *why* I didn't want to work there."

"I told you I couldn't explain. Remember I told you how I wanted to do, like, a series of paintings about it, but that it didn't even make good art?"

"No," said Kenya. "No, I don't. But you need to make a portrait of the rat in the storeroom," she said, waiting for Commodore to be shocked.

"It's cute you think it's just one," he said.

"All food places have rats," said Mary Elizabeth, not unkindly.

"Well, I'll admit I did think rats had better taste than the

Green Apple," joked Commodore. "I don't get how food can be *so* spicy and *so* bland at the same time."

"And why does everything have kidney beans and tomatoes in it?" Kenya said, laughing. She had forced herself to eat the free food at work the first week. But after a few spectacular episodes in the employee bathroom, she stopped touching everything except the sweet potato muffins, whose dry crumbles she liked to meditatively roll on her tongue. She didn't know how the students, who swarmed the place at lunch, could keep eating the chicken peanut stew and the "Health Nachos."

Mary Elizabeth shrugged. "The food is pretty bad there."

"It is," said Kenya, trying to be friendly. But then she looked away as Mary Elizabeth began practicing pliés and relevés, possibly with no underwear on. "And why won't Luther—"

"Luth! Luth!" yelled Commodore.

"—stop calling me homegirl?"

"The better question is why he won't stop calling poor Bronwyn homegirl," said Commodore. "She's just a little white girl from Narberth. What did she do to deserve that?"

Mary Elizabeth laughed in her gravelly way. Commodore cursed; he was trying to get a bit of broken eggshell out of the bowl. Mary Elizabeth twirled a long strand of light brown hair around her finger and peered at the eggs.

"You have to use a big piece of eggshell to get little ones out," she said. "Like this." She let go of her hair to scoop around in the bowl, and then triumphantly pulled out some goop.

"Wowwwwww," Commodore said. "That's clever, ain't it?" he asked Kenya.

"My mom showed me that," said Mary Elizabeth. "It's,

like, the only useful thing she knows." She rolled her eyes and smiled at the ground.

"I should probably get in the shower before Oliver gets up," Kenya said.

"That dude," said Commodore, shaking his head. "It's like using the bathroom after the Loch Ness Monster."

"What?" asked Mary Elizabeth.

"There are, like, freshwater pools on the floor," said Kenya.

"What now?" Oliver called from his doorway. He wore a navy velvet monogrammed robe that he had mocked mercilessly when his mother gave it to him. But as far as Kenya could see, he wore it at some point nearly every single day, even when it was a little warm.

The robe made Kenya think of her own mother, whom she'd thought of calling when the summer ended. For a week or so, she thought about it every day, but she was too angry. As far as she could tell, neither Johnbrown nor Sheila had figured out that she was gone. And if they had, they had not tried very hard to find her, even though the last anyone had seen of her she'd been on a Greyhound bus. Kenya imagined an alternate universe where she'd been abducted from the bus station and chained in some pervert's basement. She wanted to weep with pity for herself.

"Can I get in the bathroom first, Oliver?" she asked.

"If you tell me what you said about me."

"Dude," said Commodore. "Just admit once and for all that you throw buckets of water on the floor when you shower. Just admit it."

"Before I answer that, why don't you tell me what you're

supposed to be doing? Who taught you how to turn on the stove?"

Now Mary Elizabeth was the Cosby kid or maybe the Cosby mother, who also had to laugh at the jokes. Kenya closed the bathroom door and stood under the steaming water for as long as she could stand. She was using up the hot water and she did not care.

When she emerged, only Oliver sat at the table, reading the newspaper, eating eggs that looked dry.

"Want some?" he asked. "They're not too bad."

While she pondered an answer, a distinctly male giggle escaped Commodore's room. Someone turned up music, throbbing and wordless.

"It's not serious," said Oliver, looking at what Kenya could see were the obituaries.

"What's not serious?" Kenya asked. "Death?"

"It's never serious. But after her, there's going to be another one just like her. Commodore's endless summer of weed and white girls and never dealing with real shit."

"What's that supposed to mean?"

Oliver looked up. "I mean a lot of cats truly fall in love with a white girl. Exhibit A, my dad, rest his soul. But our friend Commodore has this idea that they're not quite real, and so he doesn't have to be quite real about his life, about the shit with his parents. Which is why he can't do his art and chase Mary Elizabeth at the same time."

"Not that I care, but where are you getting all of this?" asked Kenya, angry that she was talking to him, and because she knew that what he was saying was true.

"You know me," he said. "I'm the Watcher."

"Oh yeah?" Kenya said. "Watch this." She walked to her room and slammed the door.

"Touché!" called Oliver.

Once in fourth grade she'd had dinner at Trinity Howell's house. She had been presented with a plate of meat, applesauce, and green beans. First she ate the beans, then the applesauce. The meat, crusted in gold, white on the inside, was still there. She knew that it was not chicken. She also knew that she was forbidden to eat pork, but there was no way she was going to explain that to the smiling Howells. *If I don't ask*, she had told herself, *then I don't know that this is pork*. Later she told her mother that they'd had fried chicken for dinner and Sheila had said, "Oh, fried chicken for the little black girl. Give me a break!" Her mother had been so frustratingly smug that it had been very hard not to blab the truth at that point. That night she lay in bed, expecting her stomach to explode.

At some point Kenya had begun flattering herself that Oliver had been struck with passion when she appeared and had been slowly working his angle. She thought about him sitting alone at that first party; she imagined that he had been waiting patiently for her. As it turned out, she could explain everything more easily using logic. Oliver was just a drug dealer who had tried to use her. Now, as she sat in the cleanest-looking corner of a holding cell, filled with a colorful variety of Philadelphia's female lawbreakers, she thought, if someone would just be quiet for a moment, she could figure out how it had all gone this wrong. But—

"Bad girls," sang two young women wearing boots and shorts though it was November. One wore a blond wig. The other had braided extensions down to her waist. *"Sad girls,"* they sang.

"This ain't *Star Search!*" yelled a twitching woman with yellow eyes. "Shut the fuck up!"

"You shut the fuck up!" said the blond wig.

"You shut the fuck up, Marilyn Monroe!"

"Alla youse need to shut the fuck up," said a mountain of a woman with a strong white Philly accent and a short haircut that reminded Kenya of *The Outsiders.* Her "fuck" sounded like "feck." Then she began banging on the bars. "You need to let me out of here! I have seizures when I get stressed! I'll sue your feckin' asses . . ."

Most of the women, black and white, sat quietly on the bench and floors. Despite the singing and yelling, there remained an air of tense boredom in the small space. The woman sitting nearest to Kenya chewed on her finger. She was young and white with a dark, neat ponytail and a clear porcelain face. She looked the most normal, which was why Kenya had sat near her. Too late she discovered that the woman, who looked about her age, seemed to be sitting in a puddle of her own urine. But Kenya didn't move. Instead, she tried to make herself still and small, fearing television scenarios where one of the rowdier women in the cell noticed that she, Kenya, wasn't one of them and tried to test her.

She had watched the things going on around her in Commodore and Oliver's apartment, hoping without hoping that even if something was not right, it would be as unremarkable as those pork chops at Trinity Howell's, which had not made her sick at all. Yes, there were a lot of parties where there was a lot of weed. And once, she'd barged into Oliver's room and two white boys with wolfish facial hair jerked their heads up from a mirror on the bed, where they were cutting lines of cocaine. She had shut the door quickly and not mentioned it to anyone.

It was not that night, but sometime after she'd met Mary Elizabeth, that Kenya had the conversation with Oliver. Despite what Oliver said, it seemed that Mary Elizabeth and Commodore *were* serious. Oliver was a cheery fount of gossip about her, having been friends with her twin brother in high school. Mary Elizabeth had a terrible reputation, he said, because she was a tease.

"She doesn't seem to be teasing now," said Kenya.

"I mean, she might be giving it up to him," Oliver said. "But not really."

"I don't know what you're talking about," said Kenya. "And I told you I didn't care."

"Yes, you didn't care so much that you had to slam a door in my face. Well, you will know what I'm talking about when he starts coming around all long-faced, talking about 'I need to get back to my art.'"

Kenya had to laugh. She remembered back in high school, after the Pippa debacle, how Commodore had gone on about making his art a priority.

At the next party Oliver, who usually had only a few beers, drank what seemed like an entire six pack and sat on the couch next to Kenya, chattering too quietly. Finally, he slurred, loud enough to hear, "You know what would really fix him, right? You know what we need to do?"

Commodore and Mary Elizabeth were tossing themselves around to what they claimed was their favorite song, "Oh Bondage! Up Yours!" They screamed into empty beer bottles like microphones. Some people cheered. Oliver had once told Kenya that when they met, Commodore was listening to Keith Sweat. Now somebody was hollering to turn that shit off and put on the Beastie Boys. Somebody else countered that the Beastie Boys had "fell off."

"So you know what we should do?" Oliver was saying again. Kenya had not had anything to drink, but had let him show her for the umpteenth time how to get high. It had never worked before as far as she could tell, and probably was not working now, but she wondered if there was some connection between being high and the fact that he said, in answer to his own question, "Fuck." That what they should do to "fix" Commodore was to fuck.

"We need to fuck," he repeated.

"Maybe," Kenya said. But she hadn't meant it. It was a placeholder—like the snowy blank TV screen between channels. She wasn't even sure she was altogether there in this room, in this reality.

"Maybe, huh?" said Oliver. He laughed. "Wait a minute," he said like a confused vaudevillian drunk. "Wait a minute. Are you, like, a virgin? Touched for the very first time?" he slapped his thigh.

Kenya said nothing.

"It's *totally* okay if you are," Oliver said.

Whooooooooooooooooooo, screamed Poly Styrene, seeming to tear her throat apart. Commodore was toppling. Mary Elizabeth and Kevin, the too-old-for-the-party black dude who was always there, caught him and led him back to his room. Somebody changed the record and Kenya heard the *tingtingting* opening of "Girls," a song that she hadn't heard in years, but that had once been so ubiquitous, she couldn't believe she'd forgotten it.

"Think about it," said Oliver, suddenly sounding crisp and sober. He got up and walked away.

Kenya was afraid to stand. *Girls to do the dishes, girls to do the laundry*, everyone sang, including the girls.

She woke up alone in the dark on the couch, the apartment tidied as usual. No matter how late it was, Oliver always scrubbed the place clean after people left. But what had happened was still there: he had said what he had said. Wide-awake, she went into Oliver's bedroom and climbed into the space between him and the wall. He curled around her as if this was how they slept every night. At that, some music of flutes and strings welled up in her; she thought of trips with her mother to the Plymouth Meeting Mall.

The next night, they tried to have sex. It was difficult and embarrassing. Kenya screwed her eyes shut. The condom smell reminded her of her job at Dr. Walton's. Oliver hurt her and muttered that he would get "that jelly stuff for next time." They were not successful. She told herself there would not be a next time. But then when it was over, he hooked his arm around her and they curled into each other and she floated on music, which spoke of polished department store floors, glass walls streaming with light, a mint chip ice cream cone with chocolate sprinkles from the food court. Drifting off to sleep, she noted that his nails had been neatly trimmed.

They continued to try, and he eventually got it in, but Kenya was in it for the spooning. All she had was the Green Apple and this apartment with its musty smell of boys, the endless parties, and no family and no future and lousy memories. On top of that, her alliance with Oliver had not interested Commodore one bit. One afternoon she bumped into him as she stepped out of Oliver's room. She couldn't help it; her heart jumped in anticipation. "All *right*," he said, grinning. "My man." Then he rushed off to meet up with Mary Elizabeth and her parents at a South Street restaurant where Simon LeBon had once eaten. Everything was horrible. Everything was horrible except this, she had thought, wrapped in Oliver's arms, mercifully facing the wall.

In the police station at Thirty-Ninth and Lancaster, the prostitutes were still singing with quiet defiance. *I'll be your freak-a-zoid; come on and wind me up!* The mountainous white woman mumbled and rocked herself on the floor, sweat streaming down her face. The ponytailed girl who smelled like urine asked Kenya in a whisper if she had a cigarette.

The police—led by Kevin, who, as it turned out, *was* too old for these parties but perhaps in the prime of his undercover narcotics career—had burst into the apartment early that morning. The party the night before had raged until four, and Kenya remembered working on sex with Oliver again— they jokingly called it "penetration"—weeping as he flailed on top of her. They had pretended that this was some kind of emotional breakthrough and that she was crying because it meant something to her. But that wasn't why at all. And thank God (*the Creator?* she thought) it wasn't. Because not only did Oliver not say a word when the police, in the process of tossing her room, found what was evidently a felony charge's worth of marijuana, he also remained silent when they handcuffed Kenya along with him and Commodore.

"What is that doing in my room?" Kenya kept saying, the walls moving forward, the floor falling away. "What is that doing in my room? *Who put that in here?*"

Oliver let out a strange bark that was clearly meant to sound ironic.

She couldn't believe she'd had the poise to throw on real clothes before they burst into her room. She was grateful to her father and his riff about being prepared if the police burst in. About how they'd take you to the station naked just for fun—that is, if they didn't shoot you in your sleep. She remembered her mother stifling a snort. Kenya wondered if they had ever been in love.

As she sat in the back of a police car, absurdities threatened to come bursting out of her mouth. She wanted to say that she'd gone to the Barrett School for Girls. That she couldn't even get high properly; coffee was the drug that made her heart sing. That Oliver was repulsive, and getting close to him had been like summoning up her courage to dive into that cold swimming pool at Barrett all those years ago. That she didn't know anything about anything, which was true in so many ways.

"But you knew Oliver Gold was selling illegal substances?" asked a cop in an interrogation room, who didn't look anything like she thought a cop would look. He looked like an overweight Italian Rob Lowe.

"I knew they—he—smoked a lot of weed. But I didn't know he sold it."

"But you knew there were illegal substances in the house?"

Look, she wanted to say, *I never asked if it was pork, so I didn't know it was pork.*

"I told you all I know." She sighed. Suddenly she was thirsty. "Can I have some mother?" she asked.

The policeman looked at her strangely. "Did you want water? Or did you want to make your phone call?"

She did want water. But she wanted her mom more. Now she sat in the cell wondering about Sheila's foster sister, the one who'd gone to prison. She thought about the butler, who'd died in jail. Her father hadn't included that part in his story. Maybe he was writing it now.

She'd had time to read and reread the pages her father had given her. She had begun to think that they were some kind of apology to her for leaving. But did he really think of himself as a servant in the early 1900s? Was that what living with her and Sheila had been like? Kenya felt insulted. Other times, she thought maybe it was true what he said at the farm, as flaky as it was. That the story, which was true in its broad strokes, after all, had sprung into his head and directed itself toward Kenya. That it was the only thing he had to give her.

She wondered what had happened to the woman, "Elizabeth," who was pregnant with the butler's baby? What had happened to the baby?

It was a girl, she decided.

The police officer finally understood that she had nothing useful to say. He escorted her to a phone in a cramped room where a guard read the newspaper. The recording told Kenya that the phone had been disconnected. Not knowing what else to do, she tried the same number twice more. Then the guard told her it was time to go back to the cell.

Her quiet cellmate with the ponytail whispered at the floor. "I'm sorry," she said. "I'm so sorry."

Sheila screeched to a halt across from the police station, calculating that she would get a ticket but not towed. The late-October air was pregnant with rain, which made the shoulder in which she'd been shot ache. She knew the rain, when it came, would be cold.

Walking into the station, she tried not to think about what it must have been like for Kenya to call and get the musical tone and the cheery recorded announcement that the phone had been disconnected. When the house sale went through and Sheila had to leave, she begged the phone company to let her keep the phone number. She'd gone down there in person bearing a flyer with a picture of Kenya, and wept in the office of a pleasant but unyielding blond man. She'd toyed with the idea of trashing the office, but decided she'd spent enough time in jails as it was, between visiting Johnbrown and the fucking incompetent con artist to whom she was currently married (though not for long). And now instead of Parents' Weekend at Wesleyan, which she'd marked on the calendar when they'd gotten the admittance packet the previous spring, here she was at jail again.

There was a black officer at the desk with a look of intelligence and a gentle air that surprised Sheila. This, she saw, was the station's rather smart approach to dealing with the constant stream of anguished women—many black—who flowed through. He had a warm smile and seemed deeply concerned that someone had given Curtis an extra *s* in the paperwork.

"Was it you who called me?" Sheila asked him. "From Missing Persons?"

"Ma'am?" he said with a puzzled look.

Of course it wasn't him. "I'll just . . ." Sheila said vaguely, and sat down to wait for Kenya. But after a few minutes, she was up again. Was he sure Kenya hadn't been transferred already? Was she on her way? Officer Rivers seemed to get calmer and more assured each time she went up to the desk with a question. Sheila had just begun to feel he was truly on her side. But then a loud woman in soiled clothes with her wig askew entered, talking fast, and he treated her with the same elegant deference.

Finally her daughter was there, wearing a fancy peach-colored blouse and faded green sweatpants. Her short hair was ragged around the edges. But she was beautiful. Sheila crushed Kenya into her chest, gratefully inhaling her staleness.

"But your phone—" Kenya said.

"Doesn't matter. I'm here," Sheila said.

Sheila knew that when some women observed the progress of time in their getting-older children, they flashed back to them as infants. But Kenya's infancy was a time of blurry terror that Sheila rarely thought about. Instead, when she noticed Kenya getting older, as she did now in the police station, she remembered her at four and five, asking questions with serious eyes: questions about nuclear war, death, God, the making of babies, the color of skin. She thought of Johnbrown and his reckless conversations with the little girl. At the time, Sheila had thought maybe a preschooler did not need to know that, yes, the earth would one day be consumed by the sun, or about slaves being hobbled for trying to escape. On the other hand, she didn't want Kenya to grow up in the same ignorance she had. Sheila had known that with Johnbrown in her life, Kenya could be proud of who she was. She wouldn't grow up thinking that white people were gods or superheroes. Sheila herself had known very few white people, since none lived in the Richard Allen projects or went to her schools. From television and occasional car trips, she knew they lived in houses with lawns and station wagons in front of them. She once asked her mother if white people were better than black people. "They sure got more money," her mother had replied.

Officer Rivers cleared his throat softly, indicating forms to sign. When their business was concluded, he nodded with his smile. It occurred to Sheila that after Johnbrown had left, she should have married a man like that. She imagined Teddy at the desk, acting as if he'd done a magic trick to produce people's sons and daughters and boyfriends, after detaining them with bullshit conversation.

Teddy. She gripped Kenya's hand. Then she pulled her daughter's head to her shoulder, even though it made for awkward walking out of the station doors, and though it made her shoulder hurt even more. In all of these years, nearly ten, she had taken great care never to betray to Kenya that it still caused her pain.

"You got a ticket," Kenya said as they approached the car.

"Yup," said Sheila. She yanked the paper off of her windshield and shoved it into her purse without looking at it.

"I'm so sorry," said Kenya, starting to cry as soon as she was in the car.

Sheila wiped away her own tears. "Yeah, you *are* sorry," she said. "Do you know how many stations I went to filling out missing persons reports? Do you know your father came down here and we spent a week driving all over the fucking Greater Philadelphia metro area looking for you? I had to spend a week listening to him go on about the farm and all of his financial problems. And he kept saying, 'She's okay, I just know it.' I wanted to strangle him."

At this Kenya burst into fresh sobs that Sheila didn't understand. "What?" she said.

"Do you?" Kenya began.

"What, baby?"

"Have a tissue?"

Sheila laughed as Kenya blew her nose and dabbed at her cheeks. Before long, they were on Irving Street, in view of the small, peeling houses where all of this had started. She stopped the car directly in front of their old home, whose windows now bore lace curtains.

"What are we doing here?" Kenya asked in a panicked voice.

"Long story," Sheila said.

She knew she should walk in front because she had the key, but instead she followed Kenya's thin, sagging figure. Sheila felt as if the figure was her. She had borrowed against, and then sold, the house in the suburbs. She'd used all of her savings and much of her pension to pay for lawyers for the con man and to put up bail for her daughter. She was breathlessly awaiting a call about part-time work at a used bookstore that reeked of cats. Before Missing Persons had called to tell her where Kenya was, she'd been very close to walking out into the Philadelphia streets naked and screaming. But now that her daughter was back, she knew it was all going to work. Somehow the two of them had to make it all work.

Kenya looked at the house and back at her mother. She remembered seeing it with Commodore, their arms brushing. Her knees buckled slightly. "Am I going crazy—or having a dream?"

"Let's get inside, Kenya," her mother said in her least dreamlike voice. "For now, we're home."

That night Kenya sat in the kitchen, which now seemed tiny, listening to her mother explain how they'd wound up renting their old house. The landlord was a friend of Grandmama's; there had been a chance meeting and then a break in the rent.

"But, Mom," she asked, "why would you want to live *here* again? After everything."

"Well, it was cheap."

"Okay," said Kenya. But she didn't believe that was the reason. When she looked at Sheila across the table, she got an image of her blurring at the edges, flickering like a TV screen going snowy. Her mother felt like a ghost who had come back to haunt their old house. Kenya reached out to her.

Sheila winced. "Baby, your hand is freezing."

"Is this the best you can do for a touching family reunion?"

Her mother squeezed her hand and smiled. "This is just getting started. Wait till you try spaghetti from a can."

All Kenya had to do was close her eyes in their old house, in a new, stiff bed, to have a dream of the butler. The next morning she woke feeling horribly awake.

She tried to close her eyes, but they snapped back open. And before she could stop them, her feet had hit the ground.

You have to burn it all down, the butler had told her. She knew he didn't mean for her to set fire to anyone's home and kill anyone's child with an ax. But she knew the key to the next part of her life, the good part, was figuring out exactly what he did mean.

Acknowledgments

Warmest thanks to Ellen Levine, Miranda Popkey, Jesse Coleman, and Lorin Stein for all that they have done and continue to do.

Thanks to Alicia Hall Moran and Jason Moran for telling me about the burning of Taliesin and for cheering me on. Thanks also to Donna Aza Weir-Soley and Linda Kim for helping me pretend to know some things I did not know.

Thanks to Washington and Lee University, Trinity College, and Haverford College for their support.

Thanks to Andrew, Adebayo, and Mkale, as well as Akiba, James, and Rochelle for just about everything else.